Words of Praise for Iris and the Crew

"Readers, get ready—for the gleekin' ride of your life! *Iris and the Crew Tear Through Space* is an exuberant romp that ditches all the stale clichés of sci-fi in favour of what's fresh, exciting, and truly possible. Here is a tale that shows when it comes to accessibility, not even the sky is the limit. Buckle up and enjoy!"
Amanda Leduc, author of *The Centaur's Wife* and *Disfigured: On Fairy Tales, Disability, and Making Space*

"I simply cannot tell you how much I enjoyed this!
Best thing I've read all year."
Robert Kingett, co-editor of *Artificial Divide*

"Space… the most accessible frontier. These interconnected, intergalactic stories imagine disability as a natural part of life, and accessibility as a necessity rather than an afterthought. No matter what your body can or can't do, and no matter your species, Iris and the crew welcomes you aboard."
**Jennifer Lee Rossman, co-editor of
*Mighty: An Anthology of Disabled Superheroes***

"Cait Gordon has written a book that shows us a world where disability doesn't mean unable." **C.L. Carey, author of *Spaced!***

"High adventure, fabulous characters, and representation? Yes, please! Pew pew pew!"
**Jamieson Wolf, author of *Little Yellow Magnet*
and *Beyond the Stone***

More by Cait Gordon

NOVELS IN THE 'COSM SERIES:

The Stealth Lovers

Life in the 'Cosm

SHORT STORIES:

"Putting a Bee in Their Bonnet" (Mighty: An Anthology of Disabled Superheroes)

"Alien" (There's No Place)

"The Hilltop Gathering" (We Shall Be Monsters)

"The Silken Eclipse" (Space Opera Libretti)

"A Night at the Rabbit Hole" (Alice Unbound: Beyond Wonderland)

ANTHOLOGIES, AS CO-EDITOR:

Nothing Without Us

Nothing Without Us Too

SEASON ONE

IRIS AND THE CREW TEAR THROUGH SPACE!

by Cait Gordon

Renaissance
Diverse Canadian Voices

pressesrenaissancepress.ca

This is a work of fiction. Any similarity to any events, institutions, or persons, living or dead, is purely coincidental and unintentional.

SEASON ONE: IRIS AND THE CREW TEAR THROUGH SPACE! © 2023 by Cait Gordon. All rights reserved. No part of this book may be used or reproduced in any manner whatsoever without written permission except in the case of brief quotations in critical articles and reviews. For more information, contact Presses Renaissance Press. First edition.

Cover background image by InstaWalli from Pexels. Cover art by Cait Gordon. Cover design by Cait Gordon, Diana Galván Mejía, and Nathan Fréchette. Interior images by Cait Gordon. Typesetting by Diana Galván Mejía and Nathan Caro Fréchette. Edited for sensitivity by Robert Kingett, Eman Rimawi-Doster, and Christopher Jon Heuer. Additional editing by Allyson Throp.

Legal deposit, Library and Archives Canada, 2023.

Paperback ISBN: 9781990086496
Ebook ISBN: 978-1-990086-60-1

Presses Renaissance Press
pressesrenaissancepress.ca

We gratefully acknowledge the support of Canada Council for the Arts.

SEASON ONE

IRIS AND THE CREW TEAR THROUGH SPACE!

by Cait Gordon

CONTENT NOTE

Some episodes in this season include scenes of familial loss, whether by death or estrangement. They also include scenes of working through sensory overload and overwhelming experiences. And there are even scenes with ableism, some of which is corrected by characters learning better, but most of it is unashamedly committed by pirates. In fact, if you're an ableist pirate, then this book is definitely not for you.

To Bruce, who navigates this life with me

Lieutenant Eileen Iris faced the same issue every morning because colours mattered. That is, they mattered to *her*, ever since she had become reacquainted with them several years ago. Clarence thought paying such detail to tones and hues was overrated and didn't know why she even bothered. She did, though.

Bother. She was bothering now, in fact, because everything had to fit just so in her mind. Planning this ritual in advance would not have suited her at all, as each day presented a different essence to it.

The drawer remained open before her, displaying an array of irises. She could see the colour inserts clearly without already wearing a pair; their absence didn't affect any visual data. *Window dressing this might be, but if I feel sharp, I'll be sharp.*

A shimmering sash associated with her rank draped along her right shoulder, catching the overhead lights of her quarters. The mirror she faced reflected the gradients of violet and green flecks in the material. *Hm.*

She felt on the verge of making her choice when the comm interrupted her thoughts and resounded throughout her chamber. The lieutenant stepped in bare feet to the screen by the door. It read aloud:

"Stop primping already, princess. I'm so hungry, I can eat an entire menagerie and maybe also the zookeeper!"

She smiled and dictated:

"Davan, you misinformed soul—"

"You mispronounced magnificent."

"I don't primp; I undergo metamorphosis."

A pause, then her screen displayed and said:

"Listen, friend, if you're not out in five, I'm inhaling all the hash browns. The spicy ones you like. I have no remorse over demolishing them. No remorse, I tell you!"

She snickered while threatening his life a little and went back to select her irises for the day. *I really do love those spicy carbs, though,* she mused while gazing at the tray. *Okay, these ones will do.* As she popped a piece in each eyeball, it whirred and turned and locked into place. The lieutenant stared at her reflection with approval. Her shiny platinum hair hung down her back in a tight plait, there was a healthy glow on her rosy-beige complexion, and after putting on her boots, her uniform was textbook crisp. *Now, time to eat. Better make it a hearty breakfast. This will be a long shift.* She turned to her right. *I think I'll have Clarence stay behind today. Xey won't like it, though.*

With a wave of her hand over the sensor, the door whooshed open to reveal her fellow officer standing with folded arms and an unimpressed glare.

"Can we go now?" Davan unlocked his steel-blue arms to sign.

Iris rolled her eyes to stop herself from grinning. "You didn't have to wait for me," she signed back.

"Old habits are hard to break."

She snickered.

"Let's move," he added. "I can smell the food from here."

"You probably could catch the aroma of supper from three galaxies away."

"You're not wrong!"

Commander Davan was a Quargnan. The people of Quargayle did not speak with their mouths but when communicating audibly, they relayed a complex and melodic language using their long, trunk-like snouts. Because it had been the custom for Quargnans to keep their audible and signing languages for use only on Quargayle, Davan had become fluent in Keangal Standard Tongue and IGSL, that is, intragalactic sign language. The Keangal (pronounced like *k'yANG-ull)* was the intragalactic governing network to which their military belonged. In any case, Davan felt rather glad about having his trunk. It rarely let him down, especially during mealtimes, when he'd revel in the acute sense of smell and taste it provided.

Iris and Davan walked side by side at a quickened pace. He touched her shoulder. She faced him.

"So, what's the decision today? Which colour did—whoa!" He signed that last word with an emphatic gesture. "Your eyes! I think you might want to go back and change."

Lieutenant Iris lifted her nose in the air. "Everything is perfectly fine, thank you very much. I purposely chose two different colours. They match with my officer's sash."

Davan blinked. "Yeaaaaah." He spelled out those extra vowels with his fingers.

"Listen, Davan—ah fweep," Iris groaned, as everything went unexpectedly dim and out of focus. Her right forearm tingled as a sensory cane elongated from its casing in her uniform, then displayed a colour pattern indicating her current visual state. It was white with a red segment at the bottom.

Davan withheld the urge to place an arm around her shoulders to guide her to the wall. He knew she could manage without his help; it had been just a reflex response. He quickly typed into his wristband.

The audio rang with a lilt Davan had specifically chosen to match his personality: "Forget another upgrade, Poopsie?"

"Shut up." She playfully punched his arm, feeling smug that she'd made contact on the first try, then tapped her cane to release it from the casing and into her grip.

Whirring out of her chamber door and jetting irately into the air came Clarence, Iris's guidebot.

"Ha! Thought you could leave without me again, did you?" said Clarence in a digitized but distinctly irked tone.

Lieutenant Iris really didn't feel she needed Clarence as much anymore, what with her latest implants and how she knew every nook and cranny of the ship. She could easily move about—even during an emergency while half asleep—but the guidebot had another idea about that altogether. Xey regarded xeir efficiency fathoms above most technology and had rather a disdain for "sloppily designed" modules. When it came to assisting xeir Eileen, xey simply didn't trust other electronic and computerized devices to get the job done as well as xem. Same with people.

"Fine. You can tag along, Clarence. I'm guessing this upgrade will take about an hour."

"I told you to set all upgrades for when you are sleeping. Now they'll randomly appear when you least expect them."

"I'll do it when I get off duty."

"You say that every time I remind you."

She swished her hand. "I'm too hungry to argue."

"Here, milady," rang out Davan's input before he touched her arm and offered his elbow as a sign of affection.

Clarence swatted Davan's limb away and placed xeir aqua-tinted head under Iris's left palm. Guiding her movements had always been *xeir* job, after all. Davan's good nature took it in stride, and the three of them entered the lift that would bring them to the Officers' Mess. Inside sat another of their shipmates.

"S'up," she said.

"Morning, Lartha," said Iris.

"Hey, Lartha, having a chair day?" typed Davan.

The chief of security grunted and shook her head. Tousled magenta waves rioted down her left shoulder while the other side of her medium-brown scalp was cleanly shaved, exposing a deep purple tattoo that shouted: *Just try it!* "Shore leave was, let's say, a little wild."

Iris feigned surprise.

"Yeah, yeah, I know," said Lartha. "I hooked up with this guy on Zazeth-3. Gorgeous. Even with fangs. Knew just how to use them, too."

This was met without response.

"Anyway, we chatted over drinks, and he gave me this big gooey speech about being a 'leg man.' Said he loved mine, which was nice, considering his own legs looked top of the line. So, okay, I was flattered. Until the next morning, when I discovered mine missing."

"What a scumbag!" cried Iris.

"I'll say. Turns out this guy's the biggest seller of leading-edge prostheses on the nether market."

"Come again?" signed Davan while typing the question for Iris to hear. He adjusted his wristband setting to project a holo interpreter that faced him, so they would state aloud what he signed from this point on.

"Yeah," said Lartha. "He *really was* a leg man. A used-leg salesman."

"Wait," signed Davan. "You're the best security chief in the fleet. How did you let this happen?"

"Shore leave is one of the few slots when I get to lower my guard. But never again. Even on sexy time, I'll stay on high alert. If anybody tries to pull a fast one, they're going down, and not in a fun way."

"So, what about your prostheses?" asked Iris.

"Ah, it's all good. Herbie's been hacking up my old pair for the last month. He said he had a few ideas to make them even better than the legs that got stolen."

The lift door opened. Lieutenant Commander Horatio Herbert from Engineering lay on the floor, grasping his genitals. His usually alabaster cheeks were flushed from pain. Beside him stood the culprits: two prosthetic limbs, dressed in the standard-issue black boots and grey leggings of the security crew. They leaned nonchalantly against the wall opposite where he writhed.

"Herbie, what the living gleek?!" cried Lartha.

"They"—he gasped—"work! Next time... anyone tries to... steal... they'll fight back. The... legs, I mean."

One of the legs tapped its foot impatiently. Davan lifted Herb off the floor, attempted to dust him off, and finger-combed Herb's bed-head mop. The russet-brown locks would not obey much.

"Over there," gestured Herb to the legs. "Security Chief Lartha is your new boss."

The pair stood at attention and then walked over to Lartha.

"Hey, legs!" she said.

They sort of made a bow.

"Moving on their own, eh, Herbie?"

"Yeah," he grunted. "I was able to manage it after all. Let me send you a scanner setting." He removed a device from one of the many pockets on his olive-green coveralls and aimed it at Lartha's wristband.

She received the addition, studied the readings, and raised her eyebrows. "Well, how about that? There's an invisible me attached to them. That is me, isn't it? Only as a body-shaped field and totally bald?"

"It would take me too long to configure your hair, and I didn't think it was necessary for optimum functionality."

"Fair enough." Lartha asked her legs permission to put them on, and they answered by stepping forward. Her scanner showed the field-body disappearing. She leaned over them.

"Herbie? The liners?"

"Inside each leg. Just tap the sensor on the top rims three times or say, 'Right, release liner, and Left, release liner.' I reconfigured the voice recognition to yours."

Lartha spoke the commands and heard the pins release. She rolled each liner onto her legs, then reached out and fastened each leg to her body. Pushing herself out of her hover-chair, the security chief stood upright.

"Yeah, okay, I like these ones even more. Comfier liner, better fit, and most of all, love their attitude!" She patted each one. "Good girls. We'll get along really well."

The legs hopped with joy, which meant so did Lartha. She laughed. "Hm. Maybe I will sign up for that happy-happy dance class after all. Might be a fun way to unwind when I'm off duty."

Iris grinned, then cocked her head. "Hey, I can still hear Herb gasping. Are you okay, Herb?"

"Yeah. It's just a bit peopley out here. I think I'd prefer to go back to my station."

"We haven't seen you in a bit, though. Won't you join us for breakfast?"

"It's more people in the Mess."

Davan perked. "What about your private room? You can bring it with you. That way, we can hang together, and you might feel less overwhelmed."

"That's an idea," said Iris. "Herb, do you have it on you?"

Herb tapped the top right pocket on his loose-fitting coveralls. A metallic grey box materialized and enveloped the chief of Engineering. Even though it appeared that Herb had encased himself in a holographic tomb, the inside of his private room resembled a spacious green field. He missed the land he owned back home, and an expanse of green had always relaxed him. Herb could also adjust the scenery to suit his tastes. Sometimes he added a little lake. The thing about the private room was that he could wear it anyplace, not only when he was alone. Herb currently adjusted the audio to hear what his colleagues were saying, without any annoying ambient distortion. The program also relayed anyone's signing gestures as scrolling text in his sky. The noise filtering he'd designed was par none, and his technology had been sought and procured all over the galaxy. Another feature he'd rigged was a holoscreen on the outside of the wall that displayed whatever he said.

"Good, we're all settled and—*oh!*" cried Iris, blinking. "Gee, that was quick. Maybe only a small patch uploaded." She retracted her cane, then tried taking her hand off Clarence's head, where it had been fastened firmly with a mild tractor field.

"Clarence?"

"What?"

"You can let me go."

"No."

"What?"

"I said, 'No.' I'm not risking you falling again."

Lieutenant Iris sighed. *Anyone want to buy an overly protective guidebot?* "That hasn't happened in years, and I have my cane anytime I need it. But if it makes you feel better, you can stay by my side until my implants fully upgrade." She said this to humour xem.

Clarence hovered for a moment while xey mulled this over. Then xey released the tractor beam.

"Thank you," said Iris.

"I swear, I'll ingest one of *you* if we don't get to the Mess soon," signed Davan.

"Hey, wait," said Lartha. "Herbie, can you see what Davan signs?"

"Yeah, I've also added him in the field with me," Herb blurted without thinking. It had been the latest feature he'd been working on. He blushed, grateful that the science officer couldn't see the engineer's cheeks redden once again.

Davan straightened. "I'm honoured you're letting me share your quiet space."

Herb coughed bashfully.

"Intruder alert on the command deck, intruder alert on the command deck!" The words boomed in the air and scrolled along inlaid screens along the walls throughout the ship.

"Aw, 'nads," signed Davan, "I'm destined to starve."

"No time for our stomachs now," barked Lartha, running back to the lift. "Let's get to our stations!" Her hover-chair followed her inside.

"Bridge!" said Lartha.

"This lift does not currently connect to the bridge," replied the lift's AI.

Herb peeked at his console. "Oh yeah. This network segment is under repair and restricted to vertical travel. We can still get to the correct level, but we'll have to bolt the rest of the way."

"Hey, what about that remote 'porter patch I requested for Security? Is it enabled?" asked Lartha.

"Not yet, but you'll have it when we get to Haven. I just want to run a few more tests. But it won't be for within-ship 'porting anyway. The captain is concerned about tracking-logistics and resources if everyone's disappearing and reappearing everywhere. Might be a safety issue."

"Yeah, I get it, but what if you just limit on-ship 'porting to Security and maybe Medical?"

Herb cocked his head. "I could do that. But it's ultimately the captain's decision."

"We'll have a chat with him," said Lartha, which meant she'd push for the meeting.

"Uh, I think we should get going," said Iris. "Command-deck level," she ordered.

"Taking to Level CD," said the AI.

"Well, guess it's time to test drive these legs," said Lartha.

"You have your chair too," said Herb. "It'll go as fast as you'll need it to."

"I know, but I'm feeling adventurous with my new girls." She gently patted her prostheses, then addressed her chair: "But have my back, okay?"

The chair messaged, "Gotcha," to her wristband.

Outside the lift again, they ran through the corridors that led to the bridge, passing a silver-haired maintenance technician with a pale beige complexion, who wore grey overalls and red corrective safety goggles. She shouted, "Hey, where's the fire?" in a jovial tone while pulling an electronic spanner from the tool-kit attached to her candy-pink rollator-wheelchair. After receiving no reply, Fran shrugged her shoulders and went back to her work inside an open panel.

When Iris, Clarence, Davan, Herb, and Lartha arrived at the command deck, two security officers were aiming their weapons at a pasty soul who shook with terror. He wore faded blue coveralls and held a stick that had a large bristly implement on the bottom of it, which rested on the ground. On his chest was a white patch embroidered with *Wendell* sewn in a darker blue thread.

"Please! I'd just been dusting. I didn't know the contraption was alive!" This is what the startled intruder had said in his own tongue, but nobody in the command crew actually understood any of the words.

Captain Warq spotted Lieutenant Iris and motioned her towards him. She rushed over with Clarence jetting after her.

"Captain?"

The captain wore his speech interpretation visor but seemed at a loss. He stood tall in his pristine dark grey and gold uniform, his seafoam-green skin still glowing after his pre-shift workout. Warq scratched the back of his silvery-white crew cut, which was his "tell" when he was in deep thought. He abruptly stopped the motion to sign:

"Lieutenant, I don't understand this person's spoken language, and he doesn't know IGSL. Everything he says is coming up as gobbledygook on my visor. This looks like a job for our highly skilled communications officer." He signed the compliment with a kind smile.

Lartha, standing with two other security guards, triple-tapped a sensor on her chair, which transformed the mobility device into a massive tubular weapon. She took it into her arms like it weighed a feather and pointed it at Wendell.

"Don't shoot! I'm a janitor from NASA. I swear, I didn't know the machine worked! They told me to clean the laboratory. I was only doing my job!"

"No, I can't make that out," said Iris. "Captain, might I recommend that Lieutenant Commander Lartha and her team refrain from blasting this person into microns? Just for a sec?"

"I agree. Security, no disintegrations." Warq couldn't help but hold back a grin at Lartha's reaction. He knew a groan when he saw one.

"Yes, Captain," said the security chief, not moving from her position.

Iris dashed to her workstation. "Let me access my language archive. Maybe we'll find a match."

Davan held a scanning device and waved it over the intruder.

"Thoughts, Commander?" signed the captain.

The science officer and second-in-command switched off the device. "No internally concealed organic weapons. Vital signs indicate this being is frightened and not a threat. Yet, I'm not sure what the object is that he's clutching onto so dearly."

"Here it is!" shouted Iris. "Goodness, I had to dive deep for this one. There had been an away mission that went awry about two hundred years ago. An anomaly that sucked their ship to an unknown galaxy but thankfully brought them back to ours again. Funny, they don't say where the anomaly was located; the information seems to be redacted. Anyway, the language is Earthan. Or, more accurately, one specific Earthan tongue. Setting audio-visual translation now."

The captain walked over to Wendell and signed, "Earthan Being, how did you come to be on this ship?"

Wendell beamed with relief. "You speak English! Thank goodness."

"English," said Iris. "I'll make a note of that. Guessing he's from the land of Eng?"

"I'm so glad you can finally hear me," said Wendell to the captain.

Captain Warq paused. "I'm sorry? Hear you? I'm afraid you're mistaken. But I do comprehend your speech now. Are the people of the Nasa continent not familiar with Intragalactic Sign Language? Perhaps sign a little for us, so we can detect if we have your dialect in our system."

Wendell tried paying attention to the captain, whose appearance defied the janitor's preconceived notion of what "little green aliens" should look like. In fact, the captain was rather tall and buff, resembling a human, apart from the aqua-green tone of his skin. There were also finely drawn tattoos in a symmetrical pattern on either side of his face and neck. But as fascinating as this discovery was to Wendell, he couldn't help being distracted by a floating metallic crate that loomed nearby.

"Why is that box moving around on its own?"

"That is not a box," replied the captain. "That is my chief engineer."

"Why is he inside a box?"

"It calms him so he can focus while in a larger group."

"Oh."

"Captain, I—*fweep!*" cried Iris, cursing the unreliability of her implants. "That does it, I'm switching down for the day! And as soon as my shift is done, I'll give that manufacturer a piece of my mind!" She continued about her workstation without missing a beat, fingers reading hastily, ready to execute the required commands from her console to her earpiece. Iris's cane automatically extended, but she retracted it for the time being. Clarence tugged on her sleeve.

"I told you not to select the inferior model just because your medic said they would expedite it," xey complained. "But why should you ever listen to me? What should *I* know about technology? Oh, and by the way, you're wearing two different-coloured irises today."

"I *like* the different colours!"

Davan signed, "And some folks are born that way! The Dairym of Soadayl even have six eyes with each iris its own shade. They're quite beautiful."

"Exactly," she muttered upon hearing the interpretation in her earpiece.

"I'm really sorry about my reaction earlier," signed Davan. "That wasn't okay." He'd switched to a signing language only known to her, for private conversation.

"Thanks," she signed back. "But you need to compensate me by not doing that again to me or anyone else, and by filling my plate with spicy hash browns."

"Done!"

"Wait a minute," said Wendell, looking at the captain, then Iris and Davan. He also spotted the design of Lartha's legs. Then he glanced in Herb's direction and remembered how his own nephew often had to wear noise-cancelling headphones when in public spaces.

"You're all disabled!" the custodian cried.

The captain paused for a moment. He swiftly turned to his chief engineer and signed, "Mr. Herbert, is the ship disabled in any way?"

Herb's private room disappeared as he consulted a live schematic on a wall console. "No, Captain, all systems functioning as expected."

Captain Warq nodded. "Thank you, Mr. Herbert. Now then, my good man," he signed to Wendell, "there's no need to panic. I am not sure where you received your intel, but you are quite safe on this vessel. We are not disabled in the least."

"I didn't mean the ship; I meant you and your crew are disabled!"

The captain seemed perplexed when he read these words. He didn't want to seem rude, but a confidential discussion with his subordinates was in order. To be safe, Warq switched to a signing dialect that had been developed especially for the command crew, which would only be displayed and heard at their consoles, headsets, and earpieces, but not upon the wall screens. He addressed Davan first.

"What are your thoughts?" he signed to his science officer. "Some sort of misperception of reality whose distortion is a result of the transport process?"

"It's hard to say, Captain," signed Davan. "I've never heard anyone refer to a living being as disabled before. Lieutenant Iris?"

"I'm afraid I can only provide a basic translation of his words to our common galactic tongue. I have no idea what a disabled *person* is. Could he believe we're dead and perhaps apparitions? Therefore, we're no longer *enabled,* as in living, because we no longer exist on the mortal plane?"

"Interesting theory," signed the captain. "It would explain the alarm in his expression."

"Perhaps we should just smile politely. It might soothe his nerves," signed Iris. This got Herb's attention, who caught Lartha's eye. They signed an affirmative at Iris's instruction.

Wendell had no idea what was going on but felt a burst of disquiet as several of the alien beings suddenly grinned at him in unison. Davan's narrow mouth was concealed behind his trunk, but the Quargnan smiled warmly with his eyes.

Captain Warq approached Wendell, waving away the security officers. Warq pointed at Wendell's stick and indicated that the intruder hand over the curious weapon. Confused as to why a ship's captain would need a broom, Wendell still did as he was bid.

"Now, now, my good man," signed the captain. "Be not afraid. Every single one of us aboard the *S.S. SpoonZ* is alive. Not one of us is disabled. It seems you've had a traumatic journey. Might we get you something to eat, and perhaps a tonic to settle you?"

"*S.S.?*" asked Wendell. "But this isn't a steam ship. I should know. My grandfather was in the Navy!"

The captain signed a question to Iris.

"I don't know why his grandsire would have been immersed in a specific colour," she signed back.

"Colour?"

"Yes, Captain. Navy is some sort of deep blue, almost like a midnight sky. Also, our ship's ID seems to be translated in English as *Ess Ess Spoons*. I'm not sure of that significance, but I do find it intriguing that Earthers have discovered a way to power a ship using steam."

"I wonder if they're willing to share this tech with us," signed Herb. "Might make for an interesting backup."

Captain Warq nodded again and directed his attention back to Wendell. "The script that translates to *Ess Ess* for you stands for Science Ship. Can you please explain to me the cultural significance of why your grandsire was immersed in a pool of dark blue? And we are very much interested as to how you power your spaceships using only steam. I'm sure my chief engineer would be most enthusiastic to learn how you—"

Alas, the crew of the *S.S. SpoonZ* would not discover the secrets behind that particular technology, because before the captain could finish his question, Wendell's form distorted and disappeared from the command deck. NASA's fretting night shift had been scrambling for answers using their combined brainpower, but they finally managed to transport the janitor back home safely before the news outlets and social media geeks found out about this particular SNAFU.

"What happened?" Captain Warq demanded.

"It wasn't us, Captain," said Herb. "I believe it came from beyond our galaxy."

"Yes," signed Davan. "My readings also confirm this."

"Another anomaly?" asked Iris.

"Or something artificial," signed Davan.

"Nobody could 'port from galaxy to galaxy!" said Herb.

"Maybe the Nasa Earthers have harnessed the power of that natural anomaly to get to him," signed Davan. "Mind you, we registered nothing in this area except for readings that resemble a 'port spike." He studied his console to confirm. "In fact, it looks identical to a 'port spike, but one of honkingly massive intensity."

Herb fell silent as his brain flooded with theories. He ran a hand through his hair and fidgeted with a lock of it while pursing his lips as he thought. Finally, he said, "I wonder if those old-time Earthers tampered with the Keangal's intel all those years ago and since then, they've been building a kind of wormhole generator, so they could send all sorts of spies back and forth to learn about us." He paused and made a dissatisfied face. "Then again, this guy really seemed confused. As if we were brand new to him."

Lartha lowered her weapon, which she had raised as soon as the janitor had begun to go out of focus. "Huh. I almost feel sorry for the guy."

Herb and Davan turned their heads.

"What do you mean?" asked Iris.

"Well, it's obvious, isn't it? We're pretty sure 'porting is impossible this far away, so he's probably been disabled." She made a slashing gesture with her finger across her neck. "You know, for using their wormhole generator and sharing too much about their alternate engine tech."

"Wow," said Herb. "That's harsh. I share tech designs all the time in the Keangal."

"Yeah. That's why it's really sad. These Earthers might be like the Pirates for all we know. Poor guy."

A few of the crew bowed their heads.

"This is terrible," signed Davan. "Wendell didn't deserve to be disabled."

"One minute you're alive, then next..." Lartha snapped her fingers.

"It's mysterious indeed that the Earthers felt the need to do this to an innocent man. May he rest among the stars," signed the captain. "Now, I don't mean to dismiss the tragic nature of the moment, but I want observation reports from each of you about this incident. Lieutenant Iris, please send a message to our nearest Keangal outpost, asking if any similar intrusions might have occurred on other ships in the quadrant."

"Aye, Captain," said Iris. "Sending now."

"And Chief Lartha?"

"Captain?"

"I want Security on alert in case we find ourselves spontaneously housing any other guests from that planet."

"Way ahead of you, Captain. Already contacted Lieutenant Reez."

"Excellent."

"Captain, a small request," signed Davan. "May we log our incident reports after a quick breakfast? A few of us never had the chance to get to the Mess this morning."

Warq's expression grew slightly sterner as he signed, "You can enter your report *during* breakfast—and be prepared to be called back to the bridge without delay. There is no time to waste after an extragalactic experience such as this."

"Aye, Captain."

Iris, Lartha, and Herb also expressed their compliance. Iris, Davan, and Herb made sure they carried portable consoles that connected with their workstations. Lartha ordered her deputy security chief, who had just exited the lift, to join the other two guards who remained on the command deck, then she dashed into the lift with her colleagues. Clarence hovered by Iris's side. They all remained silent for a moment or two, mulling over this unusual start to their shift.

Finally, Davan turned to Iris and signed to his wristband interpreter, "Well, that was weird."

"Yeah."

He paused before continuing.

"So, do you think we guessed correctly? *Is* that what it means to be disabled?"

"Beats me," she signed with a shrug. "I guess we'll never know now."

These Legs Were Made for Stompin'

Chief of Security Leanna Lartha removed her newly refurbished legs and liners. She carefully cleaned and moisturized her skin, then reached for the silk tunic that lay upon her side table. Once she'd put the garment on, Lartha sat back in her worn and torn easy chair with a delighted sigh. Even though this particular piece of furniture should have been stamped with a *Condemned* notice, one would have had to have gone through her before gaining the slightest chance of recycling it. Lartha loved this chair and planned to keep it until the soft hide begged her to let it join the afterlife.

Once off her body, the prostheses trotted over to the door of her quarters and stood, facing it. Lartha smiled at them while pouring herself a drink.

The chime to her quarters rang out.

"Come in!"

The door whooshed open, revealing Lieutenant Iris.

"Evening, Lartha—whoops!" She stumbled at the sight of her shipmate's legs but recovered quickly enough.

Iris moved to one side. So did the legs. She moved to the other side, and the legs did too, blocking her entry.

"Um, a little help?"

Lartha took a swig. "Okay, girls, we like Lieutenant Iris. Let her through!"

The legs stood out of the way but pivoted in Iris's direction as she walked over to the security chief. Peeking over her shoulder, Iris saw them standing close by. The right one tapped its foot.

"Gee, and I thought Clarence was protective. Tonight xey recommended long underwear because xey know you like your cabin two degrees cooler than mine."

"Want a blankie to stave off the dangers of hypothermia?"

Iris sneered. "Don't you start!"

Lartha snickered. "And listen, about the refurbed gams? After watching over everyone all day, it's nice having my own personal bodyguards. That way, I can take a moment to tune out. Drink?"

"Something soft, please. The last time I tried your liquor, I woke up in your bed with my uniform on backwards."

"Truth. In the middle of a rant about conformity, you took off your tunic and put it back on that way. Insisted it made you feel empowered. How could I have denied you from taking such a stance against sameness? Solidarity, my sister! Whoo!"

Iris sneered.

"Anyway, you know you're always safe with me," continued Lartha. "All I did was place you on the mattress to sleep it off. No biggie. I've spent many nights a-snooze in this chair. Sometimes I prefer it to the bed."

"Well, tonight I want something mild. And fizzy."

"Yeah, I figured. That decanter over there, the one with the green liquid. It's mild and fizzy. You'll leave here as sober as you entered."

Iris spotted the bottle, whose base started out cylindrical, but halfway up, the glass had been blown into a swirling design, almost like icing on a fairy cake. "Thanks for thinking of me."

"No problem. Plus, tonight is an 'I wanna sleep in my own bed' night."

The door chimed again. Lartha's legs hopped at the sound and trotted over to the entranceway.

"Who is it?" barked Lartha into the comm fob attached to her robe.

A haughty voice replied, "It's Security Officer Bronwryck."

"O gleekin' rapture, this little turd," whispered Lartha to Iris. "In my head, I call him Beachfront. He comes from money and thinks he's entitled to promotion just because of his family."

"Promotion? He's only just joined us."

"Did I mention he's entitled?"

"Lieutenant Commander!" shouted Bronwryck.

Lartha guzzled her glass and belched. "Come in, Beach—Bronwryck." She pressed the remote by her chair to open the door.

Lieutenant Junior Grade Bronwryck stood outside, wearing the on-duty uniform of a black leatherette jacket and grey trousers. His sandy blond hair was cropped short everywhere but the fringe, and ocean-blue eyes played a leading role in the security officer's severe case of Resting Brat Face. He held his baby-blue chin far too high for someone of his rank. Iris took a disliking to him immediately. Bronwryck definitely didn't give off the same vibe as most of the crew, almost as if he fancied himself above everyone else. But she couldn't figure out exactly why that would be. It felt to her like more than just a wealth thing.

"I came to request shore leave," he said firmly.

Lartha poured herself another drink. "Request denied."

Bronwryck's chest puffed like a flotation device. "What?! Why?"

"Because request denied." Lartha smiled, showing as many teeth as she could. "Anything else?"

He huffed and took a step inside her quarters. Lartha's prostheses blocked his path. Just as Iris had tried before, Bronwryck moved from side to side, with no luck.

"Get out of my way!" he shouted.

The legs faced each other, toe to toe, then turned back to Bronwryck. Annoyed, he bent down and reached out to move them from his path.

"No, Bronwryck, don't!" cried Iris.

Too late. The air fled his lungs as he crumpled to the floor, clutching his upper-class family jewels.

Lartha shook her head in amazement. "You really gotta hand it to Herbie and his gadgets-smarts. He's good people."

Iris knelt beside Bronwryck and stroked his shoulder, feeling a little sorry for his situation. "These legs were designed with several anti-theft features. Although, this response seems to be one of their favourites when it comes to people who possess scrotums."

The junior security officer coughed his reply. Iris gently helped him to his feet.

Lartha took another sip of her drink.

Bronwryck glared at her.

She smiled again, but with fewer teeth on display. "So tell me, Bronwryck. I bet you didn't think I overheard that remark the other day, huh?"

He seemed perplexed. "What remark?"

"Oh y'know, the one about how a security chief should 'at least have legs that function properly'?"

His eyes went wide, and the colour drained from his blue cheeks, turning them almost grey.

Lartha emptied her glass again. "Well, as you can plainly deduce, young soul, my legs are in perfect working order." She grinned mischievously. "Wouldn't you agree?"

It came out with barely any volume: "Yes, Lieutenant Commander."

"Sorry? Didn't catch that. How about you sign it to me?"

Bronwryck clumsily repeated what he'd said orally, using his hands.

"A bit shaky, son," signed Lartha. "You're rusty. Get on board with IGSL, lose the superiority complex, and earn your gleekin' way into getting shore leave. Do I make myself clear?"

"Yes," he signed.

"Yes, what?" she signed.

"Yes, Lieutenant Commander."

"Good," she signed. "Now, get out."

He nodded and turned to leave, yelping when Right Leg moved to kick him again. Fortunately, Bronwryck bolted away in the nick of time.

Iris watched him leave and then looked back at Lartha with her mouth agape.

"What?" said Lartha.

"Was that absolutely necessary?"

The security chief snickered. "Oh, he'll live. It's not like I hadn't warned the entire team about my new legs. Beachfront just thought he could overtake them because he's under the impression he's invincible." She covered her hand to stifle another belch. "But in my experience, sometimes one has to be kicked in the parts in order to wake up."

Iris made a face. "I don't understand your methods at all."

"Yeah, I know. But that's why you're you, and I'm me. Here," Lartha said, holding up the swirly decanter. "Have some more fizzy green stuff. We'll put on a vid. Something with a hot romantic lead."

"Bleh."

"Ugh, fine, a documentary."

"Documentaries are my favourite!" Iris parked her bottom on the bed as the video of her choice was projected onto a wall in Lartha's room.

After only a minute did the security chief vow to herself to perhaps never suggest they watch something together again. Which she knew was an oath she wouldn't keep because she enjoyed her friend's company. *Still... steamy stuff to the rescue, the moment Iris goes back to her quarters.*

A few days later, Lartha and her team had been teleported to Haven, an ironic name for a barren moon mostly consisting of dark rock. However, Haven possessed minerals and crystals that the engineers of the *S.S. SpoonZ* could use to optimize the tech on their ship. Herb had been in charge of amassing a list of the most essential elements, along with a thorough description of each of their properties and cross-references about their usefulness. When Lartha had received this scientific tome, she'd asked Herb for the "I have to pee, tell me quickly" list. This had produced a deep sigh but also a customized spreadsheet for her use. Nevertheless, Herb had vehemently urged Lartha to study the full document.

What her team really needed to focus on at present were the Caves of Rimn, and if an away team would be safe doing excavations there.

Leading the way, Lartha moved gingerly on the craggy surface of one of the largest caves; her left prosthesis remained unclothed but for a short, flat boot.

Lieutenant Reez cursed under his breath, just behind her.

"You know I've got the ears of a Glazabird, buddy. I can hear a bug scratching its butt," said Lartha.

Reez swore louder this time.

Lartha stifled a laugh.

"Well," said Reez with a cocky grin, "since I can't hide anything from you, might as well go full volume." His attention turned to the feeble glow of his torch, which barely illuminated his deep brown features. Narrow black and grey braids rested upon his brow. "Gleek, these things are useless in here. It's like the darkness is swallowing us whole."

Lartha smirked that smirk of hers. "Not for long, old buddy. Watch this!"

He looked up. "Wait... Watch what?"

"Left," she barked, "light up my life!"

Her left leg beamed so brightly, the entire security team cried out, covering their eyes.

Lartha held a hand over her own eyes. Thankfully, the standard-issue purple gloves of Security could automatically enable light-shielding mode for such occurrences. She said to her prosthesis, "Okay, girl, let's tone 'er down to 70% intensity."

Left obeyed, and the relieved officers eventually adjusted to their surroundings once again.

Reez scratched his bristly silver beard in wonderment. The cave walls glistened like cut obsidian, and a myriad of crystals shone through the black stone like stars in the sky. Except there almost seemed to be every colour of the spectrum blinking down at them.

"I believe this is what's known as the motherlode," he said.

"Yup, we've hit pay dirt," agreed Lartha. "My scanner is going off the charts here. Hey, Right, you sensing what I'm seeing?"

Her right leg quietly whirred and fed data back to her forearm scanner. Lartha nodded, pleased with the results.

"You picked up way more than I did, girl. Proud of ya."

"What did she pick up?" asked Reez, who, like everyone, accepted the pronouns of Lartha's legs, as was the custom regarding any sentient entity, whether alive in the "standard" way or through AI.

"Not much. About a thousand sleeping ground bats, a hundred metres in."

Reez was not amused. "You know, there's such a thing as being too laid back, huh, Boss Lady?"

"Bah, it's a piece of cake."

"Piece of cake. Ground bats. Each about four metres tall with a sixteen-metre wingspan."

"Yup."

"And venom that could melt the side of our hull."

"Yup."

"So, we're not worrying, because..."

"We're gonna be super quiet."

Before Reez could get another word in, Lartha began to sign.

"Signing and thinking only. Screens on."

Reez relayed the message to their team. Everyone pushed down their protective face shields from their helmets, which also displayed messages for them to read. Sensors on an interior helmet band activated thought transmissions. A vital part of graduating advanced security training was that every cadet learned to project specific thoughts to their team. In a situation like this, it could mean their very survival.

Lieutenant Reez tapped her shoulder, and the security chief turned to face him.

"We need to get back," he signed. "There's no way we can give the all-clear for an away team."

"It's not a problem," she signed back. "Not as long as I stay here!"

What do you mean? he projected.

Watch this!

Another, 'Watch this?'

She winked at him, then touched a spot on her right leg and tapped her fingers in a certain pattern, messaging something directly to the prothesis.

A rumbling rang throughout the cave along with a series of high-pitched shrieks.

One officer shouted in panic: "They're awake! Charging right at us!"

Lartha cursed under—then over—her breath. *Stay in place!* she commanded.

But Chief! implored the security officer.

STAY IN PLACE! Lartha projected to the entire team.

In no time, it felt like the colossal cave itself would collapse from the thunderous vibrations of the trampling beasts. Reez gave the order for weapons up. The officers followed through in perfect synchronicity.

Lartha remained in front, weapon at her side, free hand on her hip.

Chief! projected Reez, also using the shorthand for security chief. *Weapons up!* He was grateful for the thought-tech. His voice would have been swallowed by the roaring of the oncoming stampede.

Lartha placed her weapon by a stalagmite and leaned against the rock formation.

LEANNA! screeched Reez into her mind.

The creatures were visible now, the black hairless skin of their bodies and wings glistening, mouths frothing, and yellow eyes glaring. They ran so close to each other, they resembled one massive being known as the Bat King, ready to dissolve the trespassers and drink their remains.

The leader of the pack snarled at Lartha and lunged right for her.

She pointed to her tattoo: *Just try it!*

Reez aimed his weapon.

The ground bat yelped as it bounced backwards. Reez's mouth hung open. He hadn't fired. Neither had anyone else.

Then, one by one, ground bats appeared to ricochet from something—hard. Each one fell against the other, until they formed a huddled whimpering mess.

Lartha commanded everyone to stand down.

Reez stood by her side now, watching the pack leader try several more times to break through the invisible barrier, before giving up altogether.

"So," he said. "Projective transparent shielding?"

"Projective transparent shielding," said Lartha. "Herbie set up the feature in my right leg."

"Huh. Cool."

"Now, go tell the away team they can 'port down here."

"Aye, aye, Boss Lady."

"Call me that one more time, buddy."

"Ah yes, I remember. You're a woman but no lady."

He smiled in that dashing way that went right to her bits. She shook it off and continued to face the tunnel where the ground bats clumsily disassembled into their retreat.

"Good girl," she said to Right.

Left blinked on and off.

"You're still a good girl, too, Left."

The leg continued to shine brightly while the security crew greeted the away team.

The ruckus coming from within the training room could have theoretically burst the woofers in an amplifier stack. Several of the newest members of Security were having at each other in sparring matches, vying for who was the best among them.

So far, Lieutenant Bronwryck was losing this latest fight... badly. Each punch felt like a belt straight to his ego, which hadn't been in great shape these days. He'd barely recovered from the humiliation of being taken down by Lartha's legs. And according to the sensitivity session he'd been forced to attend, touching someone's assistive tech required the same consent as touching a biologically living sentient. Therefore, the prostheses had acted in their own defense and were not culpable for their reaction.

He shuddered. His parents had owned canines that had behaved with less ferocity when guarding the manor. A small part of Bronwryck, very deeply buried, sort of perhaps maybe kinda felt an inkling of admiration for the legs' fighting spirit. But mostly he felt terrified in their presence.

"Duck!" shouted a colleague.

Bronwryck managed to save his jaw in the nick of time. Only to realize the move was meant to dupe him, and he ended up kissing the mat with his entire face after receiving a sucker punch to the gut.

"Ooof..."

"Get up, Bronwryck!" shouted another voice.

"I think I'll stay here. Here is... much better," he mumbled, grateful he hadn't eaten in a while.

"Whoop, whoop!" cried Tirlock, checking her tablet. "Bronwryck is down, Hannes is the winner of this round and moves up the Badass Scale." A door opened while her face was focused on the screen. "It's still anyone's guess who will be crowned our leader." She scribbled something, then continued. "Okay, let's see who's up next."

"I'll give it a go," said the latest person to enter the training area.

Lieutenant Tirlock's fingers clenched her tablet, whitening at the knuckles, and she bit her lip. Bronwryck attempted to crawl to the furthest spot from the entrance. Lieutenant Hannes wrung their forest-green fingers.

Lartha stood akimbo. "I've always been curious where I fit on the Badass Scale. Glad you folks set this up." She cast her gaze at the security officer holding the scoring tablet. "Your idea, Tirlock?"

"Definitely wasn't mine," Bronwryck said, then groaned on the floor, rubbing his stomach.

Lartha strolled nonchalantly among the young security officers, weaving through them, taking her time to assess the scene before speaking further.

"So, what is all this exactly?" she said with a naïve tone to her voice that not one newbie considered genuine. Nobody replied to her question either.

"Wow. Silence," Lartha added. "When I was outside in the corridor, I couldn't believe how much racket made its way through what are supposed to be soundproof doors. Guess I'll have to send a service request to Engineering."

She marched over to Lieutenant Tirlock, whose eyes seemed larger than ever before.

"Tirlock," said Lartha.

"Yes, Chief," she croaked.

"Explain."

"Um, well, we just thought it would be, like, we wanted to see which one of us was the toughest. You know, the best. So, we're sparring to determine who are the weak links and who aren't."

Lartha nodded, then swept her gaze over the entire group. "Interesting, this," she said. "A contest to determine who reigns as top among you, all based on who can pummel each other in a fight. Do I have the gist?"

"Yes, Chief," said Tirlock.

Lartha addressed the rest of the group, "And you all thought this was a good idea, an effective measure to find the cream of the crop?"

Once again, no reply.

"You chose this," continued Lartha, "instead of a team-building exercise to find out how well you work together in adverse conditions or circumstances." She began to pace as she talked. "You know, I've been in Security since I was a young adult, which to you might seem like millennia ago, and hey, maybe I am a little bit old school. During my training, we felt it was less important to discover who among us was the most skilled and more important to figure out how our skills fit together, so we would be an undefeatable group."

She again stared at each face, which one by one cowed before her. Lartha shook her head.

"Understand this: I can't keep this ship secure all by myself. I can't even lead Security alone. That's why I have Deputy Security

Chief Lieutenant Reez. And he and I can't run things by ourselves either. That's why we need teams of guards, each with their own strengths, so we can be cohesive, tight."

No one even uttered a syllable as a retort.

Lartha shrugged her shoulders, then removed her jacket.

"But, well, hey, if you want to find out who is the Ultimate Potentate of Badassery"—she removed her shirt, revealing a black sports tank—"I guess I'll play, too. I mean, we can't stop here! With nobody knowing for sure who's the best? Maybe we can sweeten the pot, while we're at it."

The junior security officers responded with a collection of slumped postures, sighs, and gulps.

"Great. Now give me ten more!"

"Gleek! Just how much crap did I dump on you in a past life?"

"C'mon... the unrelenting Leanna Lartha can't possibly be pooching out on me now!"

"You PT folks are vile, you know that?"

"Oh, my feelings. I said ten more—and make 'em fearsome!"

Lartha growled as her physical therapist pushed the controls to raise the seating bar to where Lartha could reach the top bar with both hands. Once she got a grip, the seat was lowered.

"You really aren't a nice person, Tildy," said Lartha.

"Boo hoo. Gimme these last ten, then we'll work on those new core exercises."

As Lartha grunted with each pull-up, her prostheses stood at the far corner of the gym, under strict orders not to do any harm to Tilda Berch, no matter how much pain the security chief seemed to be in. Lartha had explained to them that this was all part of keeping her strong and limber.

"Doing, great! Five more!"

"I hate you."

"I know."

But Lartha completed the set... out of spite. Tilda knew it, too. She brought up the seat for her patient.

"What's gotten into you today?" asked the physical therapist.

"Mostly bruises," said Lartha. "Participated in a few sparring matches last night."

"The day before therapy?"

"Couldn't resist."

"How much did you win?"

Lartha's mouth twitched. "Win? It was a friendly sport. Nothing more than drills, really."

"Uh-huh. How much?"

The security officer's eyes sparkled. "Enough to go on a spree next shore leave."

"You know gambling is forbidden on this ship," said Tilda, in *that* tone.

"Yup. But it wasn't gambling."

"What was it then?"

"Teaching underlings life lessons."

"You're kidding."

"And as we all know, life lessons come with a price!"

Tilda rolled her eyes. "Did you fight with your refurbished legs on or without?"

"Yes."

The PT burst out laughing. "Well done."

Lartha preened.

"Fair enough," said Tilda. "Now I expect two more reps of ten, killer."

"Aw, why?"

"Consider it a bribe for me not telling the captain about your life coaching."

"Wench," muttered Lartha.

"And I know you've got it in you." Tilda raised the seat again. "You were absolutely faking that those last five were difficult. I didn't meet you only yesterday."

"Ugh, fine."

"Trying to cut therapy short, huh? Gonna meet someone?"

Lartha grabbed hold of the bar. "Who, me? Why, I'm sure I don't know what you mean." She mimicked the narrator's "polished" accent from that documentary Iris had made her watch.

"Mm-hm," said Tilda. "What's his name?"

"Shaddup."

Lartha pulled herself up with ease.

At the entrance to the Clubhouse—what everyone called the ship's massive social lounge—stood an oblong metallic box. Lartha smiled at it.

"Hey, Herbie."

"Hey."

"Just hanging out?"

"Well, I thought I'd stop by to see who's here this evening."

Lartha glanced about the place. To her left, barkeeps served drinks at The Wave, named for its curvy turquoise-marbelite countertop. At the other side of the Clubhouse, the band played while singers signed and sang to a slow jam. Lots of bodies swayed, pressed together on the dance floor. She couldn't wait to be one of them.

Her eye caught hold of a steel-blue arm waving in her direction. She chuckled and waved back.

"There he is," said Lartha.

Herb cleared his throat. "Oh? Who?"

Lartha slowly tilted her head in his direction. "Really?"

Herb cleared his throat again. "I… well, it's an honest question."

"Herbie, unbox for a sec."

"Okay." The holo image dissolved, revealing the blushing engineer.

"You know," said Lartha, "Davan is probably the friendliest guy I've ever met. Just hop over there and chat him up. It'll be fine."

Herb held his breath and peered over to where Davan still stood. The Quargnan signed, "Everything good?"

"Sign 'yes,'" muttered Lartha.

Herb signed the affirmative.

"There ya go!" said Lartha. "Now march over there and get your man."

He froze. "Um… yeah. Maybe tomorrow. I think I'll feel better heading back to my quarters for now." Herb signed to Davan, "Sorry, got to run," and darted out the room.

Davan slumped his shoulders.

Aw, shame, thought Lartha, then signed to Davan, "He's okay. Just needs some quiet. He'll try again tomorrow night."

"I understand, thanks," signed Davan, who sat back down at the booth with his friends.

Oh well, nothing I can do about that now. It's time I roll out my own nocturnal activities! She sauntered inside the Clubhouse on tall glittery violet boots. Left's boot had circles of various sizes punched out of the faux leather, and soft beams of alternating colour pulsed in perfect rhythm with the beat of the current song. Lartha's sparkling silver jumpsuit had a cowl neckline that plunged to reveal just enough muscular cleavage to "tantalize, not advertise." (One of her infamous expressions.) Her hair spilled over her left shoulder like a magenta waterfall.

Someone bumped into her as she headed towards a stool by The Wave.

"Watch it!" she barked without looking to see who it was.

"Sorry, Boss Lady."

She stopped in her tracks and turned round. Reez was all decked out in a light grey tunic with a white shirt peeking out from the front slit, loose grey trousers, and pointy black shoes.

"Hey, old timer," she said.

He beamed at her, then pretended to be miffed. "If that's another crack about my growing a beard, I'll have you know this silver beauty runs in my family. We wear it with pride."

"I'd expect nothing less than pride from you. You're not exactly the type who'd have a confidence deficit."

Reez gestured with his hands. "This is coming from *you*?"

She laughed.

"And we're the same age, remember?" he added.

"We are? I guess I might have forgotten since you started your grandpa-chic phase."

"Ageist."

"Not at all. Grandpas are great. I loved mine. Anyway, you know you clean up well," Lartha said. "But then again, you always did."

He smiled handsomely. "Same with you. Who's the lucky guy?"

"Rivers. From Medical. Know him?"

Reez inhaled. "Yeah. I might."

Lartha squinted. "What?"

"Tell me it's nothing serious."

She scoffed. "When am I ever serious about men?"

Reez's smile grew wide.

"Yeah, *you* don't get to answer that, buddy," said Lartha. "My mistake for asking in the first place."

"All I'm going to say is that he's over there." Reez pointed to the dance floor, where two people seemed to be on a mission to defy physics by attempting to occupy the same space.

"Well, gleek," said Lartha. "That's what I get for earning detention in physical therapy."

"You look amazing, though. Way too good for him, anyway."

"Hm."

Reez put his hand on her arm, gently, so as not to provoke her legs into an act of war.

"Buy you a drink?" he said.

She stared at him while having a short ponder. *No, I can't*, she thought. *Never good to crap where you eat. Besides, this history shouldn't repeat itself.* Before she could answer, a young officer in a little black dress came squealing into view, making a beeline for Reez, and threw her arms around his neck for an enthusiastic snog. Her poofy ginger curls obscured his face.

"Hi, honey!" she said, when she finally let him loose.

"Hey, babe," said Reez. He smiled awkwardly at Lartha. "Um, Lieutenant Tessa, this is Lieutenant Commander Lartha."

"Tessa," said Lartha with a smile and nod.

"WOW! It's so great to meet you! Reez has told me so much about the legendary Lartha!" Her bubbly expression fell from her face the moment she realized what she'd blurted. "Oh, my goodness, I apologize! I didn't mean any disrespect"—she stood at attention and saluted—"Lieutenant Commander."

"Bah, hey, we're in the Clubhouse. No ceremony needed."

"Great!" chirped the lieutenant as if her indiscretion had never happened. She clutched onto Reez's arm and grinned. "May I just say your prostheses are awesome?"

Lartha giggle-snorted. "You may!"

"I love that you come with your own club lights!"

Reez coughed. "Uh, babe, that's not being sensitive."

Tessa's eyes went wide again. "I'm so sorry!"

"Why? It's true!" said Lartha with a casual chuckle. "They're not overly bright, the lights never strobe, the beams cast downward, and Left can tell if they bother someone, so they'll switch off in that case."

"Oooo!"

"Listen, um, can we still buy you that drink?" asked Reez.

"Silly Reezie. You know all drinks are free," said Tessa.

Reez and Lartha exchanged a look.

"What?" asked Tessa.

"You know, thanks, but I'll pass," said Lartha. "You kids have a good night." She turned and walked away without waiting for a response. *Damn, I could have used a shot, too.*

Lartha found herself in a unique place of indecisiveness. Should she stay or go back to her quarters? Her muscles and connective tissues ached something fierce, but she also felt the need to be among other people. They typically energized her. In the distance, she could still see Doctor Boy trying to perform a tonsillectomy on his dance partner—with his tongue. She rolled her eyes. *Yeah. Maybe I'll just go.*

She barely took three full steps when her eardrums got pounded by wildly excited voices hailing from behind.

"CHIEF! CHIEF!"

Lartha pivoted to the sound and found three of her underlings thrilled to bits at the sight of her.

"Officers," she said with a nod.

"OMERGERKS! YOU LOOK FANTASTIC!" they shouted together.

Yowch... synchronized shrieking much? "Thanks, folks, but let's take it down a bit. No need to holler."

Unaffected by the gentle rebuke, one boingy brunette grabbed one arm while a green-haired beauty grabbed the other. The last young woman, with hair spiralling in a sapphire updo, led the way.

"Whoa, where are we going, team?" asked Lartha.

"We just can't have you standing alone on the sidelines," said the brunette. "Let's get on the floor and do some stompin'!"

Lartha snickered. "I'm in!"

Following her troupe, she spotted the slurpy duo that included the guy who'd found it perfectly acceptable not to have contacted her to ask why she was late, but instead, had moved onto the next closest thing. Lartha stopped just before them. *Yeah, I just gotta.* She and her legs danced over and hip-bumped right into Rivers.

After he'd issued a startled expletive, being quite pissed at the interruption, the medical officer's mouth hung open at the sight of Lartha. His eyes immediately swept over her face and body while revealing more than a hint of regret.

"Later, loser," she said, then joined her subordinates and danced up a storm to the raving beat.

EPISODE 3:
Herbie Tries to Flirt

While we understand that on long-term missions such as these, relationships between crew members can occur, there are policies we must enforce to ensure the safety and wellness of the parties involved.

1. It is not encouraged for people of different ranks to become involved, as there could be a presumptive power imbalance. If anyone feels pressured or coerced in any manner, they can report unwanted advances to Crew Relations, who will ensure confidentiality. However, if there is a consensual pairing, then this must also be disclosed to Crew Relations, to assess if there might need to be a change in supervision of the partner with the subordinate rank. Again, this is for the protection...

Lieutenant Commander Horatio Herbert focused intently on the screen before him, in his private room.

"Morning Herb!" It was Iris's voice.

"Morning!"

"Heading to the Mess?"

"Nah, already been."

"Okay! Catch you later then."

"Yeah, cheers."

Again, this is for the protection of the parties involved and to maintain a positive working atmosphere in...

"S'up, Herbie?"

"Hey, Lartha."

"What's going on in there?"

"Nothing. Just reading."

"You coming to the Clubhouse later? Been a couple of weeks since I've seen you there."

"I dunno. Maybe."

"Well, message me if you do, okay?"

"Yeah."

"See ya 'round!"

"Bye."

...a positive working attitude in your divisions, and to quell any rumours of favouritism.

2. Should the involved parties get to a stage where they would like to engage in a ceremonial custom of betrothing or marriage or official partnership status, the captain has full legal rights to perform or grant...

Two hands clapped a pattern to grab Herb's attention. The engineer jumped and stared at the vision standing in the tall grasses within his private room.

"Morning, Herb!" signed Davan.

"Morning, Commander."

Davan blinked, then his eyes smiled. "Formal today, aren't we?"

"Sorry... just reading."

"Anything good?"

"Um..."

"Skip to the saucy parts." Davan's shoulders bounced up and down and a honking sound exited his trunk as he laughed.

Herb did his best to laugh too. It didn't really work, though. He could tell by the sudden switch in Davan's expression.

"Are you all right?"

"Yeah. Just reading an important thing, so... and... um, could you maybe not clap next time? I kind of get a visceral response to clapping."

The commander's expression showed remorse. "Oh, I'm very sorry. I should have known better. And to disturb you when you're researching, too. If I played a soft musical scale with my trunk, would that be better?"

"I think so. We can try it sometime."

"Great! Well, I won't take up any more of your time. Hope you can make it to the Clubhouse later. Have a good day... Mr. Herbert."

Davan punctuated his statement with a friendly wink. Herb had always felt uncomfortable being called by his rank, so Captain Warq had agreed that Herb would be formally addressed only in this manner.

He knew Davan used it now as part of his playfulness. Herb's breath caught in his throat as he gazed back at him. "Bye."

As Davan walked away, Herb's private room dissolved. He leaned against the wall of the corridor, tablet in hand, and sighed.

...the captain has legal rights to perform over a hundred types of civil ceremonies, but arrangements can be made to procure the services of religious leaders, if given 3–6 weeks advance notice. Even so, we cannot guarantee the availability of the religious overseer of your choice, so we would have to discuss postponement or an interim civil solution.

Herb raised his head and stared sadly into nowhere.

"We've triggered a proximity trap near a Piranha Brigade School!" said Lieutenant Udana of the Navigation duo, listening to the readout while his fingers tapped the elevated symbols on their console's keypad. He initiated the command to display the findings on the viewscreen and read aloud in headsets on the bridge and in Engineering.

"In this system? I thought the Brigade didn't come out this far!" said Iris.

"School imminent!" signed Lieutenant Renley, the other member of the Navigation duo.

"Go to Alert Status 5," signed Captain Warq. "We cannot stand against a School; we must flee immediately."

"Captain, aft engines are failing!" signed Commander Davan.

"Copy that." Warq tapped the comm pad on his chair to contact Engineering and signed, "Mr. Herbert, we need those engines!"

"Aye, Captain," said Herb. "We're on it. Transferring power from the forward shields."

A single shot fired across the bow. Something the Brigade often did, like a feline playing with its food before the final kill.

"We need forward shields, too, Mr. Herbert!" signed Warq.

"Forward shields holding at 50% efficacy. Suggest evasive manoeuvring in the meantime to avoid more direct hits."

Captain Warq read the words projected from his visor and tried not to shake his head. "Yes, thank you for that advice, Mr. Herbert. I'll make sure to remind Navigation."

Lieutenants Renley and Udana simultaneously inhaled when reading and hearing these words at their consoles. They thought-projected to each other, *Good luck*, and *We got this*.

"Um... right," said Herb, appearing onscreen. "Sorry, Captain," he signed.

"When can we jump to lightspeed?"

"Redundant systems should be online. I'll verify."

"Quickly, Mr. Herbert. We've not much time in our present state."

"Acknowledged, Captain. Herbert out." Herb ran his hands through his long, wayward bangs as he tried to solve three problems in his mind at once.

Lieutenant Sheena darted up to him. "Sir, the ship's got no jump."

Herb frowned. "That's impossible. What about the redundant system?"

"Dead as a doornail."

Herb felt his hackles rise as he ran towards the hyper-jump core. "You know I can't stand it when you say these flippant expressions instead of giving me data I can actually use."

"Right, sorry," said Sheena, following closely behind. "There's a break in continuity across the main circuit of the drive."

"What about the bypass circuits?"

"Nothing happening there as well. Like it's open circuit season."

"That doesn't make any sense. Checks across the bypass cleared only a few hours ago. We should have had power to reroute to secondary systems. Enough to initiate at least one jump, so we could buy time for further repairs."

The ship shook from the hit it took. Lieutenant Sheena slammed into Herb's back, and he rammed into a console desktop.

"Ow!"

"Ugh," said Sheena, righting herself. "Sorry, sir!"

"It's fine, Lieutenant," said Herb, clutching his gut. It hurt like a devil, but there was no time for self-inspection. He initiated commands at the console to give him access to the hyper-jump core.

Another blast walloped the ship. Herb went flying into the core tunnel, banging his head along the way.

"I told them evasive manoeuvres!" he cried, rubbing his scalp. "Does this seem evasive to you?"

"No, sir," said Sheena, clutching onto the side of a console for dear life.

Herb felt distinctly dizzy. And whirly. Although he wondered if dizzy and whirly could be the same thing. *No, vertigo is entirely different from dizziness.* The latter was more head-spinny and the former more as if the entire ship was rotating like a top. Then again, he wasn't sure if it was about 43% of Column A and 57% of Column B. Or maybe 45% and 55%. *No time to waste on percentages, though. Focus!*

His aching stomach careened into the unwelcome realm of queasiness. *No time for that either. Fix ship first, fall down after.*

It wasn't easy to concentrate in the swirly reality his vision presented, but Herb managed to blink his way towards the main system of the jump core and pulled out his scanner.

"Whatcha got, sir?" asked Sheena.

Herb clenched his teeth. "Nothing. Dead as a doornail."

Sheena appeared rather pleased with herself.

"Right," he said. "Get me some Elbaite."

"What? Elbaite?"

"Yeah, the away team collected some on Haven."

"Sir, I understand it's pyroelectric and piezoelectric, but Elbaite's too brittle and, frankly, too useless for jump-core tech."

"Not the one on Haven. The Mining League has classified minerals similar to these as Elbaite, but I think what was brought to us is something else entirely. Its properties seem far superior than typical expectations. It will work with the components of the core to give us the power needed for jumps, as long as we recalibrate the control panel to maintain stability and prevent surges. We want to make sure it offers us the precision required for the core drive. And it's important not to apply too much heat through this particular crystal. Or, you know, zap-boom." Herb closed his eyes and rubbed his head for a moment, then tapped a console display and an application window floated in mid-air before them. He adjusted several settings for the core while Sheena observed.

"How do you know all this?" she asked.

"I tested it myself during an experiment. That's how I shorted all the modules in my quarters."

"I thought you told Engineering it was a power source malfunction."

Herb turned to face her. "How was that *not* a power source malfunction?"

She paused, pursing her lips. "Right. I'll get the pretend Elbaite. Just one thing, sir?"

"What?"

"Try not to fry the entire ship?"

"Let's suspend the snark until after we resolve this, Lieutenant."

"Yes, sir."

"Mr. Herbert!" the interpreted voice of the captain reverberated through his skull. Herb just managed not to vomit.

Hours later, Herb awoke in a strange bed, then closed his eyes again, trying to think through the brain fog.

"Well, Lieutenant Commander," said an unfamiliar voice. "You have yourself a helluva concussion."

Herb tried to sit up and groaned. "Your bedside manner and medical acuity are mind-boggling, Doctor." The pain raged in his head and his abdomen. "Oof. What's going on with my stomach?"

"Just some bruising. Nothing serious."

"Was the nausea also from the concussion?"

"Yes, a common symptom during a head-smashing," said Doctor Rivers. "You'll be fine, but we're keeping you overnight for observation."

Herb scowled. "That's not acceptable. I have things to do."

"Well, you're not getting clearance to return to duty without my permission, Lieutenant Commander, so here you'll stay." Rivers flicked his wavy auburn fringe in defiance and left without further comment, to tend to other patients.

Herb cursed under his breath and tried to figure out how he would manage his time confined to Medical. His fingers felt fidgety, so he fished through his pockets for something to ease them. All he could find was a piece of so-called Elbaite that had been too small for their repair needs. He fiddled with the reddish-pink stone. The hue appealed to him, and Herb liked how it felt against his skin as he ran it between his fingers.

However, the noise coming from various medical consoles and utterances from other patients were beginning to irritate him. He fiddled with the stone some more. These weren't the familiar sounds of the engine room or the stations he occupied in Engineering, which Herb had mostly tolerated or could tune out with assistive tech. His private room activator had been removed because it interfered with the medical devices in sick bay. He tried covering his ears, but the pressure against them made him even more uncomfortable. It was difficult to feel at ease. Every module had their own set of blips and beeps and whirs, which all intersected or bounced off each other. Also, the timber of the voice of the patient two beds down reverberated into his sternum. Herb tried diaphragmatic breathing in an attempt to focus on something else.

It wasn't working.

He rubbed the stone faster.

Get me out of here! I need to get out!

His breath quickened, and his heart rate began to soar.

A nurse hurried over. "Lieutenant Commander? Are you all right?"

"Need... to... leave... now."

"I'm sorry, sir, but we must keep you here for observ—"

"No! I need to get out of here!"

"But sir—"

"*NOW!*"

Another friendlier face suddenly appeared into view, and a quiet melody emanating from his trunk called the nurse to face him. When she did, Davan signed, "He needs quiet. Very important."

Herb's lips parted in surprise.

Davan looked down at him. "Hi, there! Heard you got hurt. Brought some provisions!"

"Thank you," Herb signed.

"You're welcome!" From a satchel, Davan pulled out a tablet. "Loaded it with tech journals. New ones, too! I checked the logs. You haven't read these."

Herb smiled.

The commander reached in again and pulled out two earpieces. "I spoke about you with Fran, who's been working with Wellness and Tech's R&D. These are not like the over-the-head ones that bothered you so much. No painful pressure on the ears or top of your skull," he signed. "You can also set them to float by your ears if you don't want to insert them. Would you like to try?"

Herb nodded and decided to put them in, and Davan signed instructions about how to enable them. Just like that, the irritating sounds of the room vanished.

"Good?" signed Davan.

"Amazing!" signed Herb, dropping the object in his left hand.

"What's that?" Davan pointed to the stone on the blanket.

"This?" Herb held up the Elbaite.

"Yes."

"It's what powered up our hyper-jump core."

"Nice! I like the colour."

Herb just stared.

"Okay," signed Davan. "I'll let you rest. See you tomorrow morning before duty?"

"Yes," Herb signed. "Thank you again."

"Anytime for the man who saved our ship!" Davan patted Herb's hand before leaving.

Herb gently cupped the stone between his palms while watching Davan exit Medical.

When conversing with a potential partner, it helps to express an interest in their interests. In conversation, recommend a book or a vid about a topic or genre they might enjoy. Or, invite them to an outing where such topics can be discussed. Remember to listen often and not dominate the conversation.

Herb chewed his lips. *What if someone asks me about a topic I like? How am I not supposed to dominate the conversation? "Thanks for asking, honey. Now brace yourself for a two-hour presentation with slides and charts. Also, here are some sandwiches, so your blood sugar doesn't dip too low. Feel free to ask questions. I'd like for this session to feel interactive. Please let me know when you have to pee!"*

"Morning, Herb!" said Iris's voice.

"Hi, you."

"Going to the Mess?"

"Um... okay. Sure." The metallic box dissolved.

Iris's face showed her surprise. "Great! It'll be nice to have you join us!"

"Us?"

"Yeah, myself and—hey. Where did he go?"

"Who?"

Davan jogged around the corner, signing, "Sorry! Got sidetracked!"

"You mean I was talking to myself for how long?" asked Iris.

"Not too long," he signed. "Honest!"

"Serves me right for not signing to you. I tend to look straight ahead when I'm walking and talking aloud."

He bowed contritely, then stood erect. "Again, so sorry, Princess. I will accept the smiting of your choice."

"You doink."

Herb steeled himself and asked Davan, "What was it that piqued your interest?"

"Ah! Someone posted they're virtually teaching a *Snarr-cha* class, starting next week."

"What's that?" asked Iris.

"It's like a martial art," signed Davan. "Very big in the system where I come from. It's been too long since I sparred, so it wouldn't hurt to take a refresher class first. Wanna come with me?"

Iris shook her head. "I'm a lover, not a fighter." She paused. "Actually, I'm not really a lover either!"

Davan snort-laughed. "But you're the fairest in the land!"

She stuck out her tongue at him.

"You know," she signed, "you can ask Lartha! I'm sure she'd enjoy learning another way to beat someone senseless."

He scratched his trunk while thinking things through.

Herb cleared his throat. "Or, you know..."

Davan looked at him.

"Uh... maybe... I... can join you?"

The Quargnan's eyes brightened. "I would love that!"

Iris seemed pleasantly surprised. "Well, good for you, Herb! I bet you fellows will have a great time."

"Yeah. Actually, for now, I think I'll just grab a snack from the kitchenette near the 'Port Parlour, then go and be good at stuff," signed Herb.

"Which I'm sure you can do in your sleep," signed Davan warmly.

"Thanks. I am rather productive when sleeping."

Davan honk-laughed.

Herb bashfully signed, "See you later."

"Bye!" signed Davan.

"Have an uneventful day!" said Iris, which was the best thing to wish anyone in charge of the technical operation of a ship in space.

"Thanks."

Herb left them signing animatedly to each other as he headed down the corridor to start his shift. Once inside the lift, he opened his tablet and said, "FindIt, tell me about *Snarr-cha*."

Back in Engineering, Lieutenant Sheena dashed over to her superior officer with exciting news.

"Sir, the results confirmed it! The stone we call Elbaite is 85.98–86.92% more efficient than the recommended crystals we typically use in our jump core. Most impressive. You've once again made a discovery that could change the way—"

"Thank you, Lieutenant."

She froze, somewhat taken aback at being cut off. "Sir? We can gather the data for a report, should you wish to be published on this finding."

Herb crossed his arms, uncrossed them, then decided crossing them felt better. He stared at Sheena, unblinking. For perhaps long enough to make her feel uneasy.

"Sir? Is something wrong?"

Her superior officer resumed blinking and appeared to come back online. "Oh, um, right. Yes, I'll want to publish for sure. But, um, Lieutenant?"

"Yes, sir?"

Herb stared off to the side, appearing to find fault with a monitor reading. Sheena studied the screen in an attempt to analyze the problem. When Herb woke again from his reverie, he grabbed the stone from his pocket and rubbed it between his fingers.

"It's pretty, isn't it?" said Sheena. "Would make for a lovely ring or brooch."

Herb watched the stone as it caught the light.

"Sheena?"

"Sir?"

"Would it be all right if I asked you a personal question?"

Sheena put a finger to her chin. "I think so. Depending on the question."

"Oh. Well, how do I know if my question will be suitable to you before I ask it?"

"I suppose you can always ask the question, sir, and then I can decide whether or not to answer it."

Herb nodded. "That's sensible."

Sheena waited.

Herb looked at the stone again for another long minute.

"Um, sir?"

"Yes!" He lifted his head. "Uh, Sheena"—he cleared his throat—"Have you ever... the thing is... there's this person... um... okay... have you ever... liked... a person... who... what I mean to say... if there's an inequality of rank... but... I'm really fond of this person... I respect them... and you see—"

Sheena's eyes lit up. "Oh, sir!" She threw her arms around his neck and hugged him closely. "I feel the same way!"

Herb blanched. "You—you *what*?"

She let go of him and gazed tenderly into his eyes. "I care about you, too. I admire you so. Working with you each day has been the sweetest torture!"

Herb's jaw dropped.

"Why do you look so surprised? How could you not think I'd be attracted to such a brilliant soul?"

"I... I—"

She put her fingers to his lips. "Don't worry, darling! We'll go together to Crew Relations and disclose our feelings. It will be difficult for me to be assigned to another department in Engineering, but it will be worth it if we can be together when we're off duty!"

"No, no, Sheena, you see—"

"We must be separated, my dearest Horatio. It's for the good of the team. And don't worry. I'll make it perfectly clear to CR that this relationship is absolutely consensual. Oh, you've made me so very happy!" She took his face in her hands and pressed her lips to his. "Just as I thought. You're a wonderful kisser!"

Herb gulped.

"I'll set up the appointment for us; I don't mind!" said Sheena. "But for now, it's back to work for me. I'm going to send you the data from the core so you can write your report." She saluted with a smile. "Sir!" Then she giggled with glee and trotted off to her workstation.

Lieutenant Commander Horatio Herbert stood motionless, clutching onto the Elbaite as sweat filled his palm.

"Aw, gleek."

"HONK!"

"ARGH!"

"HONK!"

"UGH!"

"HONK"

"ACK! WAIT! WAIT!"

Davan paused the holographic instructor when Herb held up his hand while gasping. The engineer clutched the Snarr pole with his other hand as he leaned against the wall, then slid right down it.

"I'm sorry," Davan signed. "I think I might have gotten carried away."

Herb dropped the weapon. "Mercy on the noob, mercy on the noob!"

The Quargnan chuckled. "Your problem is that you are a natural. I forgot the entire newbie factor!" He switched off the lesson, set aside his pole, and sat down on the floor beside Herb.

"Is it okay with you if I speak out loud?" asked Herb. "It's just that my arms can't arm at the moment. My muscles are presently contacting my attorney to sue me for divorce."

"Sure. I don't mind," he signed.

"I mean, I'd rather switch to your audible language, but as you can see, I'm currently trunk-challenged."

"A shame," Davan signed with a grin. "It's a rather beautiful language, in my humble opinion. We do have several signing dialects of it, but they are rarely used off-world. IGSL is convenient, but I sometimes miss communicating in the language of my planet, whether spoken or signed."

Herb felt the polished wood of the Snarr pole, the smooth surface soothing his fingertips, and pondered what Davan had said.

"Quargnan don't travel much outside their system, do they?"

"No," signed Davan. "Most are quite content to stay where they are. And if I do say so myself, Quargayle is a paradise all on its own. I wish I could be lying on white sand near the purple falls of home, under an amber sunset. It's so quiet apart from the rushing of the water, when the birdsong starts to fade as the avian creatures settle in for the evening. I suppose that particular spot is like my very own private room." He elbowed Herb playfully.

Herb smiled. "It sounds wonderful."

"It is. I've never shared that spot with anyone either." Davan looked ahead for a moment before turning back to Herb and adding, "Maybe I've been saving it for someone special. I mean, we can't ask just anyone to share our private rooms, can we?"

Herb blushed, zealously hoping Davan forgot Herb had programmed the Quargnan to appear inside his virtual private room. Not trusting his own voice and willing to risk more aches in his arms, Herb replied by signing:

"Right."

"Herb, I was wondering—"

"Commander Davan, report to the command deck. Commander Davan, report to the command deck," the announcement repeated, whose text also scrolled along the walls in their sparring room.

Herb cursed in his thoughts.

"Well, duty calls," signed Davan.

"Mr. Herbert, report to Engineering. Mr. Herbert, report to Engineering," sounded and scrolled another message.

"Yeah, same," said Herb.

Davan stood up and reached out a hand to help Herb onto his feet. The head of Engineering whimpered and mewed in protest.

"Holy fweep, I am just one mass of OW!"

"I'm sorry. I feel terrible about this," signed Davan. "Let me know how I can make it up to you, and I will, okay?" The commander touched his wristband and typed, "On my way."

"Oh, don't worry about it," said Herb. "I had fun. Up until it got massively frightening and intensely painful."

More honking chuckles ensued as Davan waved goodbye and dashed into the corridor.

Herb stared at the closed door.

"Mr. Herbert, report to Engineering. Mr. Herbert, report to Engineering..."

"Arg." He opened a channel on his wristband. "Herb here. On my way."

He stopped by the door, noticing Davan had left his weapon in the room. Herb ran a digit along the varnished surface before making his exit.

It is very important for one to be honest with one's partner, and misunderstandings should ideally be cleared up straight away, to prevent further distress. One method is for partners to go to a setting that feels non-threatening and, in fact, pleasant to the senses. And one's tone should be gentle, apologetic, stressing the good qualities of the other person while expressing that any hurt caused was unintended...

Herb rubbed his eyes and held his aching head. Things couldn't have been worse if he tried. Or perhaps if he *had* tried doing what he wanted in the first place, things would have been... better? *Maybe they would have just been a different kind of worse.* He covered his eyes altogether.

The CR appointment was this afternoon, but Lieutenant Synthie Sheena, in her utter joy, had already disclosed their "relationship" to most of the ship. Herb couldn't enter a lift, a corridor, or even a lavatory without someone congratulating him on being paired with such an amiable woman.

And how did I reply? I said nothing, or as close to nothing as possible. Every fweeping time! The words just couldn't form in his mouth, no matter how much he longed to tell her. Even his arms would feel numb, so he couldn't sign out the truth. *Maybe I'll be lucky, and she'll die before me. About twenty to thirty years into our marriage.*

He immediately felt horrible at even imagining that situation and wanted to slap his hands down really hard, grateful he had learned how to stop that physical reaction to stress years ago. These days, he'd first remind himself that he deserved comfort, not pain... although he wasn't sure how to avoid inflicting emotional pain in this situation. Either Sheena would be hurt, or he would be. *And after we're together long enough, won't we both be miserable? Is there a win here at all?*

With his eyes still covered, he inhaled deeply, trying to envision the shape of a huge Elbaite, cut like a glorious sparkling jewel worn in a crown by royalty. He concentrated on each contour and imagined tracing his fingers along it. Although colours had never really left a mark of interest on him, he had to admit the mineral's hue was rather stunning. The piece had become sort of a talisman for him these days. Herb continued to breathe from his diaphragm while concentrating on the image of the floating gem.

Fingers softly tapped upon the table, cutting into his meditation. Herb groaned. If one more person offered their most sincere happiness for him, he'd respond with projectile vomiting. For now, he simply spread his fingers apart to see who'd come knocking.

Davan waved at him. "May I sit with you?"

"Sure."

"I heard today's a milestone day."

Herb closed his fingers over his eyes. He felt his body tremble from deep within. *It is very important for one to be honest with one's partner, and misunderstandings should ideally be cleared up straight away, to prevent further distress.*

"I... I can't..." was all he could manage, then he began to cry. Herb couldn't stop it; The Overwhelm had finally taken hold. In no time, his tears became heart-wrenching sobs.

Davan dashed to the chair beside him and put his hand on Herb's arm. Herb looked at him but couldn't speak or sign yet. Davan nodded and opened his arms.

No CR manual or self-help book mattered anymore; their contents didn't even run through Herb's brain. He had no energy to overthink his next thought, sentence, or motion. All he wanted was the comfort offered to him. Herb dived into Davan's arms and wept against his neck.

The Quargnan rubbed Herb's back with a tenderness that only made Herb cry louder. People in the Mess wondered what was happening to the head of Engineering, but Davan waved off anyone who approached. He just let this engineer be how he had to be right now.

Herb had lost track of time, and for a moment, this alarmed him because it wasn't like him to be late for duty. He pushed himself out of Davan's embrace and focused on his breathing. When Herb felt calm enough to gaze in the vicinity of Davan's eyes, he signed, "Thanks. I'm sorry for that."

"Sorry for what? Crying? Crying is good for you."

More tears spilled, preventing Herb from seeing Davan clearly, which in a way, gave Herb more courage. His hands flew into a fervour:

"Davan, I messed everything up. I wanted to tell someone I really like them, and I accidentally told the wrong person instead. Well, I didn't really tell them it was them—I didn't say who it was at all, but she thinks—but it's not her, it's someone else, and I don't know how to tell her!"

Davan handed Herb a handkerchief. When Herb wiped his eyes and blew his nose, he peered up shyly.

"I wanted to tell someone else," he signed.

Davan sat still, his expression kind.

Herb took a deep breath. "I wanted to tell you…" he said aloud. He quickly stared down at his lap, then pulled the Elbaite from his pocket.

Davan lifted Herb's chin. "What did you want to tell me?" he signed.

Herb placed the stone in Davan's right hand.

"This stone becomes an unstoppable power force when heat surges through it," signed Herb. "My heart is this stone… and you're the one who ignites it. I feel energized enough to jump from quadrant to quadrant whenever you're near."

Davan's eyes sparkled. "Why, Horatio, are you flirting with me?"

Herb smiled back. "I genuinely don't know. I don't think so, though. It feels like I'm honestly telling you that… nobody makes me feel the way you do."

Davan nodded.

Herb waited patiently.

"Same," signed Davan.

Herb gasped. "You never said anything."

"I wanted to, after our *Snarr-cha* lesson, but then I thought you were already cared for, so I stepped aside. It meant more to me that someone made you happy, even if they weren't me."

"I've not been happy at all. Quite miserable, actually."

Davan nodded again. "Would you like company when you tell her?" he signed.

"No," signed Herb. "I think it's best I take her to a non-threatening setting that's pleasant to the senses and speak in a gentle, apologetic tone."

Davan tilted his head. "What?"

"Never mind. Thank you. I think I've got this."

"Okay. Would you like to meet me at the Clubhouse later?"

"Sure, but can we head directly to the Zip-it Zone? It would be better to spend time without all that racket. We can have a long talk. I'll sign back, so as not to disturb the others who need their downtime."

"Perfect!" Davan returned the stone to Herb, then squeezed his other hand. He stood up. "I'm glad you told me everything."

Herb got up as well. "I am, too."

"Meet you at 2100? I'll place the order, then bring the drinks to you at Double-Z."

"Great, thanks!"

Davan leaned in and pressed his cheek to Herb's. They stayed like that long enough for Herb to close his eyes and let out a contented moan.

"Bye for now," signed Davan when they drew apart.

"Bye."

And for the first time in what seemed like forever, Herb's chest didn't ache when he watched Davan walk away. Instead, he sighed dreamily.

His forearm buzzed. A message from Lieutenant Sheena:

-- Hi, darling! Want to get together so we can talk before the CR session?

Gee. She really is a lovely person, Herb thought. *I hope she can forgive me.*

-- That's a good idea. Let's go someplace nice and have a chat.

-- By the aquarium?

-- Sure. Meet you there.

It had been far too long since they'd all been on leave at the same time for a three-day run, but Iris and her shipmates buzzed with anticipation for what lay ahead. Captain Warq had felt his command crew deserved a bit of rest and relaxation, but he himself remained on board with the secondary team, assuring everyone that the Barquinn system posed no great threat. It consisted of eight planets, all dedicated to recreation in its various forms.

After alighting their transport on the moon of Garjex, Lartha immediately noticed a dozen recreative forms as they passed in front of her.

"Ooo, pretty men are pretty! Don't ya think?"

Iris passed a glance over the tourists dressed in flowing white shirts, plaid-pleated skirts, and mid-calf soft leather boots. "They are, um, aesthetically pleasing?"

Lartha fixated on the array of skin tones of the proudly displayed chests, since the fashion for the men of this culture was to fasten their shirts just above their navel. "Sooo very pretty. Hm. You know, I feel I should thoroughly infiltrate this group of individuals, to determine security risks, of course. It's the responsible thing to do, really." She cleared her throat. "Yeah... Bye now!"

"Lartha, wait!" cried Iris, clutching onto her arm. "I thought we were going shopping!"

"But the men are so pretty. You gotta understand, I'm sacrificing myself and my time off by engaging with them... to... ensure they're not a threat to our safety." She fake-coughed. "Yeah, that's what I'll be doing."

"Lartha."

"Don't interfere with security protocols, Iris. It's you I care about, not me." She looked down at her legs. "C'mon girls, help me sashay over there fetchingly!"

Iris grabbed her arm. "Wait a sec, lovergirl. You said today would be just for us! I believe you described it as a heckin'-fun friend date?"

Lartha whimpered. "But the men are so pretty."

"You can have all the pretty men tomorrow. You promised me a lovely outing. It's the only reason I came to this location!"

"Oh, fine." Another man passed by whose white shirt revealed a ruddy chest with dark curly hair just begging for fingers to run through it. He spotted Lartha and gave a friendly wave and smile.

She lifted up her hand and longingly waved back. "Bye, bye, pretty man."

Iris grunted. "Gracious, woman! Are you planning on a shopping spree or a whoo-hoo fest?"

"The second thing sounds nicer."

"Pardon me for interrupting," said Clarence, "but do you each possess enough prophylactics for all the sexual encounters you wish to engage in this weekend?"

"Have you met me?" asked Lartha.

"I have exactly none," said Iris, "which is the precise number of sexual encounters I want to have."

"You don't have *none*," said Clarence.

"What are you talking about? I didn't bring any!"

"But *I* did." A slot emerged from xeir chassis, filled to the brim with sheaths in an assortment of sizes, colours, and for a variety of appendages.

"Jackpot!" cried Lartha. "Where do I get me a Clarence? Now *this* is the perfect guidebot!"

Clarence's head lifted high off xeir neck. "Why thank you, Lieutenant Commander. It's nice somebody finds me useful!"

Iris rolled her eyes. "Do you think maybe you can close that slot now? People are going to think you're a kiosk."

"Yeah," said Lartha. "A kiosk of luh-vin!"

"I don't understand why you're embarrassed, Lieutenant. It's prudent to be prepared for such opportunities, should they arise."

"Close the slot, Clarence!"

"Hey," shouted a dark-skirted fellow who approached them. "What a great idea! Having a safer-sex bot."

"I know!" said Lartha.

"Xey're not a safer—" tried Iris.

"Shaddup, woman," mumbled Lartha. "Hey, there, what's your name?"

"Roddy, why?"

"You gonna be here tomorrow?"

He chuckled. "I can be."

"Good. Maybe I'll see you around."

"I'd like that... officer." He gave a flirty salute, then turned when his friend called him over to the entrance of the Market.

"Hm," said Lartha, then she leaned forward. "Hold still, Clarence. I'll just take a few of those ticklers."

"Lartha!" cried Iris.

"What? It'd be a shame to let them go to waste!"

"Oh, for the love of..."

Lartha inspected the packets. "I have to hand it to you, Clarence. You're a resourceful little thing. Did your research, too!"

"Again, I'm glad to be of service to those who appreciate me." Xey let out a digitized huff.

A loud honk trumpeted behind them. Iris turned around.

"That's one way to announce your presence," she signed to Davan.

"I feel sorry for all of you who aren't aware of this most distinguished way of communicating," he signed.

Herb touched Davan's elbow. "Don't be so quick to discriminate against the trunkless, dear!"

Davan's face expressed his curiosity. Herb removed a small oval-shaped device from a pocket on his brown microfibre jacket and squeezed it to a certain rhythmic pattern, resulting in a curious series of honking noises.

The Quargnan's eyes welled with tears. He grabbed onto Herb and held him closely, pressing his cheek to Herb's hair.

"Hey, what just happened?" said Lartha.

"I'm guessing Herb said something really nice," said Iris.

"Aw, whatcha say, Herbie?"

Herb nuzzled into Davan's neck. "It's private."

Davan lifted his arms off Herb's back to sign, "And really nice."

They gave each other one last squeeze before letting go.

"Would you look at these two? Such mushy-mush cakes," said Lartha. "Adorable, even if a little pukey."

Davan signed something crass, which made the security chief bend over with laughter. Then Herb honked out a response that made the Quargnan double up.

"I have a feeling I don't want to know the translation to that one," said Iris.

"Are you certain?" said Clarence. "Because Lieutenant Commander Herbert said something rather strange about the implementation of a plunger that I'm sure isn't medically possible."

"Yes, I'm certain," said Iris.

Lartha leaned over the bot. "Tell me later."

"Anyway," said Herb. "We're here, we're together, so what's say we try out the Market?"

"I'm game," signed Davan. "Do you have your earpieces?"

Herb fished them from another pocket and put them in his ears. "Thanks for the reminder!"

"Okay," said Iris. "Let's see what all the fuss is about!"

"Great," said Lartha. "Only keep your forearm monitors on and enable location tracking. We want to be able to find each other in case we wander off."

Iris, Davan, and Herb checked their settings and gave Lartha the "all-good" sign when they were done.

"Excellent," said Lartha. "Let's rock Shore Leave, Day One!"

The Market was actually an exhibition hall about the size of an average city block where vendors from around the galaxy displayed their wares. It had everything from food and beverages to clothing, art, entertainment, and inventions of all kinds. The place was teeming with customers roaming through, stopping at booths, chatting happily with each other, or haggling prices with the booth-keepers.

Davan checked that Herb didn't feel overwhelmed by the crowds, but Herb said he appreciated the natural lighting from the sky-dome roof and explained if he just focused on one booth at a time, he should be comfortable enough.

"But you still have your private room, right?" signed Davan.

"Yup. I don't leave my quarters without it."

"Good."

They waved at Iris and Lartha, indicating they wanted to go down another aisle. Iris signed, "Have fun," and took Lartha's arm as the women and Clarence headed towards a row of fabric vendors.

Herb cocked his head at a display in a tech section and reached for Davan's hand. As they strolled closer, the crowd parted to reveal a man wearing a complex, hulking bionic suit, who stood by a staircase to nowhere. He resembled a type of machine of old, like a vehicle had transformed into massive metallic arms and legs, their bulk managing to move gingerly enough up and down those stairs. The people gave a little "Oooo" at the demonstration.

"And with this suit, we can explore ancient ruins with ease!" said the vendor, smiling with almost too-perfect teeth.

Herb stared incredulously at the man, who caught his expression.

"Ah, a doubter. I see one in every exhibition," said the vendor with a phony smile, but in a tone where butter wouldn't melt in his mouth.

"This is... Just no. Not the best solution," said Herb.

The smile dimmed for a flash, but the vendor recovered quickly. "Yes, well, hover-chairs don't have the propulsion to move up stairwells this steep, my good man. So, therefore—"

Herb opened the flap on the upper left pocket of his jacket and removed an object from it.

The vendor gasped. "What is that? Weapons are not allowed in the exhibition!"

Some of the crowd panicked.

"Not a weapon. But get out of the way." Herb aimed the device at the stairs.

The vendor clumsily leapt away from Herb's path, landing with a loud clunk on his metallic bum.

A beam emitted from the device, morphing the stairs into a system of ramps and landings.

"There," said Herb. "Fixed it."

"What? How dare you transform my exhibit? And your solution is ridiculous. Why, it would ruin historical buildings throughout the galaxy!"

Herb shrugged his shoulders. "Well, they never should only have stairs in the first place. Anyway, your suit is cumbersome and only works with a certain build of person."

"Why you—"

Davan gently pulled Herb away, then signed. "Excuse us folks. We have to go... now."

"Wait!" cried a person who used a wheelchair. "Where can I buy this morpher? I'm an archeologist. Is there a way to have it beam a ramp that could be set to the side or over the stairs if we wanted to preserve the ruins?"

Herb took a moment to consider this. "Yeah… yeah, sure. Could tweak it to project weight-bearing shielding. Give me some time to really work out the details, but I'm quite sure it can be done."

"May I have your contact information?"

"Oh, and me!" said another.

"And me, too!" said yet another.

In no time, Herb was surrounded. He explained that he was a member of a Keangal science vessel, and not a merchant, but once he figured out the solution, he would publish it, so it could be manufactured all over the galaxy. It was his passion for problem-solving and inventiveness that gave him satisfaction, and not monetary gain. Especially not for products involving accessibility and accommodation. Herb deeply felt that profiting off those things was abominable. He said as much, and the resulting growls from that particular vendor indicated that he and Davan better move along to another booth.

The couple said and signed their goodbyes to the small crowd and made their way over to the painters and sculptors' section.

Davan had a love for art, and while he respected digital works, he much preferred the vivid tones and textures of paint on canvas. The first vendor they approached was an intriguing soul with an unusual headpiece.

Herb couldn't help but stare at the person who seemed to be wearing some sort of barn fowl sporting a pale-pink mesh skirt that fanned out around the waist. It baw-bawked at them and flapped its wings. Davan also felt taken aback, but before they could move on, the vendor grinned brightly as he greeted them.

"Hello! Are you having a sparkly day?" he said aloud.

Even with his earplugs on, Herb could still hear nearby voices clearly because of the settings he'd configured. He replied, "Uh, I'm not sure what that means, but hello."

"Why, sparkles make the universe expand!" The vendor tossed up a mass of glitter into the air. It landed all over the couple. Davan tried not to sneeze while dusting it off his trunk.

Herb smacked his lips. "Yeah, okay. Uh, so what kind of art... like... can you describe your art... no wait...this is what I really need to know: Why do you have a bird in a tutu on your head?"

"Why not? She's content to be there, and I'm glad for the companionship!"

Herb honked to Davan: "How can anyone argue that?"

Davan laughed. He signed to the vendor, "Hello, I'm Davan and this is Horatio."

"Welcome! I'm Jamieson," the vendor signed. "How can I make your day more sparkly?"

Davan held up both hands. "No more sparkles, please!"

Jamieson's jaw dropped.

"What I mean is," Davan signed, "I think my partner and I can agree we are quite blessed already by what you've given us."

"Yeah, a scorching case of the craft pox," trumpeted Herb.

This was met with a scolding honk from the Quargnan. Herb bit the inside of his cheek.

"Although," said Davan to his beloved, "I am impressed with how fast you're picking up the language."

Herb smiled shyly and pressed a specific phrase on his linguistic device. It had been the first one he'd learned.

The Quargnan's heart leapt. "I love you, too," he signed.

"Awww," said Jamieson. "Isn't that lovely?"

Remembering they weren't alone, Herb and Davan jumped at the sound of the vendor's voice.

"Would you mind telling us about some of your pieces, Jamieson?" said Herb, cheeks flushed, as he tried to hide in Davan's shoulder.

"Of course!" signed Jamieson. "Now, this first series is about the elements of earth, fire, and um—"

"BAWK!"

"Yes, Jezzy-belle, I know it's water. I was going to say that!"

Not particularly into this form of art, Herb decided to write a stream of code in his head while Davan carefully listened to the artist's descriptions of every painting on display.

Several aisles away, Lartha and Iris were also about to have an unusual interaction upon approaching a table filled with breathtakingly beautiful textiles.

A rather dapper gentleman in a suit, waistcoat, and colourful bowtie conducted himself with a most proper demeanour. He kept his chin slightly elevated as he spoke through full lips, as scarlet as the rest of his well-oiled head. A clear contraption was wrapped around the gills jutting from his shirt collar, supplying him with oxygenated fluid so he could breathe with ease. Bulbous eyes blinked with semi-translucent lids.

"Officers," he said with a watery accent. "I am Nat, and this is my sister, Kat."

"Ah, so you're siblings," said Iris.

"Indeed, we are not. We're Squidblings!" said Nat.

Kat, who resembled her brother except her skin was neon orange, appeared rather unimpressed with the customers, vendors, and the Market as a whole. She had refused to dress up for the occasion and instead wore her silver cut-off T-shirt under a black tank top with the phrase, *The squid is hawt tonight,* in gold lettering. She also wore bands around her slimy wrists with metal studs protruding out of them. Her drumsticks lay on the table near a swatch of black leatherette.

She took one look at Lartha and said, "You in a band?"

"Me? No, why?"

"Leatherette, shaved head, wicked tatt, bitchin' legs." Kat pointed to Right. "That one gotta woofer?"

Lartha smiled. "Yup."

The Squidbling stared at Left now, the leg uncovered but for the short boot. "This other one light up?"

"Yup."

"You sure you don't front a band?"

"I front the security on my ship. We're a band of kickass, so that's close enough."

"You sing?"

"I do, but it's been a while."

Kat pursed her lips, fished out an e-card, and handed it to the security chief. "Open mic tonight. Come on by. You're hot, too." She turned to her brother. "Gotta trek. Later, sib."

"Wait a second, young lady. You said you would host this booth with me all day," said Nat.

"Feels like all day. Must be all day on some planet's rotation."

Nat gave her The Eyebrows. Because Squidblings had no hair anywhere, the brows were actually gelatinous protrusions, but the expression was effective enough to make Nat's point. Kat sighed.

"Fine," she relented. "I'll grab snacks, then drain some urine. Be back in fifteen."

Iris made a face. "You know, I play a little harpsichord!" she shouted to Kat's back as the Squidbling walked away.

"Probably already has that band member, Iris," said Lartha.

"Yeah, that must be it."

"Anyway, my good people," said Nat. "What might I procure for you on this glorious day?"

"I'm just searching for some soft silks for house-robes," said Iris. "I enjoy relaxing in—"

"Oh yeah!" said Lartha, holding up a sequined bolt of cloth that ran in a gradient from fuchsia to orange. "Iris, you need this."

"So, that's the opposite of what I want…"

"Yeah, but there are things we want and then there are things we need."

"Where am I going to wear this?"

Lartha smirked and grabbed another bolt that changed colours depending on how the light caught the fabric.

"I don't like that look on your face," said Iris.

"I got an idea," said Lartha. "A big one!"

At an aisle not that far away from their shipmates, Herb and Davan encountered Chef's Row.

"This is what I've been waiting for!" signed Davan.

"Food?"

"Not just any food. Chef's Row is renowned all over the galaxy, even Quargayle! Every season, the culinary professionals try to outdo each other, not only with the flavour of their dishes, but also the presentation!"

They approached the first table, and Herb scrunched his nose. "This is weird."

"What is?"

"I swear I smell pastries, but there's nothing here but electro-mech tools."

The chef behind the table giggled pleasantly. Her uniform was the faintest shade of pink, from her comfy shoes to her cap, complementing her celadon green skin.

"Your nose is correct," she said, "but your eyes deceive you!" She cut into a huge electro-spanner, revealing it to be a red cake with a light buttercream icing.

"Wow!" signed Davan.

"Would you like to sample this? I can tell by your friend's outfit he might be a mechanic of sorts. So, how much fun would it be to sink your teeth into these treats?"

Herb watched as she sliced into the spanner again. He shuddered and turned his head from her, grabbing the small piece of Elbaite from a pocket on his sleeve. "Yeah. That's just wrong," he said, rubbing the stone, and promptly walked away.

The chef seemed perplexed. She just stood there, holding a plate of sliced spanner, unsure of what to do.

"He... he likes his spanners to be actual spanners," signed Davan, taking a piece of the cake and inhaling it. "Mmm, yummy! If it helps, I think it's a really impressive deception." He nodded to the chef, who seemed barely pacified, then followed his partner to the next table.

This other chef stared at Herb, concerned at the expression of this potential customer, who had pulled out a device from a trouser pocket and waved it over each dish.

"Excuse me," said the chef. "My ingredients have already passed all quality assurance and safety standards. I didn't realize we would still have random inspections during the exhibit."

Herb nodded to himself, satisfied. "No, it's not that. I just wanted to make sure these samples were actually what they appear to be. I don't want to try something savoury only to be met with puff pastry."

Davan said quietly, "Please lower your voice. You'll hurt the other chef's feelings."

Herb signed in their command-crew language, "She knew the risks. Cake should be cake. Who wants to bite into a JL-28 SuperTorque anyway? I don't get the appeal."

Davan honked a little sigh.

This new chef leaned in towards the couple and said, "You know, it kind of creeps me out, too. How about I distract you with a savoury plate? What do you fancy?"

"Thanks!" said Herb. "I'll try this steak. I like the aroma."

"I do, too!" signed Davan.

The chef proudly offered them two plates and Herb and Davan each grabbed a sample and pretended to toast each other with them, like glass flutes. As they were about to taste/inhale the savoury treats, two hands grabbed each of them, causing Herb and Davan to drop everything on the floor.

"Hey!" said Herb to Lartha. "You're denying me sustenance!"

"What's going on," signed Davan. "Is there trouble?"

She let go of them and offered a naughty grin. A custodian bot had already come around to clean up the mess, muttering in their own dialect about the sloppiness of bio sentients.

"Everything's fine," said Lartha. "I'm here with a proposal. Wanna do something completely spontaneous and off-track?"

"No," said Herb.

Davan gave her the side-eye before signing, "What do you have in mind?"

The audience was jumpin'. That was a saying, but many people were bouncing to the beat. The pit in front of the stage included music lovers who spun or pulsed in their hover-chairs. One woman's chair was outlined with neon glowsticks, and its jets rose her slightly above the audience to catch a fluorescent ball and toss it back into the crowd.

Glitter reigned supreme at this festival, refracting specks of light in every direction. Between their skin, scales, or fur, hair or head-tentacles, and the effervescent materials of the costumes, one could almost feel this crowd put the most detailed colour wheel to shame.

As the lead singer belted out her multi-harmonic voice to the driving distorted strings over a pulsating kick, her counterpart signed his heart out while maintaining a head-banging rhythm.

Then the music abruptly stopped. The singer of Morbidd screamed her final note, the lead-signer emphasized the gesture dramatically, and the band received peals of appreciation in return, along with a ground-quaking rumbling of applause.

"Who's the best gleeking audience at SpectraFest?" shouted Sydney Morbidd. Percy Dreggs signed the same question.

The audience roared and waved their hands.

"That's right! You are! Catch you next year, babes!"

As they exited the stage, the audience booed or signed their disappointment. Nobody wanted them to leave.

Sydney glided in her thigh-high boots to the backstage area. Her gold lamé halter dress clung to her dewy form, and she pushed her sweat-soaked ebony and red-streaked bangs from her head. The rest of the band followed her, not even pausing to glance at the members of the following act, one of whom appeared absolutely terrified.

"Okay, no! I'm not doing this!" Iris cried. She tried to flee with Clarence, but someone gently touched her shoulder.

"Iris, hold on—" said Lartha.

"That Squidbling-sibling person said this was an open mic!" cried Iris. "I thought open mics were for amateurs! That was obviously an established band!"

Lartha let go. "Listen, you need to calm down—"

"When has telling anyone to calm down ever worked, like, in the history of time?"

"Will you just come with me?"

Iris closed her eyes and took deep breaths to ground herself, reaching out and grasping Lartha's arm. The security chief escorted Iris to the full-length mirror, which had been propped up for anyone wanting to do last-minute touch-ups.

"Okay!" said Lartha. "Open your eyes!"

Iris did as asked but gave no reaction to her reflection.

"Well?"

"Oh, nice. Very stylish."

Lartha's lids lowered half-way. "You like the shade of eyeshadow I chose?"

"Very much!"

"Subtle, isn't it?"

"Which is always my favourite way to go."

"And the barely-there lip gloss?"

"Really understated. Lovely!"

"Iris?"

"Mmm?"

"Turn your eyes back on."

"H-huh? What do you mean?"

"Turn. Them. Back. On."

Iris sighed. "How did you know?"

"Call it intuition."

The communications officer made a little whine, then a grring sound, but she reactivated her implants.

"OH MY *WHAT?!*"

"That's how I knew," said Lartha.

"What have you done to my... my everything???"

Iris liked having the option to shut down her eyes whenever she had felt overwhelmed. It often relaxed her during stressful moments or prevented visual sensory overload. Sometimes, she turned them off just because she wanted to. Today, however, she'd been thrust way out of her comfort zone, and happily relied on Clarence and her cane. During the makeover, she had been aware that her waist-length platinum hair had been freed from its plait, but she'd never expected it to become a poofy crimped mane. It surrounded her frame like a follicular halo of sorts, with huge rhinestone clips holding it up on the sides. Nat's tailoring wizardry had produced a one-shoulder wrap dress in that fuchsia-orange material within the hour of purchase. Iris's waist was cinched with a silver belt that picked up the hues of the fabric. And Lartha had done her makeup with artistic flair—replicating the gradient with a band of eyeshadow that went from fuchsia to orange from right temple to left. And Iris's lipstick went in the same gradient, but with the colours in reverse.

"I can't go out like this!"

"Are you kidding me? You look balls-achingly gorgeous, my friend! I mean, I don't have balls, but I'm guessing."

Lartha herself wore the same outfit she'd had on when Rivers had stood her up in the Clubhouse, so she felt more than ready.

Iris's breath quickened. She grabbed onto Lartha's shoulders. "You don't understand. I've terrible stage fright. Ever since I was a little kid. That's why I switched my eyes off. I just needed some peace, so I could get from one moment to the next, and I didn't want anyone to know it because I was embarrassed."

"It's gonna be great, trust me. When we're old hens, we'll laugh about this."

"Not if I die of fear!"

"Just focus on your playing. You remember how the song goes?"

"Yes. I play by ear."

"Then we've got this!"

Davan entered the backstage area, clad in a sparkling silver and black waistcoat and orange silk trousers. Clarence accompanied him.

"Everything programmed?" asked Lartha.

"We're good to go!" signed Davan. "You're both looking terrific!"

"Hey, Commander, I thought you were one of my best friends," signed Iris. "How could you let her do this to me?"

"How could I let who do what?"

"Never mind," said Lartha. "She's just having a hard time adjusting to life on the wild side."

"More like life on the Lartha Side," muttered Iris.

"Hey, where's the next act? Delays are death, people!" cried Taig, the cranky stage manager, irately tapping his schedule.

"That would be us!" said Lartha.

Taig pursed his lips. "I've got no band name. Who even *are* you people?"

The trio froze. Nobody had ever thought of inventing one before registering for the open mic.

The stage manager sneered. "You!" he barked at Iris. "What's your name?"

"Lieutenant Iris, and we're from the crew of the—"

"Got it: *Iris and the Crew*. I'll tell the emcee. Now get on stage behind the black shield. It'll be deactivated after they announce you."

"Eep!"

Lartha kissed her cheek. "We got this!"

"Remind me never to go on anymore friend-dates with you. I should have let you play with all the pretty men."

The crowd whooped and punched the air, indicating in no uncertain terms they wanted the next band to perform. When the spotlight appeared on the emcee, the audience roared with excitement.

"And now, we've got a group making their debut at SpectraFest. Let's give it up for Iris and the Crewww!"

The shield-curtain dissolved. The band onstage stood motionless for more than an awkward pause. Audience members murmured and signed questions of confusion to each other.

Then Lartha's left leg lit up and light swirled around her. She sauntered over to the amplifier stack on the stage by her and said, "Right, hit the beat!"

Her right leg, communicating with the amplifier, pumped out a thrusting kick that reverberated into the crowd, who began to cheer again.

Iris picked up the cue and started playing the electric harpsichord, overlaying the melody with other pre-programmed instruments to create an elaborate wall of sound.

Davan opened all of the nostril slots on his trunk, then placed his fingers to close them in specific patterns, effectively creating his own horn section.

Clarence projected an enormous hologram of a woman from the top of xeir head, who would sign whatever Lartha sang for their set. Xey also twinkled the lights on xeir chassis for further effect.

Lartha stepped to the microphone and extended a soulful vocal run.

The audience roared with recognition.

Then Iris and the Crew had everyone in the palms of their hands; the jumpin' and hovering resumed on the floor and in the seated rows.

But towards the back of the arena, after taking the lift to go way up into the nosebleeds, a solitary metallic box also hopped up and down to the beat while recording the performance for posterity.

"Mr. Herbert, status report."

"All systems go, Captain."

"Thank you, Mr. Herbert. Lieutenant Udana, set course for the Vorgan system, using these coordinates."

The Navigations officer listened to the coordinates on his headset, plotted the route, and checked for possible obstructive anomalies. "Course set. All clear."

"Fly us there, Lieutenant."

"Aye, Captain."

As the ship headed away from Garjex and the Barquinn system, Lieutenant Commander Lartha entered the command deck and stood at post. The captain caught her eye, and they exchanged a friendly nod.

Iris looked over at her and mimed playing the harpsichord at her communications workstation. Davan spotted this and pretended to trumpet out a tune on his snout. Lartha stifled a laugh and lip-synched lyrics while moving to the unheard beat.

Upon instinct, the captain turned his head.

"Glad you all had a good R&R, people. But I'm going to need Iris and the Crew to get back to work."

The trio went suddenly bashful—yes, even Lartha.

"Aye, Captain," they signed in unison.

Captain Warq snickered. "And let me know when you'll be dropping your debut album. I'll be the first to buy it." He initiated a command, and Herb's video recording resounded throughout the primary speakers and vibrated through the chairs of the command deck, displaying the performance with the band and Clarence's holographic lead signer on consoles and the main viewscreen.

For the duration of the tune, absolutely no one kept still; not even the captain.

EPISODE 5:
Beachfront Learns a Thing

Lieutenant Junior Grade Marq Bronwryck wasn't a happy prince. Not only had the mission been a total bust because they hadn't been able to rendezvous with a new supplier of security tech, but also the two-person transport he shared with Lieutenant Sasha had become hopelessly lost from the rest of the convoy. He stared at the viewscreen and groaned.

"And now what the fweep is *that?* Some sort of nebula? Sasha, I thought you said this course was all clear."

"Seemed clear," she replied.

"Does that look clear to you?"

"No, it looks like a nebula."

Bronwryck clenched his teeth as his cheeks flushed a deeper shade of blue. "Get us out of here!"

Sasha turned in her seat and raised a yellow-green hand in a mock salute. "Aye, aye, man-child!"

"Hey!"

"You know you're not the same rank as me, right, Junior?" said Sasha, her antennae pointing forward through her greenish-white locks, indicating her annoyance. "Don't ever speak to me like that again, Beachfront."

He was taken aback. "Beachfront?"

She returned to the controls. "Never mind."

"No, wait a minute, why did you call me that?"

"Forget it." Sasha tried another course, but their transport recoiled as if slamming into something. Lieutenant Bronwryck, who had been standing, was flung backwards.

The small vessel began filling up with what looked like smoke but smelled more like a dank mist. Sasha retracted her antennae, grabbed her helmet, and initiated its safety shield, which rid the air she breathed of toxins. She whipped her head around to notice Bronwryck lying on his back, annoyed, nothing seeming hurt but his pride.

"Put your helmet on, quick!" she cried. "We don't know what this thing is!"

He folded his arms, remaining on his back.

"I'll do it when you get us out of this mess."

Sasha willed her antennae to stay put. "Yeah, okay, Junior. Breathe in whatever you want." She swore quietly in her own language, then plotted another course.

One of the navigation pilots of the *S.S. SpoonZ* listened intently to the readings. "Captain," said Lieutenant Udana, "it's not even listed on the charts." *Can you see anything, Renley?* Udana thought-projected.

"This is weird," signed Lieutenant Renley, the other member of the navigation duo, whose signs appeared as text and audio within the command deck. "Technically, it's not on the visual charts either."

"Yet, I can see it on the viewscreen," signed Captain Warq. "Commander Davan, any ideas?"

Davan scrutinized his workstation, checked another reading, then scratched his trunk.

"Commander?"

The science officer jumped. "Yes, Captain," Davan signed. "Well... it would seem that this is not a cluster of gases, but rather..."

"Yes?"

Davan looked up again. "A swarm of sorts."

"Swarm?" signed the captain. "What's the species?"

"Unknown, Captain. Microbial, though. Possibly parasitic."

"Parasitic?"

"Yes, Captain. Suggest we modify our shield configuration to a broader range of anti-microbial coverage."

"Understood. Thank you, Commander." Warq turned to sign at the video console at the command chair. "Mr. Herbert?"

"Already ahead of you, Captain," said Herb, placing his hands at the controls. "Keeping teensy creatures out... now!"

Captain Warq smiled at the paraphrasing of the situation. Herb's being in love was having an effect on how he broadcast information. Summarizing with colloquialisms was not typical for the engineer.

"Thank you, Mr. Herbert. We heartily appreciate our newly engaged teensy-creature barrier."

There was a pause.

"You're welcome, sir."

Davan honked a little laugh.

Warq now addressed another unit: "Captain Warq to Medical…"

"Dr. Rivers, Captain. How might I assist?"

"Doctor, we are bracing for a potential infestation, but we are trying to avoid this. Shields have been modified, but the organism is unknown. Commander Davan will be sharing his findings directly." Warq looked over at Davan and signed, "If you please, Commander."

The Quargnan nodded and sent the transmission.

"Engineering to Captain Warq!"

The captain noted the exclamation mark on his readout. "Yes, Mr. Herbert?"

"Sir, we've finally located Junior Security Officer Marq Bronwryck and Lieutenant Teena Sasha."

"That is good news."

"Aye, sir, but they've flown through what we're calling the parasitic nebula. Lieutenant Sasha reported that she engaged in hazmat protocol, but Officer Bronwryck had not."

Lartha had just arrived through the lift to hear Herb's update. The face she made could have been interpreted using at least a hundred different curses from a cluster of planets.

The captain caught her expression as he signed at the comm, "And what prevented him from doing that, Mr. Herbert?"

Another pause.

"You've not really engaged with Officer Bronwryck before, have you, Captain?"

Warq stared quizzically at Lartha, who unclenched her fists to sign, "Leave him to me, Captain."

The captain exhaled and resumed with, "Sending a team from Medical and Security to assess. Isolate the area of the bay where Lieutenants Bronwryck and Sasha docked, Mr. Herbert, and take all required safety precautions."

"Yes, sir."

Warq pivoted in his chair, and Davan signed that he was already contacting the most qualified personnel for the task.

"And Chief?" the captain signed to Lartha.

"Yes, sir?"

"Let's focus on ridding this ship of any unwanted entity that might make us ill."

Her eyes had that glint. "That was my plan, Captain."

"No, Chief, I meant the microbial sort."

"Aye, aye, sir. No yeeting Beachfront into the cold vacuum of space. Got it." She darted towards the lift and exited the command deck.

Warq stood motionless for a moment, then turned to Lieutenant Commander Iris. "Beachfront? What does that mean?"

"I really don't know, Captain," she signed, then bent over her console, pretending to study something particularly intriguing.

"Huh," whispered the captain while scratching his chin.

At the landing bay, Sasha remained in full protective gear, while Bronwryck tapped his foot, arms still folded. They both stood in isolation from each other within transparent cylindrical enclosures. Herb had also initiated a barrier between them and the crew who worked in the bay, where Doctor Rivers and his team were busy collecting physiological metrics from several scanning methods.

Dr. Rennick hovered in his chair, wiping at the screen floating before him, parsing the readouts for better assessment. He scratched his black goatee before running a hand over his newly shaven scalp. Piercing deep brown eyes studied the data in earnest.

"Hm."

Rivers turned to his right. "That doesn't sound like a good *hm*."

Rennick gestured in the air to expand a data window. Rivers studied the information Rennick highlighted.

"Hm," said Rivers.

"Oh, for gleek's sake…" muttered Bronwryck. "How long is this going to take, anyway?"

"Cool your hoovies, Beachfront," said Sasha, a sheen on her skin from the humidity of her helmet.

"Why do you keep calling me that?" he shouted.

"Okay, simmer down, Lieutenant Bronwryck," said Dr. Rivers. "We need to hold you here just a little longer."

The tubular enclosure disappeared around Sasha.

"You're clear, Lieutenant Sasha. Report to Security Chief Lartha—"

"Sorry I'm late. Counting to ten and maybe several hundred iterations took a little longer than I anticipated," said Lartha, her gaze slicing her subordinates like lasers.

"Chief—" began Sasha.

"Not hearing it. I gave orders for you to leave with us. Disappointed in you, Lieutenant."

"But the precious prince here wanted to investigate—"

Lartha indicated for Sasha to *zip it and get lost,* so the security officer did just that. Not without gesturing some colourful opinions, but only in her mind.

Lieutenant Bronwryck unfolded his arms but challenged his superior officer with a superior-than-thou stare. Lartha pointed to her tattoo. Bronwryck had enough sense left in his brain to wipe the look off his face.

She addressed Dr. Rennick, since Rivers was so dead to her. "What's he carrying? Virus? Parasite?"

"Neither," said Rennick. "There was a blip on his brain scan, but then it returned to normal."

"What even is normal, anyway?"

"I mean, it appears as expected," clarified Rennick.

"Does he pose a danger to the ship?"

"I'm not getting anything to indicate that to be the case. Although, I'd like for us to conduct further tests at Medical."

"I agree," said Rivers. "I've just given instruction for safe transport of Lieutenant Bronwryck to an isolated intensive care room."

"Oh, come on. I feel fine. Is this really necessary?" whinged Bronwryck.

Lartha turned her head. "Ask me that again."

Once more, he had the sense to shut up.

While the junior security officer reluctantly did his time in Medical, in the canteen sat Lartha, Davan, and Herb.

"You know, I'm close to reaching my limit with that kid," said Lartha. "He's just not getting it. Obstinate, defiant, entitled. I'm really left with no choice but to cut him from Security. His attitude is affecting the entire team, and who knows what he could have brought into the ship by refusing to wear protective gear?"

"Too bad there's also not a hazmat suit for toxic personalities," signed Davan.

Herb froze, staring ahead. He slowly put down his mug, the expression in his eyes unchanging.

Lartha caught him in her gaze.

"Herbie?"

Davan raised a brow and turned to his partner.

Herb cocked his head and squinted. Then he raised his hands and after pointing one finger, began gesturing, still staring at something unknown to Lartha and Davan. Finally, a little gasp exited his lips, and he bolted from his seat, the sudden movement causing his colleagues to nearly jump out of their skin.

"Herbie, what the gleek?" cried Lartha, wiping hot fluid from her legs. She felt no pain, because the girls had instantly detected the elevated temperature, and shut off any sensory responses while affecting a surface coolant. The spill was more of a nuisance than anything.

"Gotta run," said Herb. "See you later!"

Davan chuckled through his trunk.

"What was that about?" said Lartha.

"Three guesses," Davan signed.

She stared.

Davan chuckled some more.

Lartha's shoulders fell. "You can't be serious. He's not actually going to try to design a detector... for toxic personalities?"

"I wouldn't put anything past the man I love."

The security chief's comm fob tingled. She opened the communication.

"Lartha here."

"Leanna?"

She cursed under her breath. Rivers. "What is it, Doctor?"

"Leanna, listen to me—"

"It's Lieutenant Commander, Doctor. Even Chief. And I'm not interested in anything you have to say except the status of one of my kids. Is he going to be okay?"

Rivers huffed. "Seems so. Except for that momentary glitch, which might have been a faulty piece of equipment on our part, there's nothing wrong with Lieutenant Bronwryck."

"That's a matter of opinion, but okay. So, is he ready for duty?"

"We'll keep him here the full twenty-four hours, but it seems he escaped unscathed."

"Good. But stand by because about thirty seconds after I see him, he'll probably need Medical again."

Rivers snickered. "I know you don't really mean that."

"I don't?"

"Leanna, could we just give it one more—"

"It's Lieutenant Commander and thank you for the update. Lartha out."

Davan leaned his cheek on his hand and snort-laughed.

"What?" signed Lartha.

"Rivers? Really?"

"Yeah, I know. Believe me, I'm going to have a long discussion with myself about my man choices lately. Am strongly considering just having a fling with me for a good long while."

Davan honked jovially.

"Anyway," she took a long final gulp of her hot beverage. "I gotta get back at it. Admiral's coming soon enough."

"I know," Davan signed, then finished his drink. "I admit, I am both excited and a little nervous. They are quite impressive."

"And worth impressing," signed Lartha. "My team needs to be exemplary."

"We all do. Well, good luck with your preparations." Davan stood up.

"You, too, Commander." She got up and waved, but her smile faded the moment she turned her back.

"Beachfront…" Lartha said to herself. "What sin did I commit in my youth to deserve you?" She paused as a memory hit her, then laughed. "Oh yeah, that was probably it."

After being released from Medical, Marq Bronwryck was fortunately not sent back there by Lartha, but was threatened with a dishonourable discharge—through an empty weapons bay. It had been made abundantly clear to him that because of some admiral's impending arrival, Security Chief Lartha had no time or resources to dedicate to Bronwryck's dismissal. This discourse had even been done remotely through a comm because she had been so busy. However, she would have no problem bringing up a discharge plea to the captain once the soon-arriving admiral had been escorted to their destination.

So, his only option was to smarten up. He definitely couldn't face his family after a dishonourable discharge. What would everyone say at the club? The shame upon him and his family would render them social outcasts.

Bronwryck wandered about random corridors since he would only be on duty in an hour. He moped inwardly, blaming everyone but himself for this current situation. Sasha, for veering into that weird nebula-turned-swarm thing; Rivers and Rennick, for overreacting and keeping him in sick bay; and Lartha, for being such a grouch all the time.

He shuffled around a corner and without warning, collapsed to the floor, clenching his thighs. The air fled his lungs and when he looked up, he saw his superior officer chatting into her arm band, a short distance away. Her back was to him.

"Yeah, we're gonna have to step it up when the admiral comes on board. We'll be a flagship when they arrive, and I want no sloppiness,

Reez." Lartha rubbed her thighs with an almost imperceptible wince. "Absolutely. Let's get on that for sure." She limped over to a reddish-orange horizontal stripe that spanned the corridor wall, one of many that were ubiquitous on the ship. She placed her right palm on it and said, "Chair."

"What type?" said the AI.

"Hover."

A hover-chair materialized in front of her. Lartha sat down and continued her conversation with Lieutenant Reez as she zipped away.

The pain in Bronwryck's legs vanished. *What in the worlds?* He stood up and leaned against a wall, watching her.

Down the far end of the corridor, a woman with a walking stick exhaled with a whistle, then tapped her cane in a certain pattern. The corridor's Accessible Tech stripe illuminated by her. She signed, "Chair."

Text appeared on the stripe. "What kind?"

"Motor."

A motorized wheelchair appeared before the woman, and she sat in it, just as Lartha approached her. The security chief signed her greeting, and they high-fived each other with a laugh as their chairs passed.

When the woman neared Bronwryck, she greeted him, and he signed back. But as soon as her chair got closer, a sensation overtook him that felt like searing vibrating rods had been impaled in his hips, knees, and ankles.

The other officer didn't notice as she had stopped to text into her armband. Then she rapidly turned the corner.

Bronwryck's cheeks streamed with tears. And suddenly, again, the pain disappeared. *Did I work out too hard this morning? I've never had muscle and joint stuff that just came and went, though.*

"Good morning, Lieutenant Bronwryck," said Iris.

He yelped, not expecting her to be there, turned to face her, then immediately clutched his head.

"Are you all right?" she asked.

Bronwryck closed his eyes and opened them. "Ahh!" He blinked a few times and tried again. "Okay, what *is* this? What's going on with me today???"

Iris took his arm gently. "Whatever it is, I'm here! What can I do to help?"

"First pain, like lots of it. Then none. And now, everything's like, hyper-clear—my vision, I mean. It's making me really dizzy!"

"Right, I'm calling Medical." Iris pressed her palm against the AT-stripe and said, "Transport chair."

Once again, a chair appeared.

"I got a transport one because I'd like to take you there myself," Iris explained.

"Help me! I don't want to open my eyes 'cause I can't focus without wanting to barf!"

"Don't worry," said Iris, then spoke into her forearm band. "Urgent Care, this is Lieutenant Iris."

"Receiving, Lieutenant Iris. What is the nature of your urgency?"

"I'm bringing in Lieutenant Marq Bronwryck. He's experiencing severe dizziness from what appears to be sudden onset visual hyper-acuity."

"Copy that. We'll be ready for him."

"Thank you. Iris out."

Bronwryck trembled. Iris patted his shoulder.

"Don't be alarmed," she said. "We'll figure this out."

"I'm not scared," he lied. "I will beat this!"

Iris made a face. "Or you'll adapt. I did."

"Lieutenant Iris, report to the command deck. Lieutenant Iris, report to the command deck."

"Oh, fweep."

"You're not going to leave me, are you?" cried Bronwryck.

"Um, just hold on a second." Iris peered from side to side, then smiled with relief as she spotted Davan down the corridor. She called out to get his attention.

He smiled with his eyes, then switched to an expression of surprise, noticing Bronwryck in the transport hover-chair. "What is going on?" he signed while running toward them.

Bronwryck tried to respond but found he couldn't create audible words with his mouth. His eyes fired out his alarm.

"I can't speak, I can't speak," he signed.

Davan titled his head, perplexed. "No, you're doing just fine. I can understand you completely."

"No, no," Bronwryck signed. "I can't form words with my vocal cords!"

Iris frowned and held her chin for a moment before signing, "Davan, I have to go to the bridge. Will you please escort Bronwryck to Medical? And better update them. It started as pain, then his vision, and now his oral communication is affected."

"Sure. I can take him," signed Davan.

"Good, thanks!" she signed. "Okay, Lieutenant, you're safe as houses with Commander Davan. You'll get answers soon enough, I'm sure of it," she said.

"Thank you," he signed miserably.

Iris and Davan exchanged a glance, then she darted off to the nearest lift.

As soon as she left, Bronwryck's vision returned to how he'd always experienced it. He sighed with relief. He tried telling Davan, but his vocal cords would still not obey. He reached out to touch Davan's arm.

Davan stopped guiding the transport chair and stood in front of Bronwryck.

"You want to tell me something?" the commander signed.

"My vision is okay," signed Bronwryck.

"I'm not sure what that means."

"My vision is normal."

"Uhhh…" Davan spelled.

"I still can't talk out loud, though. I can only sign. This sucks."

"I beg your pardon?"

"Wow, you're really a winner, aren't you?"

Bronwryck jolted in his chair. "Who said that?" he signed. "Did you hear that?"

"Hear what?" signed Davan.

"That voice!"

"I didn't hear anything. Is your thought-receiver activated?"

Bronwryck checked. "No. But it felt like it was."

"Let's get you to Medical."

"Can you please explain to me what you're experiencing?" asked the triage nurse.

"Well, I had this weird nerve thing in my legs, but then it disappeared. Next, my vision made me feel I could see through time, but then it got back to usual. And now I can't communicate," Bronwryck signed.

"You're communicating fine," she signed back.

"No, I mean out loud."

"Can you show me what happens when you try to speak orally?"

Bronwryck opened his mouth. "Right, I... hey! I can talk! What the gleek? Why is everything stopping and restarting for me?"

"I can't say for sure," said the nurse, "but we'll keep you here for observation. I know Dr. Rivers will want to perform some tests and give you a full examination."

"But I had one when Sasha and I got quarantined. No virus or anything. Can't I just return for duty now?"

"Sit tight," said the nurse. "I'll get the doctor."

"Fine," he said and folded his arms yet again in a right sulk.

"Caught on yet, genius?"

Bronwryck yelped and glanced around the room. He removed his pocket scanner and searched for life signs. It seemed like it was just him in the room. Then he remembered that Engineering had tweaked the capabilities of Security's scanners, under the new configuration Lieutenant Commander Herbert had designed. Bronwryck modified his settings to allow for the fullest detection of organic sentient life.

Instead of one reading, his own, there were now two.

"Hello, you razor-sharp thing, you!"

The junior security officer leapt off his chair.

"HELP, HELP ME!" he screamed.

The voice inside his head merely groaned.

"Well, this is peculiar," Dr. Rivers muttered while studying the readings in his examination room. Holographic, floating touch-displays eased the pressure on his finger joints and could be brought to whatever position he was at, whether sitting or standing. And this afternoon, the equipment had been modified with the parameters gleaned from Herb's upgrades of Security's hand-held scanner.

Bronwryck lay very still on the cot. He was afraid to move.

"I still can't make out anything," said Rivers. "Are you sure you got two readings?"

"Of course I'm sure!"

"No need to shout. It's just that I'm not picking up a secondary life form."

"Oh, fine."

Rivers jerked his head. "Ah, there we go!"

"And did you hear the voice?" asked Bronwryck.

"Voice? No. But I can make out a blip on your anterior insular cortex. In your brain configuration, it plays a strong role in helping you process things like compassion, empathy..."

"Should I explain what those are? Because it's like a void in here."

"Hey!" said Bronwryck. "That's not very nice."

"What did I say?" said Rivers. "This is actually the location on your brain scan."

"No, not you. I was talking to the thing."

"The thing? Now who's not being nice?!"

Bronwryck clutched his head. "You're sure you can't hear it, Dr. Rivers?"

"I am not an 'it.'"

"Sorry. What's your pronouns?"

"He/him," said Rivers.

"Not you!"

Rivers gestured like he was about to give up on the conversation. "What is going on? Who are you addressing?"

"We refer to ourselves as 'I', or 'we' as a group, but we never refer to other individuals of our species with a pronoun. Only by our name. You may call me Maddox."

"Lieutenant Bronwryck?" asked Rivers.

The security officer took a deep breath and slowly let it out. He raised his head to face the doctor. "Yeah, okay, so I'm talking to Maddox."

"Who's that?"

"The blip on my brain scan."

"Of all the beings to cohabitate with in symbiosis for life, this is the brain-meat I end up with."

"So, you're telling me you are speaking directly with an entity in your head?" said Rivers, jotting notes in the air.

"Yeah, I—wait, what?!" said Bronwryck. "You're with me for the rest of your life?"

"I'm sorry?" asked the doctor.

"No, the rest of your life," said Maddox. *"I can live for millennia. I'm presently 2578 years old."*

Bronwryck's heart rate soared. "Get this thing out of my head!"

"Get this genius off my body!"

Rivers injected Bronwryck with a mild sedative to calm him, then opened a channel to the command deck. "Rivers to Captain Warq?"

"This is Warq," scrolled the words on the display.

"Captain, I think I need a consultation with Commander Davan. We might have an undiscovered species aboard our ship."

"Species?"

"Yes, Captain. Lieutenant Bronwryck is hearing voices in his head, but my deduction is that there's a life form communicating with him. I'll need the data acquired on the swarm that had come through Sasha's and Bronwryck's shuttle."

"Understood. I shall accompany Commander Davan. We're on our way."

The patient was gently awakened to the sight of his captain and the first officer staring down at him. The room had become very quiet, not even the slightest ping from all the machines. He could feel vibrations, though, running through his cot and along the skin of his arms, even against his temples.

"How are you feeling, Lieutenant?" signed the captain.

Because his hands felt heavy from the sedation, it was hard to reply. He decided to speak in hope that the commander would translate for him. Yet, once again, the words wouldn't form in his throat.

"I can't speak!" he signed.

"There now, don't be alarmed," signed the captain. "I can tell your arms are weak, but I understood you perfectly."

"No, I mean, I can't talk out loud." He paused, then clapped his hands. "I can't hear, either!" But before he would allow himself another round of panic, he tried thinking a thought, without his projector: *Maddox, are you doing this?*

"Doing what?"

Are you changing me every time I come into close contact with someone who... who... um...

"I can hazard a guess on what you mean to say, but for my people, it's considered rude to close ourselves off to the physiological and psychological reality of those we encounter. Empathizing with those we share the universe with and offering compassion are our prime motivators of existence. This is how we can better offer a friendship that has true meaning."

Empathy? Offering compassion? Friendship? You've been rude to me this entire time!

Captain Warq tried getting Bronwryck's attention, but the lieutenant junior class signed for him to wait because he was presently conversing with someone. Warq looked at Davan, who shrugged and signed that perhaps they should give Bronwryck a few more minutes.

"Rude? Well, maybe a bit snarky," Maddox continued. *"About five hundred years ago, I lived inside a sardonic comic. Ze kinda rubbed off on me. Anyhow, what I've observed about my latest host is this: you're a particularly cherished someone who's been handed his entire life on a gilded tray, yet thinks he always deserves more. You're constantly complaining about everyone else, always playing the victim. I've only been inside your mind a couple of days, and frankly, it's exhausting. Oh, by the way, I'm on the side of Security Chief Lartha. I might have even hoorayed a little at the time."*

Bronwryck slapped his thighs in frustration. *I didn't sign up for being used this way!*

"I didn't expect the cluster I was communing with to be rammed into by your shuttle, leaving me sucked into your sinuses. At least I have previous know-how of your species and found my way to your brain before I died. I can survive in the cluster or in someone's brain. Nowhere else.

"Also, I'm not 'using' your body. You just experience the empathy I feel because we are now joined."

Bronwryck growled.

Commander Davan waved at him, then signed, "Lieutenant?"

Bronwryck sat up slowly. "It's okay, Commander. We don't need your data," he signed. "Maddox is a being who has to live in my brain until I die. Maddox is only referred to by name, not by pronouns, and is hyper-empathetic and compassionate. Although I'll believe that when I actually experience it."

"Be compassionate yourself, and you might receive it in return. The trick is not to expect it in return."

"And Maddox might also be my own personal motivational speaker because I'm just that lucky."

It could have been his imagination, but he thought he felt something like laughter in his mind.

Rivers' brows furrowed as he signed, "Is there a way we can safely detach you both?"

Bronwryck mentally focused on the question. After a few seconds, he slumped his shoulders. "Nope. We'd most likely both die. So, yay."

"Don't worry, brain-mate. I'm sure we'll eventually get used to each other."

Do you actually mean that?

"I have to. The alternative is unbearable."

Whoopee.

"You know, you can continue to do that oh-so-charming thing where you feel sorry for yourself, or..."

Or?

"You can use this circumstance to learn a thing."

Learn a thing? What could I possibly take from being stuck in this mess?

"If I had eyes, I'd be rolling them."

Six days later, Lieutenant Junior Grade Marq Bronwryck meandered about the ship on the way to his psych appointment, which he and Maddox had nicknamed "couple's counselling." He hoped he still had a career in the military and really wanted to remain part of the security team when the distinguished admiral arrived. Bronwryck had listened to several of his shipmates share stories, and it would be a rare privilege to have Admiral Jaq Miran aboard their vessel.

Miran had joined the Keangal at age eighteen, and after years of receiving decorations for heroism and fast-tracked promotions, they had ended up becoming the youngest in the Keangal's history to rise to this rank. Many felt they highly deserved it. Apparently, Miran was a force to be reckoned with, particularly when it had come to the Piranha Brigade.

Bronwryck felt qualified to meet them, since he'd experienced another force to be reckoned with—on this ship—and her disappointment in him still looped in his head.

"You know, I bet all is not lost," said Maddox.

I dunno. I think I'm toast.

They passed a familiar intersection off the main corridor. Bronwryck stopped and stared down the hall.

"I don't think it's a terrible idea, if you ask me."

I didn't ask anything.

"No, but I can sense you musing. Why not try it?"

Maybe not. I'll only say the wrong thing.

He could feel what passed for a sigh from Maddox.

"Have you really not grasped anything that's happened to you? I mean, that first day, when you experienced the realities of several of your superior officers, what did you learn from them?"

Bronwryck shrugged.

"Okay, let's break it down," said Maddox. *"What did you learn about Lieutenant Commander Lartha that day?"*

She's loud.

"Really though?"

Fine. She's got pain in her legs. Sometimes so bad, she needs a hover-chair.

"What else?"

He continued to stare down the hall. *She hates me.* He shook his head. *I don't know, maybe not hate. Maybe she's giving me a last chance or something even though I drive her up the wall.*

"Right. She's had it up to here with you because of your blatant disrespect to her and the team, but she's still being a good leader by pushing you to be better."

Maybe. I guess.

"What about Lieutenant Iris?"

She can see through time and space when she has her vision turned on.

"So, you think she only sees with her eyes? They are her only vision?"

Well, no. I know she sees with her hands, too. And her stick.

"She also sees with her heart, as the poets have said. She's perceptive of others' needs. Lieutenant Iris called for a transport chair instead of a hover-chair that she could have programmed to send you to Medical. She understood you needed to be with someone because you were afraid. When duty called her away, she panicked momentarily, scouted the corridor, and was so relieved when Commander Davan showed up."

She was relieved?

"Very."

You know, she was also kind to me when the Chief's legs kicked me in the 'nads. I didn't appreciate it at the time. On account of how two prostheses had just kicked me in the 'nads.

Maddox paused. *"Yeah. That's a story I need to hear, but later. So, let's talk about Commander Davan. What did you realize about him? And if all you say is something about vocal cords, I swear I will tell your brain to make you slap yourself."*

Bronwryck huffed impatiently. *Okay, fine, he's also very caring. And so is the captain. Captain Warq also has a way of conveying a nurturing manner through his face and his gestures as he uses IGSL.*

"So, in conclusion, genius?"

Well, I guess all of them showed me their concern right away. Chief Lartha because she wants me to get my crap together, and the other three because I was scared out of my wits that my body had changed so dramatically.

"And they also showed you that you would be fine even if what you temporarily experienced had ever become a permanent state. You could still move about the ship, still communicate, and you would have mentors and medical staff to guide you and provide you with the accommodations you require."

So, in theory, even if all those changes remained, I could still be a security officer, no matter what!

"I wouldn't go that far. There is one thing you need to actually repair first."

Bronwryck folded his arms. *You're going to say my attitude.*

"If I had a nose, I would be pointing to it. If I also had fingers, too, that is."

How do I even do that? Everyone always scolds me about my attitude, but it's not like I can flip a switch and instantly be another person.

"No, but you can become the best version of yourself."

Ugh, there you go being a motivational poster again.

"Hey, all you have to do to start is just two things."

This ought to be good. What?

"Apologize, then listen. Begin with those."

The chime rang on Lartha's chamber door.

"Who is it?"

"It's Lieutenant Bronwryck, Chief."

"Come in."

The door whooshed open. Lartha was once again sitting in her nearly dilapidated easy chair. Bronwryck slowly peered in, to check for the whereabouts of her other legs.

She couldn't hide a smile. "You're safe. They're in maintenance for some upgrades. I'll be picking them up the day after tomorrow.

"Ah, okay."

"What can I help you with, Lieutenant?"

Bronwryck wrung his hands self-consciously. Lartha raised her eyebrows in surprise. This was new for him.

"Um, well, Chief... Well, you see, it's... uh." He suddenly looked annoyed and turned his head to the side. "Don't rush me! I'm gonna tell her!"

Lartha almost spoke but remembered Bronwryck was no longer alone in his brain.

He cleared his throat. "Um, so Chief, I've been thinking, and uh, so, you know, I'm really sorry I was kind of a bag of douches."

"You mean a douchebag?"

"Yeah, that."

"Of course, a bag of douches is still an acceptable account of your conduct."

He looked alarmed, but relaxed when he saw the twinkle in her eyes.

"Do you hate me, Chief?"

Lartha's mouth went slightly ajar.

"Okay, never mind," he said.

"I'm just surprised at the question, son, because it should have been me to ask it. Do you hate me, your team, this assignment? Because you've done nothing to show us otherwise."

He stared at his boots. "I don't know how to be a part of a team. I've never really had to be. I mean, yes, I'd gone through training, but I only think I graduated and got promoted because my parents pulled some strings."

She folded her arms and waited for him to continue.

He slowly raised his head. "I'd like to learn how to be a part of a team, Chief. I'd like to stay."

"You'd like to stay?"

"Yes, Chief."

Lartha exhaled, leaned forward in her chair, and pointed her right index finger in the air. "Then listen very closely. You got one chance—only this one chance. I can't afford to expend more effort than that on you. The safety of the crew of this ship and anyone else we're assigned to protect is paramount. I need you to be dead serious about this because I won't have you wasting our time."

"I am, Chief. I swear on everything. Even my trust fund."

That got a hint of a smirk out of her. "Mm. In that case, I'm putting you under the wing of Lieutenant Reez. For some reason, he told me he's willing to take you on. But mind him, Bronwryck, because like me, he won't tolerate any more of your garbage."

His face beamed. "Thank you, Chief! Thank you so much. I won't let you down."

She leaned back in her chair. "Don't tell me. Show me."

Bronwryck saluted enthusiastically. "Yes, Chief!"

"You're dismissed."

He remained in place and wrung his hands again.

Lartha cocked her head. "Something else?"

"Um, yeah. Lieutenant Sasha called me Beachfront. And so did a few others. Do you have any idea what that even means?"

Now Lartha lowered her head, but only for a moment. "I'm afraid I was overheard. I call you that. It's a nickname I dubbed you out of frustration because you acted like your financial privilege made you better than all of us. And you also severely lacked any sensitivity for the diversity of bodyminds on this ship."

He said, almost whisper-quiet, "Fair enough, I guess."

Lartha sat up. "No. It isn't. I mean, I'm sorry for calling you that. I put a big stamp on your forehead, which won't help matters in the end. I'll tell the others to stop it as well."

Bronwryck considered this a moment. "Don't, Chief. It's okay. Really. I want to claim the nickname, for two reasons. One, because it does represent my past behaviour, and two, my parents owned a home on a beachfront. The best thing I found about standing on a beachfront is looking out at the horizon and wondering all the possibilities of what lies beyond it. I want to aspire to more." He grinned at his superior officer.

She grinned back. "Okay, Beachfront it is. Go beyond the horizon, Lieutenant."

He saluted again. "I will, Chief!"

"Dismissed."

He nodded and left to catch his and Maddox's psych appointment.

In her quarters, Lieutenant Commander Leanna Lartha opened the report on her tablet, the official recommendation for a dishonourable discharge of the junior security officer, and deleted the file.

The 'Port Parlour had been scrubbed and polished to a gleaming state. One would have thought the ship was undertaking her maiden voyage, what with everything looking so brand new. Not a seam nor wrinkle appeared on any of the uniforms of the crew assigned to this station. Even Herb's multi-pocket olive-green coveralls, which he wouldn't have given up wearing, not even for a deity, had been pressed and pristine. As head of Engineering, he'd also been asked to be present, so he stood by the main transport console, in a supervisory role.

Lieutenant Commander Lartha, Commander Davan, and Captain Warq also stood in the 'Port Parlour, awaiting this much-anticipated VIP. Davan and Warq wore matching grey and gold uniforms, with Davan's tunic remaining sleeveless, and the tall right boot and short left boot on Lartha's legs had been polished like black mirrors. She still sported her grey leggings but wore her silk black jacket and undervest instead of the typical leatherette.

No one spoke or signed a single word. Everyone was uncannily motionless as if in suspended animation. You could cut the tension in the room with a knife.

Finally, a transport engineer at post said, "I have the admiral, Captain."

The phrase jump-started the team back to life again. Herb and Davan exchanged a glance; Lartha engaged a protocol on her scanner.

"Very good, Lieutenant," Warq signed. "'Port them aboard."

The air rippled on the transport pad and within seconds, Admiral Jaq Miran appeared. They stood tall with a commanding grace in their dress white uniform and smiled brightly at the team who greeted them. Their face was chiseled and remarkably handsome: pale grey skin, grey eyes, and dark grey hair with a silvery-white streak just to the left of centre, tied in a low ponytail.

Captain Warq stepped forward while the officers in the 'Port Parlour stood at attention. He saluted, and once Miran lowered their hand, he signed, "Welcome aboard, Admiral Miran. It is such a great honour to meet you. Your reputation precedes you." He extended his left hand, which Miran heartily grasped in both their hands.

"And you, Captain," they signed after releasing Warq's hand. "It's a pleasure to make your acquaintance. It pleased me beyond measure to know it would be the *S.S. SpoonZ* that would escort me to my destination."

"You are far too kind, Admiral. It is our pleasure to host you," signed Warq. "Please allow me to introduce you to my second-in-command, Commander Davan."

Davan stepped forward and signed, "Greetings, Admiral Miran! I can add with confidence that the entire crew is simply thrilled to have you aboard!"

"Thank you, Commander," they signed with a kind smile. "I also look forward to discovering more about you and the crew of this vessel."

Captain Warq now indicated to his security chief and signed, "And this is the head of Security, Lieutenant Commander Lartha."

"Admiral," she said aloud, her eyes fixed upon the scanning device. Her response appeared on the captain's visor.

The admiral looked taken aback. Warq held his breath and smiled awkwardly.

After an uncomfortable silence, followed by some bleeps, Lartha nodded at the results and raised her head, directly eyeballing this senior commanding officer.

"Yeah, okay, they check out."

Warq glared at her.

Miran laughed loudly. "How could I expect anything less from the formidable Lieutenant Commander Lartha? I'd been warned you'd never accept my presence at my word alone."

The security chief snort-laughed. "For that remark, I have decided I could possibly like you, Admiral. But I'll wait a bit before I'm sure."

"Oh, Leanna," mouthed the captain, forgetting himself.

"It's perfectly fine, Captain Warq," signed the admiral. "Honesty sits well with me and creates a trustworthy environment. And I promise I shall return it in kind."

"That's a relief," blurted Herb, then covered his mouth.

"And this is our head of Engineering, Lieutenant Commander Horatio Herbert," signed Warq. "But he prefers to be addressed no more formally than Mr. Herbert."

"Admiral," said Herb while saluting with flushed cheeks.

"Mr. Herbert," said Miran, returning the salute. "And they say *my* reputation precedes me. Why, your innovations have been transformative across the fleet. I should like to converse with you about your work sometime. Pick your brain, as they say," said Miran.

"Are you sure, Admiral? Because I often warn people not to ask me about a topic that interests me."

Miran's brows raised. "And why is that?"

"Because I'll answer them?"

The admiral snickered. "I assure you; you will find I'm a keen listener, Mr. Herbert."

"That'll be a new experience for me!" Herb chuckled. "That was supposed to be a joke."

"Taken as such!"

Warq's shoulders eased. "Would you care to follow me, Admiral? I'll escort you to your quarters. We've offered you the best of our VIP suites."

Miran hesitated. "Thank you, Captain Warq, but might I first visit the bridge?"

The sudden shy expression did not go unnoticed by the captain, Davan, Lartha, or Herb. The security chief's brown eyes popped for just a moment, until they settled into a naughty glint. After all, it was part of her role to jump to conclusions... or at least be prepared for a plethora of possibilities.

The admiral cleared their throat and tried resuming their confident stance. Lartha smirked, Davan quickly opened the door to where the lifts were, and Warq gestured for the admiral to follow him.

At her station, Iris's fingers danced away at her console. Her implants had been offline as she awaited upgrades from a much more reliable manufacturer that Herb had recommended. But it was the subtle scent of dried wildflowers that made her aware of their presence. Her heart caught in her throat, despite mentally preparing for this reunion ever since the captain had announced their upcoming arrival.

The sound of the slight gasp leaving their lips caused her heart to beat faster. *Just breathe, Iris. Breathe.*

"Admiral," signed Warq, which could be heard over the helm speakers, "this is my navigation team, Lieutenants Udana and Renley."

The pilots stood at once and saluted.

"How do you do?" said and signed Miran.

"A great pleasure to meet you," said Udana. He then extended his hand in the direction of the admiral's voice.

After Miran and Udana had shaken hands, Renley signed, "It's an honour, Admiral." Her eyes and the radiance of her fuchsia complexion revealed how she was not a little starstruck.

"I am honoured to be aboard," Admiral Miran signed in return, then also offered their hands to her for the same greeting.

The captain gave leave to the pilots, and they resumed work at their stations.

"And now, Admiral," signed Warq proudly, "I must introduce you to the woman I simply cannot live without, our Lieutenant Eileen Iris."

Upon hearing the interpreted IGSL, Iris stood up from her station, her cane automatically extending from her forearm band.

"No," said Miran. "Let me come to you."

She scowled in bold font, if that could be a thing.

The admiral paused in their tracks and let out a little chuckle. "Forgive me, Lieutenant Commander." They remained at a distance, and Iris walked around her station to greet them.

"Admiral," she said with a salute, not exactly sure if she had regulated her breathing just yet. "And it's Lieutenant."

Captain Warq paused at the curtness of her demeanour. This wasn't like her.

But Miran's features softened. "I'm afraid it is you who are mistaken, Lieutenant Commander, for you have not yet been made aware of your promotion."

"Yes!" signed Warq. "My commendation was accepted. Congratulations, Lieutenant Commander Iris!"

Iris's mouth hung open. She could hear an unrestrained "WHOOP!" from Lartha as applause rang out on the command deck.

"May I replace your epaulets?" asked the admiral.

"What? Oh yes, yes please." Iris felt herself tremble as Jaq gently removed and exchanged them from each of her shoulders. She turned her head in the direction of the captain's chair. "I... I don't know what to say... thank you, Captain."

"It is well deserved, Lieutenant Commander," signed Warq.

"And I was especially pleased to deliver this news to you myself," said Miran.

She could feel her cheeks burning, and her eyes went downcast in reflex. "Thank you, Admiral." Iris inhaled and extended her hand.

Miran cupped it with both hands for a little longer than they had done with the others they'd greeted. The tenderness of the gesture did not go unnoticed.

"Congratulations, Eileen."

The use of her first name *really* didn't go unnoticed, as it was the practice within the fleet to address everyone by their surname, if they possessed one. Calling someone by their first name was commonly only done by close friends and intimates.

Iris smiled nervously, withdrew her hand, and walked back to her station. Miran never took their eyes off her.

The captain coughed. The admiral reluctantly turned to face him.

"Shall I escort you to your quarters now?" signed Warq.

Miran nodded, turned away, but looked back to gaze upon Iris once more.

"Do you want me to escort you both as well, Captain?" signed Lartha.

"No, I do not think that will be necessary. Thank you, Chief."

"No problem," signed Lartha. "My team is available to you around the clock, Admiral. There will also be someone at post outside your quarters, even now."

"Thank you, Lieutenant Commander." They took yet another glance back at Iris.

Once the captain and the admiral entered the lift, Lartha darted over to Iris's workstation.

"Friend, I will ply you with that green fizzy soft drink and a ton of sponge cake, if you'll tell me everything!"

The brand-new lieutenant commander exhaled heavily.

Lartha and Iris raised their heads and remained still for a few seconds. Then their torsos seemed to dissolve in perfect synchronicity.

"Mmmmm!" they said together.

Iris tore into the spongey slice on her plate. "How did you procure this delectable creation?"

"The pastry chef and I are sparring buds. Isn't she a genius?"

Iris took another bite. "I need to be best friends with this person. Like, set this up, okay?"

Lartha laughed. "No, she's *mine!* All mine!"

"No fair hogging the friendship of a pastry chef!"

Lartha took another bite. "I think I could marry her. Honestly."

This surprised Iris. "Oh, I didn't realize you also liked women."

"I like cake, Iris. She loves baking. I'm convinced this is enough to keep a marriage together."

Iris shook her head with a grin.

"Well, I don't *not* like women," said Lartha. "Just haven't dated any." She put down her fork. "So, enough about my upcoming marriage of confections. Spill your truth."

"Well, I..." Iris also put down her fork, most reluctantly. "You know I grew up on a large farm with eight other kids?"

"Yeah. You were fostered, weren't you?"

"I was. And I was one of the lucky ones, too. Denny and Darren were the most amazing parentals. It really mattered to them that we thrived. Put us kids before themselves. I guess that's why we still have reunions and why I visit them whenever I can get a longer leave." Iris felt the pangs of nostalgia as the memories seemed to flood her mind all at once. "Admiral Miran... Jaq... was brought to the farm when I was fifteen. Huh, 22 years ago. Anyway, they'd been cast out of the Piranha Brigade and branded with the word 'soft' across their forehead."

Lartha blinked. "What the actual—"

"I know. It's one of the worst insults those pirates can cast. My dads scrimped, saved, sold some precious antiques, and even held fundraisers to be able to afford the cosmetic treatment to remove the word from Jaq's skin."

"But—"

"There was no free medical on my planet before it became part of the Keangal. We had to pay for it."

"That's messed up."

"I know. And in the meantime, Jaq was a living mass of undiluted anger. They never outwardly yelled, screamed, or became violent, but I could feel it. That energy surged right off them. The other kids had been afraid of them, but I wasn't for some reason."

Jaq sat on the wide stump by the cluster of towering trees up the hillock. Their dark grey hair was a mottled mess, most likely because of how many times they kept clutching their head. Their light grey eyes stared at the fields in the distance, a storm brewing in their gaze.

The sound of a twig snapping thrust them out of their brooding. Jaq turned around. It was her again. Why was she always there? Never too far out of reach.

"You stalking me?" they asked.

She swept her cane along the grasses to move closer to them.

"No," she said. "Just checking if you're okay."

Jaq underlined the word on their forehead with a quick stroke of their finger.

"Does it look like I'm okay?"

Iris pulled a face. "Is that supposed to be a bad joke?"

They paused. Then face-palmed.

"Oh fweep. I'm sorry."

Iris laughed. "What did you do, anyway? I could make out some kind of movement."

"I pointed to the branding on my head."

"Oh, right. 'Soft.' Huh. Funny, to me, soft is really not a bad word at all."

Jaq growled, "Ah, what would you know about it?"

She sat on the grass near the tree stump. "I know that soft things are my favourites. The feathers on birdlings, my snuggly fleece blanket, cotton candy from the fair, the fur of baby mammals. Soft is soothing, makes me feel secure or just happy. Soft is the best, really."

There was a prolonged silence.

"Soft is weak," said Jaq, barely above a whisper.

Again, Iris made a face. "Who told you that?"

"My people."

"Well, they're wrong."

She'd said this so resolutely and with such confidence, Jaq allowed themself to believe it, even for a brief moment. They watched her remove a wisp of gleaming platinum hair that the wind had blown across her face. They also couldn't help but find the freckles on her nose endearing.

"My moods," Jaq said. "They can go up and down, like peaks and valleys. I was supposed to run contraband for my siblings, but I couldn't get off my cot. I just couldn't move. I felt so low. I couldn't…"

Iris heard them sniffle. She stood up and let her cane guide her to the stump.

"Is there room for me to sit beside you?"

Jaq wiped away some tears and shifted over. "Yes. It's a big stump."

"Yeah, it was a really old tree, the dads had said." She sat down beside them. "You smell like wildflowers."

"What?"

"You do. You smell like wildflowers."

"Oh. I think it's this oil the dads gave me for my skin. It helps reduce the scars, but I like the scent of it."

"Me too."

They sat in silence some more.

Finally, Iris asked, "Is it all right if I hold your hand?"

"Why would you want to do that?"

"Because you're sad. And friends should care if friends are sad."

"You... you want to be friends?"

"Sure!"

"But my... my brain is all weird."

"I think my brain is a little bit weird, too. Let's have weird brains together!"

Jaq couldn't hold back a little snicker. Iris held out both hands, and Jaq offered theirs. She cupped the one hand with both her hands.

"I like to call this a hand-hug. Isn't it nice?"

They smiled. "Yeah." And after even more silence added, "So, I'm basically living in greyscale."

"Is that a metaphor for your moods?"

They laughed more easily. "No, everything about my appearance is in shades of grey."

"That's kind of awesome. Like a super antique photo."

"Is everything this positive to you?"

Iris paused. "No. There. That's a negative response."

Jaq felt something in their chest, like a slow heat rising in their sternum. "I think you're a bit silly. Silly, but kind."

"I'll accept that. And I think you're kind, too."

Jaq froze. "I'm a Piranha Pirate. How can I be kind?"

"Because you probably didn't want to be a pirate. Maybe that's what made you so low at times."

"I'm not sure. I've always been like this. I might always be this way."

"Oh. Well, maybe the dads can help find you someone who knows about peaks and valleys. Then you can understand yourself better and go out into the worlds and do non-piratey things."

Jaq shook their head, unable to resist smiling. "Who are you, really?"

"Eileen Iris."

They placed their other hand on top of her hand. "Jaq Miran. I think it's nice to meet you?"

Iris laughed. "When do you think you'll know for sure?"

"Aw," said Lartha. "That's sweet. So, you were an item as kids?"

Iris sighed. "It's... it's complicated. We were close friends, but then they wanted another kind of commitment, and friendship was what I could offer. I... I can love someone as a friend"—she flushed—"quite fiercely."

Lartha laid her hand on her own cheek. "So, you love them fiercely as a friend."

Iris nodded. "Very much so."

"And they love you fiercely in another way?"

"Maybe. Not sure anymore."

"I am. The way they look at you and the tone of their voice—you realize it changes the moment they speak to you."

"Yeeps."

"Yeah."

Iris rubbed her right thumb over her left in a repetitive motion.

"Eileen?" said Lartha, which startled Iris enough to stop fidgeting.

"Yeah?"

"You need to make a decision."

Iris gulped.

"And that decision," said Lartha, "is to finish this cake, and maybe get some more."

Iris's shoulders lowered with relief. "I love you, Leanna."

"I know," she said, lifting some cake with her fork. "I'm pretty amazing."

"All right, everything seems to be ideal," said Dr. Meridys, an ophthalmologist at Wellness and Tech. "I'll dim the lights, and we can test things out. Agreed?"

"Agreed." Instinctively, Iris closed her eyes. When she could perceive the change of illumination in the room, she opened them again.

The doctor watched her patient as Iris scanned the room. Then Iris set her gaze on Herb, who stood off to her right.

"You called it, Herb. This program is much better."

"Not too overwhelming?" he asked.

"No, I think I'm fine. Still ultra-definition, but much easier on my brain."

Dr. Meridys slowly increased the room's lighting until it was set at its typical standard. Iris nodded at each interval.

"Yeah, I feel good," she said. "Not too piercing at all."

"Very well, but consider this a new prescription. You might feel dizzy if you turn your head quickly, for just the first few days. I would recommend your guidebot stay close by, as a backup."

Iris moaned. Clarence had been extra Clarencey with Clarence-sauce these days. She felt like she couldn't make the slightest decision without xeir overbearing opinion. Iris had even lied to xem about where she was going this morning, and she'd hated doing that. But she'd reached her limit with xeir botsplaining.

"Come and visit me again if you're still having difficulty adjusting after a week," the doctor added. "Sooner, if you're experiencing discomfort."

"Will do. And I can still manipulate the implants at will, right? Set them to a lower acuity?"

"Absolutely. Anytime you wish."

"Good, because I can find myself overwhelmed from visual noise, and I prefer to switch off when that happens."

Herb's face showed he completely understood. Dr. Meridys gestured a thumbs-up.

"Right-o, off you go," said Meridys. "And as I said, let me know if you need adjustments."

"Will do. Thanks, Doctor."

Herb walked ahead and opened the door for Iris, touched her shoulder, then offered his elbow.

"It's fine, I'm good," Iris said.

"I can just escort you a little, in case you feel some vertigo."

Iris huffed. "You know, I could have just brought Clarence with me if I thought you'd be like this."

Herb put up his hands in his own defence. "No, not trying to be overly guidebotty. Just did the research, and there is a strong possibility you might feel pretty swoony on the first day."

"Listen, I appreciate your concern but—"

A voice coming from down the corridor to the left caused Iris to whip her head in that direction. There stood Admiral Miran, dismissing a subordinate.

Everything swirled about for Iris, almost violently.

"Whoops, I got you!" cried Herb, holding her shoulders.

"Oof," she said, clutching onto his hands. "Dr. Meridys wasn't kidding, was she?"

"Eileen, are you all right? Shall I call for aid?" said Miran, running to her.

Iris blinked the pattern to set her implants to minimal acuity. Her cane extended from her armband, fully white this time. She inhaled deeply as she held onto it. Usually, she'd feel calm in this state, but everything still swirled as if she'd been catapulted smack into a Class Infinity tornado.

"Iris?" asked Herb.

"I'm okay, just a bit woozy." She asked the cane to escort her to the closest inset bench. It wasn't too far away, and she was glad to sit down again.

"What do you want me to do?" asked Herb, his voice letting her know he was squatting in front of her.

"Nothing. I'll just sit here for a bit," she said. When he paused, she assumed he was making The Herb Face™, so she added, "Fine. I'll hail Clarence. Just say a prayer for me."

"Yeah. Yeah, I know," said Herb, "but I think it's wise to have xem around."

"Engineering to Mr. Herbert," rang out the general comm, with words and signing holos displaying the message along the hall walls, "Engineering to Mr. Herbert..."

"Ah, fweep," said Herb, then jumped when he remembered Miran was still standing beside him. "Uh, sorry... Admiral."

"It's fine, Mr. Herbert," they said, and sat down to the right of Iris. "Answer the call. I shall remain here with Lieutenant Commander Iris. That is, if it suits her."

"Yes... it does," she said.

Herb looked from Iris to the admiral, then back again, and one more time. "Uh, yeah. Thanks, Admiral. I'll check in soon, Iris?"

She nodded. Herb activated his wrist comm to let Engineering know he was on his way and rushed towards the lift.

The admiral and lieutenant commander sat in silence for a few minutes. Then Iris cleared her throat.

"So, um, how are the peaks and valleys?" She stiffened, surprised that of all the things she could have started with, these particular words had left her mouth. "I just realized I have no right to ask you that anymore."

Miran smiled. "You of all people in the galaxy are more than welcome to ask me that."

Iris exhaled slowly. "How are they then?"

"Good. Easy to navigate. I have a wonderful therapist who really listens. These new meds are spot on."

Relief swept through her. "I'm so glad! We also have great therapists on board, should you need to speak with anyone."

"Splendid. I will make sure to introduce myself."

"But for sick bay things, avoid Dr. Rivers. He's a bit of a skanky tool."

Miran roared with laughter. "Eileen, that doesn't sound like you at all!"

She giggled. "It's not. That's what Lartha calls him. She and I spend a lot of time together. Guess she's starting to rub off on me."

"Oh," said the admiral. "Is Lieutenant Commander Lartha… somebody… special to you?"

"Very much so."

A few seconds passed before they replied, "I understand." There was the slightest hint of sadness in their tone.

"Oh, no. Lartha is one of my best friends," said Iris. "And she's pretty much solely focused on menfolks."

"Ah."

"But maybe also female pastry chefs."

There was a sustained silence, just like the old days. It felt comfortable, familiar.

"There's not been anyone," said Iris. "Well, you know."

"I see."

"I see, too… sometimes!" Iris chuckled awkwardly. The admiral's face must have been painted with an enormous question mark because now the quiet felt super loud.

"Yeah, I'm not really that funny," Iris continued, "but I do have these implants. Sometimes I activate them fully, and sometimes I set them to an acuity I'm more comfortable with. Depends on how I'm feeling."

"Do you still play music?"

At this, Iris honked-laughed, almost imitating Davan. "I do. In fact, I'll have you know that my new band, Iris and the Crew, hit SpectraFest this year."

"What?! Isn't that the show with all those edgy performers?"

She could hear the laughter in their voice.

"Are you being serious?" Miran added.

"As a hurricane," said Iris. "Which I feel is an apt metaphor for Lartha's pushiness throughout that day. She really is kinda bossy sometimes. But she means well. Always wants me to step out of my comfort zone. It was great fun, though, after being so absolutely terrifying at first."

"Would you consider playing a little for me? I always loved it. The less edgy melodies, of course."

"Sure! There's instruments in the Clubhouse. I suppose we can head there off-hours."

"I would like that. Thank you."

"Great. Um, I think I'd like to return to the command deck now. Fran, one of our techs, wanted me around to config a few new modules at my workstation." Iris stood up and enabled her implants. Her cane asked her if she wished to continue using it, and she answered by inserting the handle in her forearm sheath, where it retracted.

Miran watched this process with interest, then said, "I'll join you."

"Okay."

They faced each other. It had been so long since they'd stood this close. The soft grey tones of Miran's skin had a deeper hue in the cheeks, but she decided her favourite feature of theirs was the streak of bright white hair among the charcoal grey locks, which they'd slicked back and bound in a long tail. She remembered how soft their hair had been to the touch whenever they had let her braid it. "Like a baby kit's fur," she used to say.

"Your eyes are definitely grey," she blurted.

"They are indeed," they said with a wink. "So is the rest of me. Like I once told you, I exist in greyscale."

"I remember. And I think the beauty of grey is highly underrated." She swallowed. "Anyway, my irises are whatever I want them to be now. Sometimes I wear two different colours."

"Today they are sea-blue and hazel," Miran said.

"Yeah. I couldn't decide which one I wanted."

They grinned at this, then took a deep breath. "So."

"So?"

"Now that you can see me, what do you think?"

Iris smiled. "I always saw you. More than you know." She cast her eyes down.

"No, I do know," they said softly. "I know."

She lifted her head again. Miran took in another breath. They remained locked in each other's gaze, and might have stayed there much longer, only...

"AHHH!!! HELP, HELP, THEY'RE GOING TO KILL ME THIS TIME! I KNOW IT, I JUST KNOW IT! HELLLP!"

"What in the worlds?" Miran bolted to the intersecting corridor to see what was going on. Iris followed.

A security guard with blond hair and blue skin fled for his life, chased by a pair of sentient legs that tore after him without even being attached to a person. Miran wondered how that was possible, but the legs ran like the wind after their quarry.

Scooting out into view on her hover-chair was Lartha, who had most likely stopped by the electro-mechanical medical unit for a quick adjustment. She flew after her legs and shouted, "Girls, girls!

Stop! Beachfront is not our enemy anymore. He's one of the good guys now. Halt, halt! No attack! No attack!"

Iris put a hand on the admiral's forearm. "Sentient legs. Security officers in their own right, really."

Miran let out a confused little sound.

"Bronwryck and Maddox will be okay," said Iris.

"I only saw one person being chased," said the admiral.

"Ah, yeah, that's because Maddox is a microscopic empath who Bronwryck snorted from not wearing protective gear and Maddox just lives in Bronwryck's brain until he dies."

Miran blinked.

"Anyway, Lartha has everything under control," said Iris. "Shall we go to the command deck?"

The admiral strained their ears to make out, "Okay, okay, yeah, I know, deep breaths, Lieutenant. You can relax too, Maddox. You're both fine. Now then, come here, my girls. Let's get you on and ready for duty."

"Jaq?" said Iris.

They quickly turned to her and grounded themselves back to the reality they understood best by patting her hand. Iris gave their hand a squeeze, and Miran's eyes poured affection.

"Yes, right," they said, clearing their throat. "To the bridge."

"Captain, we're being pursued!" said Udana.

"By whom?"

"Not identifying. They just came out of nowhere!"

"How many, Lieutenant?"

Udana swore under his breath, feeling the elevated points rising from their console screen. "I know this pattern. It has the making of a Piranha School."

"Understood, Lieutenant. Go to Alert Level 3."

The alarm for level three resounded throughout the ship deck and scrolled on screens and walls.

"Are they targeting us with intent to fire?" signed Warq.

"Negative," signed Renley, reading his words projected from her own visor as text underneath the viewscreen. "But they are attempting to scan us."

"Commander Davan, is the block holding?"

"It is for now, Captain. Contacting Mr. Herbert for a consultation."

Admiral Miran and Lieutenant Commander Iris exited the lift. A bell and message immediately indicated the presence of the admiral on the command deck.

"Admiral," signed Warq, "it appears we have company. An unwelcome escort."

Miran looked over at Davan's screen, which was the closest to them. "It's indeed a School. I was afraid this would happen."

"Afraid of what?" asked Iris.

They placed a hand on her shoulder, tapped it twice, then walked past her to the captain. Iris tried unsuccessfully to hide her irritation. They had always done that shoulder move whenever they wanted to shelter her from worrying about them.

Not this time, my old friend, thought Iris. *I am part of this crew, too.*

Miran signed, "Captain, you'll find it's the highest-ranking pirates of the Brigade. This is no minor threat."

Warq's eyes widened. "I don't understand how we managed to attract the Brigade! We've taken all security precautions to conceal—"

Miran raised his hand, asking to interrupt. Warq conceded but with furrowed brows.

"I am not questioning the capabilities of Security and Engineering, Captain. I don't think the issue lies with any oversight on their part."

"Do you have any theories on where a breach of security might have occurred?"

They shrugged, then signed, "I suspect the Brigade cut a deal with one of the way stations I used when shuttling to our rendezvous location. The reach of the Brigade is far and wide."

Lartha entered the command deck. "Captain, I just got informed about a security breach. What the ever-lovin'—we scoured and vetted that rendezvous location!"

"I'm afraid it could be the security on one of the way stations, Chief," signed the captain.

She huffed. "Dammit, I pushed and pushed those people to double up on their checks. Admiral, I'm sorry I didn't do more. We have limited jurisdiction over way stations that are not part of the Keangal. Still, that's no excuse for me to let you down this way."

"I do not blame you in the least. It was my decision to chart a path through those stations. And asking how this happened is a luxury we do not have at present. What we need to ensure the safety of the souls on board is for the Brigade not to discover me aboard this vessel. They consider me enemy number one."

"They once cast you out and expected you to die, and they've never forgiven you for defying them by thriving," added Iris.

They stared knowingly at each other.

"Lieutenant Sheena to the bridge."

"Warq here," signed the captain.

"Block is not holding, Captain. They are going to get through!"

"Reinforce, Lieutenant. Even if you have to reroute power from our shields. Absolutely no trace of the admiral must be detected aboard!"

"With all due respect, Captain, our shields are not something we want to reduce right now."

"Yes, but they do us no good if Admiral Miran is found. The Piranha Brigade will send reinforcements, and we won't be able to stand against them."

"Indeed," said Miran. "They track, find, and move in for the kill. And always with a school of fighters at the ready. Often hundreds of them at once against one ship. I know those pirates well." They paused and looked at Iris. "They raised me."

"And you broke away," she said.

"And they'll never let me forget it, especially now that I'm a senior member of the Keangal forces. We're sworn to uphold the free distribution of scientific and medical advancements where needed. My destruction alone would send a message that they're furious with the billions of coins they're losing. All because we won't allow the exploitation of essential aids and rights."

They looked down for a moment, then raised their chin and signed to the captain:

"Prepare a shuttle for me, Captain Warq. I will not endanger the souls on this ship."

"NO!" shouted Iris.

"Admiral, respectfully," signed Captain Warq, "I am under direct orders to protect you at all costs."

"And as your commanding officer, I relieve you of such duties."

"The gleek you will!" cried Lartha.

"Lieutenant Commander!" signed the captain emphatically, revealing the anger in his expression.

"I will apologize maybe another time, Captain," signed Lartha, "but not this moment." She turned to the most senior officer on deck. "Admiral, you'll have to step over my dead body before I will allow you to sacrifice yourself. We didn't bust our behinds for weeks preparing for your safe passage only to hurl you into their clutches. We can figure out a way."

Miran smiled ruefully. "You are diligent in your duty, and I'm probably more afraid of your wrath than that of the Brigade. However, I must insist—"

"Block is breaking down! At 15% efficacy. We've got seconds, maybe a couple of minutes if we're lucky!" cried Sheena over the comm.

"That's it. I must go," said Miran. "Chief Lartha, please escort me to the landing bay."

"Jaq!" cried Iris.

Miran turned about. "Goodbye, Eileen."

"Block is at 10%!" cried Sheena.

"Aw, frik it, let's go," said Lartha, heading towards the lift doors.

"BLOCK AT 5%!"

The lift doors opened. Bolting out of them and nearly knocking Lartha off her heels was Herb. He slammed into the admiral, took something out of his pocket, clipped it to Miran's lapel, and gave it a desperate wallop.

"BLOCK BREACHED, BLOCK BREACHED!" shouted Sheena.

"We are being scanned, Captain," signed Davan, who turned his head as something caught the corner of his eye. Then he did a double take.

"Captain, we're being hailed," said Iris.

"Connect us, Lieutenant Commander."

"Aye, Captain."

A holo appeared of a someone who could have been an older version of Miran, but this person sported a long silver and white beard. He was dressed in the black shirts and trousers with red fluo piping of the Brigade. Long dark grey hair, streaked with silver bands on each side of his part, flowed past his shoulders.

"This is Captain Dustin Warq of the *S.S. SpoonZ*. To whom am I addressing?"

The pirate signed, "I am Joz Miran. We were informed my younger sibling was aboard your ship."

"I am afraid you have been given incorrect intelligence, Joz Miran. We are a science vessel, and too low of importance to be deemed a flagship. Our next mission is to Planet Aveen, to observe the medicinal practices of the high priestesses."

Joz's expression was one of great distaste. "Bah. False wizards, party tricks at best. They are of no interest to us." He turned away from the captain, looking to one side, then spoke to a member of his own crew. "What? Are you certain?" He let out a low growl. "Check again." There was a tense wait for the results. "Your life depends on that accuracy, lowling." He cursed under his breath and muttered, "Someone will pay." Joz stared into the screen again. "I am being told that our scan shows my traitor sibling Jaq is not on this ship. Perhaps I shall accept this as fact, and maybe I will kill my entire scout team for their gross incompetence."

Warq swallowed. "I'm sure even a stern warning will have the same effect. You do have a motivating demeanour, if I sign so myself."

The pirate raised his eyebrows, and chin as well, standing a little taller. "You show great wisdom, for a member of the Keangal. Yes, even the threat of death will do quite well. You are most correct, Captain Dustin Warq. I shall do that instead."

"Oh, but what I meant was—"

"I have no time for further banter. We are on a hunt. Miran out." And with that, the top pirate disappeared from the screen.

"All Brigade ships have jumped out of this system, Captain," said Lieutenant Udana.

"Thank you, Lieutenant. Set Alert Status 2."

"Aye, Captain."

Warq swivelled his chair and stood up. Lartha had her arm around Herb, who stood cheerfully with his hands in two of his pockets. Davan stepped away from his workstation to the wall of consoles and readouts.

He signed, "Are you okay in there, Admiral?"

After a second or two, Miran replied, "This is surprisingly spacious. And there's the loveliest lake. Quite serene, really."

Iris clasped her hands. "Herb! Your private room!"

"Yup," said Herb. "I just had to disguise it as one of the wall panels and activate stealth mode. I messed up some of the positions of the buttons and screens, but there really wasn't enough time!"

Iris laughed. "Shame on you, Herb. You could have done way better than that."

He seemed crestfallen.

"I'm so kidding. That was a fantastic idea!"

He smiled. "I thought so. Sensory tech to the rescue!"

Davan honked a phrase. Herb blushed.

"Erm, may I leave this place now?" asked the admiral.

"Oh sure," said Herb, trying to hide his red cheeks. "Just press the centre pad on the activator attached to your uniform."

Immediately, the panel of consoles and blips and beeps disappeared, revealing the admiral once more.

Miran smiled. "Well, I must say I never thought I would ever escape while standing in place. I can't thank you enough."

Herb nodded shyly, then unclipped his private room device from the admiral's uniform.

Iris flew into Miran's arms. "I know this is breaking a million protocols, so you'll just have to put me in the brig."

Jaq embraced her warmly. "I'm sure I could excuse this breach of conduct just the once."

Her fingers gingerly moved upon the keys of the harpsichord. The delicate melody brought Admiral Miran to tears, and they wiped their cheeks as Iris played.

She stopped abruptly at the sound of sniffling.

"Oh, please, don't. Keep playing," said Jaq.

"Are you okay?"

"Never better," they choked on the words and removed a handkerchief from their jacket. "I've missed this so much."

Iris placed her hands just above the keys, but then removed them, and folded them on her lap.

"What is it?" said Jaq.

"I was just thinking. I was fifteen and you were sixteen. We lived on that farm together for only two years, then you left for the military. In only two years we formed such a bond..."

"And I fell in love with you almost right away. Well, not that long after our tree stump discussion."

"The first of the many, you mean?"

They laughed. "Yes."

She bit her lip and tilted her head. "You know, Jaq, I do love you very much. I want you to be happiest of all people. But, like... if you want a spouse and a family, then—"

Jaq reached for her hand. "Hand-hug?" they asked.

Iris grinned and extended her hand.

"Eillie, we're soul friends," said Miran. "Yes, I will probably be in love with you until I die, and I'm content with that. The only thing I propose to you is this: Will you be my dearest, cherished Iris for the rest of our days?"

She beamed. "Yes! This I do solemnly vow! And you will be my favourite Jaq in the entire universe!"

They glowed. "Wonderful! Now then, can you please continue with that aria? I have my hankie in hand, and it's wanting to help me through a good weep."

"Aye, aye, Admiral. This is my plan for the evening. First, I shall induce a right good sob from you, and then... the sponge cake!"

Jaq's eyes perked.

"Yeah!" said Iris. "Lartha's maybe-who-knows wife will totally set us up!"

"Perfect! Play on, then, my beloved friend."

Magically Suspicious

Assistant Chef Eyrena Figwell was the newest member of the *S.S. SpoonZ* catering corps. Xyr job would be to work for the head chef to program recipes into the databanks so everyone on the ship could order meals according to their specific dietary needs. The catering corps had some of the best dietary experts in the fleet, and they constantly exchanged information with cooks and chefs throughout the galaxy. Not only for meals, but also for customized utensils and other tools that aided with the consumption of food and beverages.

Because of the size of the ship, meals were prepared by a host of machines that constantly went through quality assurance testing. Many crew members volunteered to be tasters during these sessions. It had been a much-coveted role.

Davan was one of them today. The tissues inside his trunk contained an abundance of highly sensitive taste buds, and so did the thin tongue that could extract from the mouth under his trunk. Food was one of his favourite things to embrace. His other favourite thing, or person, really, had kept forgetting to eat anywhere near to a schedule, so Davan often prompted Herb to take meals and keep hydrated, which Herb really appreciated. In fact, Herb had given Davan an open permission slip to figuratively tackle the engineer out of his hyperfocus in order to maintain his nourishment.

Today, however, Herb had been a bit grumpy at the notion of being a taster. He would have preferred to further explore the properties of the stone known as Elbaite for space travel and had since discovered several more crystals like it. The more he learned, the more Herb was convinced that Elbaite was the incorrect classification because it was far different than the standard. He'd put in a request with the Mining Guild to rename it Davanite, since that's what Herb always called it in his head. Sadly, Davanite was already the name of another mineral.

But here the couple sat, and Assistant Chef Eyrena had xyr hands full—all six of them—in the chef's dining room. Tendrils of silky teal hair had escaped xyr white cap, and a glow of perspiration radiated from xyr aqua skin. Xe had been busy this morning, preparing these dishes manually to ensure the ingredients were palatable, and that the cooking and baking instructions optimized the results.

At their side of the table, to the right of Herb, hovered one of the civilian tech support personnel assigned to the ship. Davan had once seen Mx. Gawyn calibrating the AT-strips in the main corridor. It had been amusing to watch them shout the names of all sorts of accessibility devices as part of the test to ensure the strip was generating properly. About a dozen or so had cluttered up the hallway beside them. But in no time, Gawyn dissolved and reintegrated the assistive tech back into the strip.

"Mx. Gawyn," said Eyrena. "Here are your samples for the day."

"No bikzax?"

"None at all. I know your allergies, and none of the samples have been prepared with it."

"Thank you!" Their deep purple face tentacles extended to take a portion of the food on their plate into their mouth. "Mmm, exquisite!"

Eyrena smiled. "Thank you!" Xe moved on to Davan and Herb. "You two specifically wanted to try the same things, so here are your identical samples." Xe laid the large plates in front of them.

Herb winced. "One of these things might feel ucky in my mouth."

Davan signed, "But you haven't even tried it yet."

"I know," he signed back. "I can just *tell* how it feels."

"Ah. Well, how about we begin with one that you think might feel nicer?"

Herb touched a warm triangular pastry with his finger. Then he bent his head to smell it. He grinned. "This one!"

Davan chortled. "This one it is!"

Herb took a bite and Davan inhaled it. Their eyes lit up, and they applauded the assistant chef.

"A triumph!" signed Davan.

"Yeah, and the spices tingle my tongue in the most perfect way," said Herb.

"Bridge to Commander Davan, Bridge to Commander Davan."

The Quargnan let out a little expletive honk. Herb covered his ears in feigned shock.

Davan touched his wrist band and signed, "Davan here. Hi, Iris."

"Hi. Sorry to interrupt your delicious date, but there's an unknown vessel hailing us. Captain Warq wants you and Herb at post."

"Understood," Davan typed. "We're on our way."

Herb grabbed both plates and got up.

"What?" he said, to Davan's expression. "We can walk and eat." He turned to the assistant chef and said, "Don't worry, I'll get these back to you later."

"Captain, there's a distress call on loop," signed Iris.

"Thank you, Lieutenant Commander. Commander Davan, any indication of life?"

Davan nodded. "Yes, Captain. One. But their lack of responsiveness could possibly mean they cannot communicate at present. Perhaps they are injured or unconscious."

"Understood." Warq opened an internal channel and signed, "Warq to Medical."

"Dr. Rivers here, Captain."

"Send a med team to the 'Port Parlour."

"Aye, Captain. We'll be there directly."

"Security Chief Lartha—"

"I'm already here at the Parlour with Lieutenant Reez."

"Thank you, Lieutenant Commander. Warq to Engineering."

"Herb here, Captain."

"Mr. Herbert, one to 'port aboard."

"We've got a lock on them, Captain. 'Porting now."

"Thank you, Mr. Herbert." Warq got up from his chair and indicated that Davan should accompany him. "Lieutenant Commander Iris?"

"Yes, Captain?"

"You have the conn until our return."

"Aye, Captain."

Lartha and Reez had weapons aimed at the whirly image of the person materializing on the 'port pad. The security chief pointed her menacing tubular cannon, the one her personal hover-chair could transform into. It was clunky to hold, but powerful to shoot, and the sight of it was enough to intimidate the gleek out of those she targeted. Reez held a typical lightweight shooter. Each weapon was set to stun but could change to kill mode in an instant.

When the 'porting completed, a person fully appeared. Their pastel purple skin, orange-red hair, and flowing robes—that perhaps had once been a creamy white—were caked in mud, dirt, and dried fluid that might have been blood.

The officer at the 'port console beside Herb uttered a slight gasp at the sight of them.

Reez and Lartha had not changed their stance. They didn't even blink.

A nurse and Dr. Rivers entered the Parlour.

"Stay back," grunted Lartha at the med team, still not taking her eyes off the newly transported being.

The stranger on the pad put a hand to their chest, saying just above a whisper, "Oh, please. Help, help me!" They fainted rather gracefully onto the platform.

"Lartha," cried Rivers, "let us through!"

"Stay back," she repeated, keeping her aim on point. "Reez?"

"I got this, Chief. Cover me."

"You know I will."

Security Deputy Chief Reez slowly stalked over to the form stretched prone on the platform. He barked to his wristband, "Status on unidentified person."

The AI rang out: "Species unclear. Person not registered with any known identification. Outward appearance resembles a priestess of Aveen. Samples required for further analysis."

"And the health status?" said Rivers, still stuck with Nurse Quilliard behind Lartha's back. "You know, if you don't mind me asking?"

Reez bent down and put a hand on the person's shoulder to give them a little shake.

"Mm? What?" they moaned.

He pointed his gun at them. "Can you turn over?"

The person opened their eyes. "I think so." As they managed to roll onto their side, they saw Reez's weapon and cried, "What? Oh, please don't shoot! Why, haven't I been through enough already?" They collapsed into a sea of tears.

Reez raised an eyebrow. "Uh, Chief?"

Lartha kept her weapon up. "Okay, whoever you are. Switch off the melodrama, and I might consider lowering my launcher."

The person raised their head. "Ah, how could you speak to me this way? And a woman to another woman, too?"

"Yeah, I'm not standing down until you identify yourself. Woman-to-woman."

"I am Argathia, Priestess of Coryn from Planet Aveen." She lifted her hands with the flowing movements of a dancer, awaiting some sort of adulation.

"And I'm Lartha, Queen of I've No Time for Your Crap."

Argathia burst into tears and fell upon the platform again.

"Spare me," muttered Lartha. "Okay, Rivers, you and Nurse Quilliard might as well do your thing."

As the doctor moved past the security chief, he said, "What is wrong with you? Can't you tell her nerves are frayed?"

"She keeps up this act, it'll be my last nerve you should be worried about."

The doctor gave Lartha the side-eye and darted over to his new patient.

Captain Warq and Commander Davan entered the Parlour.

Argathia pushed her way out of Rivers' and Quilliard's grasps and leapt off the platform, staggering towards the senior officers.

"Which one of you is the captain? I must speak with whomever is in charge!"

Warq read her plea on his visor. "I am Captain Dustin Warq," he signed. "How might I—" He had to stop his response as he needed his hands to catch the woman collapsing into his arms.

Very rarely did the captain speak aloud, but he said to Rivers, "A little help, Doctor?"

"Right away, Captain," signed the doctor with Nurse Quilliard by his side. "AT-stripe, hover-stretcher!"

The stretcher appeared and the doctor and nurse gingerly lifted Argathia onto it.

"Poor thing," said the nurse as Argathia laid her hand over her forehead with a soft moan of despair. "I can't imagine what she's been through."

Lartha stood with one hand on her hip. "She's fine."

Captain Warq turned his head at her words on his visor.

She signed, "There's nothing really wrong with this one, Captain. Well... she'll live, I mean."

Rivers scowled at her. "Wow. You know, I never pegged you as apathetic. Guess all your years in security have put your heart in deep freeze."

"You watch it!" barked Reez.

Lartha turned her head to the deputy chief. "Do I look like I need defending?"

"Nope. This one's on the house."

She shook her head, a faint smile on her lips. *Loyal to a fault, stubborn as all out,* she thought. *Always has been.*

"That's enough," signed the captain with curt movements. "Doctor, tend to your patient and report to me with the findings."

"Yes, Captain."

"Lieutenant Commander Lartha and Lieutenant Reez, come with us."

"Aye, Captain," they signed in unison.

For some unknown reason, no one addressed Herb at all during this encounter. He walked around the 'port console and stepped to the platform where Argathia had lain. Then he stared at a smattering of crystallized granules on the pad.

"Huh." He opened one of his pockets and removed a small thin sheet of tacky acrylic, pulled away the backing, and pressed it to the 'port pad.

After two hours, the patient had been examined, washed, and was resting in a private recovery room on fresh sheets, wrapped in a pink linen robe, lent to her by Nurse Quilliard. The nurse not only had felt especially sympathetic for this genteel soul, but she had also been the same height and build, so that was convenient.

"There, how are you now?" asked Quilliard, fluffing this latest pillow choice.

"So much better, thank you. My poor head. This has all been such a trial!" said Argathia.

"We have trauma counsellors in our Mental Wellness unit. With your permission, I can speak to Dr. Rivers about assigning one to help you."

Argathia waved her hand dismissively. "No, no, don't trouble yourself, my dear. You are too kind, though. So much so, I would very much like you to accept this little token."

The priestess made a motion as if to cup her hands together but kept her fingers from touching. She moved her hands in opposite directions, as if she were feeling a sphere of sorts. The air sparked the gap between her hands, revealing a glowing object forming in the air.

Quilliard was transfixed.

Argathia placed her right hand under the object as the illumination ended, and a perfectly cut gem resembling an amethyst landed into her palm.

"Here, my dear," she said.

The nurse gasped. "But it's huge! This can't all be for me!"

"Why, of course it is! A gift from this priestess to a divine caretaker."

Quilliard held the gem in her palms with complete disbelief. "I understand the Priestesses of Aveen believe in mysticism, but I never knew they could perform... erm..."

"Magic?"

"Well, yes, for lack of a better term."

"Magic is indeed the correct term, my child. But yes, a select few of us can." She placed a hand on her head as more tears threatened. "That is why *they* were after me. To keep me as their own personal... oh, I just cannot speak about it right now!"

"They? Who? The vandals who hurt you?"

"Please, my dear woman. I must rest."

"Of course." The nurse patted Argathia's forearm. "Do get some sleep. Another nurse will tend you on their rounds."

Argathia sunk into her pillows. "Too kind." She closed her eyes.

Nurse Quilliard slowly stepped back and dimmed the lights before exiting the room.

The corner of Argathia's lips curled as she sunk into a deep sleep.

Back in her own quarters, Jenna Quilliard placed the stone on a floating mantel. She admired it for a few moments, then decided to head to the niche that contained her bed. Putting the blackout mask over her eyes, she snuggled under the covers and said, "Reader, resume with Chapter 7 of *The Mist Upon the Morrow*."

She turned on her side, toward the wall, as the narrator read the text of her book.

The gem upon the mantel began to glow.

Herb tossed and turned upon his cot. No matter how many times he tried deep breathing or imagining a story in his head, so he could relax enough to go to sleep, he'd stayed awake.

"Time?" he asked aloud.

The numerical reading projected onto the ceiling and a voice said, "It is 03:00 Keangal Standard Time."

"Bleh."

He removed the coverlet and got up, scratching his head, realizing he could use a haircut. Herb glanced around his desk, found a cable tie, and fastened it, to keep his long bangs out of his face. *Good enough.*

A yawn escaped, which gave him pause. Should he try to go back to bed? He was tired, but his mind also still felt too full to sleep.

"FindIt, open last file," he said to his computer.

The Mining Guild's analysis of the crystal dust was still pending. Herb knew this file would dynamically update, so he read how the data he'd sent them kept being passed to various individuals. Apparently, the elements weren't readily identifiable. This would happen, of course, as new gems and minerals were always being discovered.

He decided to check on another of his requests and smiled. They had agreed with his findings on the other crystal and had approved of renaming it Davatio, for Davan and Horatio. Herb would save that news for Davan's birthday.

He toggled back to the first report, and it refreshed. The screen read:

> Unknown. Sending out to Xeth Division of the Guild.

Herb blew air out of his lips. Once again, he'd have to wait for answers.

The next day, Argathia walked about the halls of the Med wing on the arm of none other than Dr. Rivers himself.

"Oh, for the love of..." trailed Lartha, who was just on her way to visit the patient, and to relieve the security officer on duty. For some reason, that officer had not accompanied them.

That's not like Parren, Lartha thought. *She's always by the book. Where the gleek is she now?*

Upon seeing the security chief, Rivers raised his chin, as if to parade the priestess as some sort of trophy, for Argathia shone resplendently as an incomparable beauty. The flow of her scarlet waves glistened in the overhead lights, and the silver gossamer-like dress covering a simple white silk shift gave her an almost other-worldly appearance. Even the soft purple hues of her skin glowed, very closely matching the gemstone on a brooch she wore.

Lartha stood akimbo in her black and grey uniform with her right hand close enough to her holster.

Argathia lifted her determined little chin. "Why, Todd, it's that woman who treated me so horribly yesterday. I don't even know how a person like this could be responsible for the safety of other souls!"

Rivers glared at Lartha. "I normally trust our captain implicitly, but even this one is proof that he doesn't always get it right."

"Are you done?" asked Lartha. "Because my poor bruised feelings."

"Why are you even here?" he asked.

"Assigned to protect the drama queen."

"Oh, Todd!" Argathia leaned into his chest.

"How can you speak to her this way?" said Rivers.

Lartha watched Argathia slump into his arms, weeping. "Yeah, it boggles the mind, doesn't it? What was I thinking? Gee, my boots will get all worn from jumping to such conclusions."

Argathia raised her head off Rivers' chest and shot darts from her eyes at the security chief. But just as quickly, she turned to the doctor and said, "Not everyone is as kind to me as you, my dearest man. Allow me to give you a small token of my esteem."

She gently pushed out of his arms and waved her right hand in a circular motion over her palm. Just as the night before, sparks flew from her fingers and a bright light appeared, then dimmed to reveal an amethyst ring. The priestess removed it from her left palm and put her right hand out, reaching for his hand.

Lartha's eyes narrowed. Rivers, entranced, offered his hand. Argathia moved to place the ring on his middle finger.

"Nope!" Lartha slapped Argathia's hand away.

"Owch, you brute!" cried the priestess.

"Lartha, what the—that's assault of my patient," said Rivers. "I'm putting you on report!"

"Did your brain fall out of your skull?" she cried. "This woman pulls rings out of the air, and you're just going to let her slip it on you? What if it's a mind-control device?" Lartha tapped her right leg. "Right, what can you find, girl?"

With a hiss, Argathia waved her hand at the prosthesis. The readings on Right Leg's scanner stopped transmitting, then the leg buckled. The security officer managed to grab hold of a wall railing before she fell.

"Oh, *gleek* no. If you hurt one of my girls, you're going down."

"Is that a threat?"

"It's a promise, babes." Lartha straightened up, leaning on her left leg for support. "Well, doctor, still think your dream girl's so innocent?"

Rivers stared at Argathia, who had recovered the ring, and she pushed it into his palm.

"She—she—" His eyes glazed over. "She was just defending herself."

"At least *you* understand me, Todd." Argathia glided the ring along his skin and slipped it onto his finger.

Lartha tapped her wristband. "Security to the bridge, this is Lartha—"

Argathia waved her hand again. The wristband stopped functioning. Then Lartha's left leg went offline.

"AT-stripe! Chair!" Lartha shouted.

Nothing happened.

Argathia had placed both hands on the Accessible Tech stripe. Then she took Rivers by the arm and said, "Let's go this way instead, Todd. You mentioned taking me to the command deck? I should very much like to visit it."

Lartha carefully slid her back against the wall until she parked her bottom on the floor. She removed each leg as the couple walked away, then pressed a sequence of buttons in a hidden panel. In no time, they were standing on their own.

"Thanks, Herbie, for the fail-safe. Girls, I need you to run like the wind. Left, blink out a message. Right, you transmit it on this covert channel. Then, I want you to meet me at another location."

The legs hopped in agreement.

Lartha gave them the message and coordinates, and they took off. She opened a tiny, shielded pocket inside her jacket, and grabbed a small comm that connected with a specific device in her chambers.

"Rose! I'm in Med-Wing C!"

"Chief!"

It amazed Lartha that he would be the first of her team to arrive as backup. Her sentient legs ran beside him in solidarity. She presumed they finally considered him an ally.

"Beachfront!"

He handed her a new comm band. "What else do you need? Is this hover-chair in top working order?"

"Rosie's never let me down yet," said Lartha, patting an armrest. "What I need is for you to get to the bridge!"

"But Lieutenant Reez is headed there. He said for me to assist you!"

"No, I want you both on the bridge. Assist him instead. I'll follow shortly."

Bronwryck turned as if to bolt, then quickly spun around and asked, "Are you absolutely sure?"

"Dead sure. You need to be in the room with her. It has to be you."

He smiled widely. "Ohhh. Got it. On my way!"

Lartha and her chair dashed in another direction while she issued various commands to her team through her new wristband.

Rivers and Argathia entered the bridge. Commander Davan frowned at the sight of them.

"Doctor?" he signed. "This is highly irregular."

"Dr. Rivers," signed the captain. "We do not know the origin of this person, and you are fully aware it breaks security protocols for you to bring her here. You must leave the command deck at once!"

Rivers stared without response.

"Doctor?" signed the captain.

"Dr. Rivers, are you all right?" said Iris.

A malicious glint flashed in Argathia's eyes, but it was immediately replaced with a demure gaze.

"I am hurt you all think the worst of me," she mewed. "I was told the crew of the *S.S. SpoonZ* were inclusive and caring. And I had also been under the impression you upheld the priestesses of Aveen in the highest regards. But alas, I now see your true colours."

Security officers Reez and Bronwryck entered the bridge together.

"You misunderstand us," signed Captain Warq. "We mean no offense, but until we have confirmation of who you are, I must insist you return to your quarters. Lieutenant Reez?"

"Yes, Captain?"

"Remove our... guest... from the bridge."

Reez indicated for Bronwryck to take her arm. The junior security guard moved forward as Reez kept his weapon aimed.

"Please, come with me, Priestess, and—*YEOW!*" cried Bronwryck. "Hey! Do you even know you're being poisoned?"

Argathia wrinkled her nose. "I'm sure I have no idea what you mean."

"Ugh, I'm so queasy," he said. "Maddox, can you please stop this sensation?" Bronwryck listened for a reply. "What?" He stood still and watched Argathia. "Wait, you're not a priestess from Aveen! You're a—"

She whirled both hands at him. A pulse knocked him on the floor, unconscious.

Reez fired his weapon, but the beam bounced harmlessly about several centimeters in front of her.

"Oh crap. Projective transparent shielding."

"Alert Status 4," signed the captain. The alarm and accompanying text were transmitted throughout the ship.

The priestess put up her palms and made a fanning motion, as if to pacify. "Now, now, you have it all wrong, my sweet children. I am no threat."

Reez was on one knee, weapon still raised at Argathia while pressing two fingers of his other hand against Bronwryck's neck. "He's alive, thank the heavens. And as for you not being a threat—"

"Oh, that? Well, he was speaking utter nonsense, and he is so much brawnier than little me. Why, I was the one who felt threatened!"

Reez gritted his teeth. "Rivers, why in the worlds are you not down here, attending to Lieutenant Bronwryck?"

Dr. Todd Rivers had been staring rather vacantly ahead during the entire confrontation. Finally, he blinked, turned to Argathia and said, "Did I hear correctly? Are you being poisoned?"

"Rivers!" shouted Reez.

Commander Davan raised a scanning device at the priestess, but Argathia caught the motion out of the corner of her eye and waved a hand. It was automatically deactivated.

Iris, who seemed to be of little interest to the priestess, covertly signed a phrase behind her back, using the language only for the crew of the command deck. The captain read it on his visor, and subtly raised a hand to his ear. There had been no need for pilots Renley and Udana to do as he did, since they always had this tech activated when on duty. Argathia's eyes remained on Davan, so the captain threw down his visor in a rage.

She and the commander turned their heads. The captain made a sign. Davan touched behind his ear.

Argathia's suspicion was evident. "I'm afraid I don't know that one, Captain."

"My apologies. A dialect from my planet. I meant to say I am sorry for losing my temper."

Good one, Captain, thought-projected Davan.

Can everyone receive me? asked Warq.

Receiving, projected Iris.

Receiving, projected Udana and Renley, one after the other.

I'm here, too, projected Reez. He reached down and subtly inserted a finger to tap behind Bronwryck's ear. *Maddox? Are we reaching?*

No response.

I don't think we can speak to Maddox, projected Davan. *Only to Lieutenant Bronwryck, and he's out cold.*

"What's happening here?" said Argathia, slyly moving about the deck. "You've all gone suddenly quiet."

Captain Warq noticed her speaking, picked up his visor, and straightened. "You have placed this crew in a position where we cannot trust you," he signed. "What choice do we have, what with your abilities to render our equipment useless. Now, enough of these games. State your true intentions!"

"Once more you misunderstand me, Captain. I am but of magic. As science vessel personnel, you must rely solely on acquired facts and evidence, which is a shame, since there is an entire universe you're missing out on." She swirled her fingers about, and sparks generated a mass within the space between her palms yet again. The result was an even larger purple gem. It floated in the air, then she pulsed it to land upon the captain's chair, at his console.

"A peace offering," she added, "to make amends for any miscommunications."

Before the captain could question what appeared out of thin air, the command deck lift doors whooshed open. Another security team stepped in, led by Lartha with Herb behind her.

Argathia's eyes widened at the sight of the security chief standing on what appeared to be the same legs the priestess thought she had destroyed.

"What are *you* doing here?" she snarled.

Lartha, without a weapon in sight, had her hands cupped and her body in a submissive stance. After a second or two, she moved forward, ignoring Reez and Bronwryck, her head slightly bowed.

"Argathia, Priestess of Coryn, I was a doubter, but now, I believe. Won't you please forgive my unspeakably rude behaviour since your arrival?"

The priestess raised a brow suspiciously.

Lartha uncupped her hands and revealed an item. It was the gem Argathia had created for Nurse Quilliard.

"Where did you get that?" asked the priestess.

"In the nurse's chambers. I was going to interrogate her, but when I saw this beauty, I just had to have it. And from the moment I held it in my hands, I began to have a wider understanding of you. You want to make all things magical and serene, and I, for one, want to believe."

Lartha? What's happened to you? projected Iris. *You don't even sound like you! Your voice pattern has changed!*

No reply.

Lartha put the stone down on Davan's console. She stepped closer to the priestess.

"Please, my lady, can we not take hands and be friends?"

Argathia eyed her suspiciously but only for a moment. Not being able to resist the notion of controlling the security officer, the priestess stretched out her hands, palms down. Lartha put her own gloved palms underneath, then pressed them against Argathia's.

The priestess inhaled sharply. Her nail beds buzzed and seared. She cried out, but found she couldn't release her hands, as if they'd been held in place by a tractor beam. Soon, the polish of her dark fingernails melted and ran down her fingertips.

"Noooo!"

Lartha smirked and stepped back. "Okay, Right, you know what to do!"

Her right leg whirred. Argathia, despite the pain in her hands, lunged at Lartha, only to be thrown back. She bounced off an unseen barrier and tried charging to the left and right only to be hurled back again. She screamed with frustration.

"Yeah, well, boo-frikking-hoo, lady," said Lartha. "I vowed you were going down, and I don't break my promises." She turned her head slightly. "Herbie?"

"Yup?"

"Do your thing."

"'Kay." Herb touched Rivers' hand with a device and rendered the gem on his ring inert. The doctor blinked a few times, as if awakened from a dream. Before Rivers could speak, Herb said, pointing to Bronwryck, "Tend to your patient, Doctor."

"What? Patient?" He looked down. "Oh, oh, yes."

Herb moved over to the captain's console and seemed to enact the same protocol with the huge gem, but it took a bit longer than with the ring.

Mr. Herbert? projected the captain.

Will explain soon, Captain. Right now, this stone is being used as a conduit. Not to manipulate us, but in this case, to track the ship.

"There's no damage to Lieutenant Bronwryck's brain," said Rivers. "The pulse just knocked him out. I'll give him a mild stimulant." The doctor injected Bronwryck with a hypodermic solution.

The security officer's eyelids quivered, then opened. "Where am I?"

"The deck, kid," said Reez.

"Remove me from this hold at once!" cried Argathia.

"What am I, new?" said Lartha.

Bronwryck slowly sat up, then focused on the priestess. "She's not an Aveenian! She's a Piranha Pirate!"

Lartha cocked her head, still staring at Argathia. "What? She doesn't look like the Pirates we've encountered. Could she be a mercenary recruit?"

"No, she is Virobian. Her grey skin only looks purple because she's poisoning herself!"

"What tripe," groaned Argathia.

"It's true," said Bronwryck. "Maddox told me!"

"Yeah," said Herb. "She's covered in crushed Mauvenite. It dyes her skin but also seeps into her pores. It usually makes folks terribly nauseated but perhaps Virobians might not experience that side effect. Anyway, she'll definitely die in a few days unless we provide an antidote."

"Lies," said Argathia. "Lies to intimidate me."

"Also, the conduit gems are for mind control and tracking. I had to disable three more on the ship, given to security guards who were assigned to her. She's trying to lure the Brigade."

Captain Warq turned round to their prisoner. "Is this correct? You are a member of the Brigade?"

Argathia folded her arms and turned away. "I am not."

"Oh yeah?" said Lartha. "Hey, Beachfront?"

"She's lying," he said simply, adopting a similar smirk to his superior officer, but aiming it at the pirate.

"But why would you do this to us?" signed Warq.

Argathia turned to face him. "Why would *you* grant safe passage to one of our own, the one who betrayed us to the Keangal?" she signed.

Iris managed to keep as still as a rod. She held her breath.

"I do not know to whom you are referring," signed the captain.

"Ha!" barked Argathia, in a deeper, gravelly tone. "We tracked Jaq Miran to a rendezvous point that intersected with this vessel. Then, all traces of them disappeared. My brother, Joz, accepted you at your word, but he's a little too trusting for my liking. So, I killed him."

Warq's lips parted.

"One has to be firm as a leader, and he was weak. Trying to speak *reasonably* with subordinates. Where in the galaxy he got an idea like that, I'll never know."

The captain inhaled slowly, knowing it was he who had given that instruction. He steeled himself and signed, "Tell us who you are, exactly."

She leaned one arm against the invisible wall of the shielding and put the other on her hip. "I am Jozelyn, now Prime of the Brigade. And you... are all surrounded." She pressed a brooch on her breast and barked, "School, attack!"

The command crew directed their attention at the consoles in order to gather readings of the multitude of ships that would uncloak and batter down on the *S.S. SpoonZ*.

They waited.

And waited.

Then waited some more.

"Captain," said Lieutenant Udana, "I'm not picking up any vessels in the area.

"Neither am I," signed Lieutenant Renley. "Are they still cloaked?"

Jozelyn blinked. She tapped her chest again. "Prime Jozelyn Miran to School 8V. Uncloak and attack!"

"Status!" signed the captain.

"I'm reading nothing," signed Davan.

"No incoming communications," said Iris.

"Still no indications of the presence of enemy vessels," said Udana.

You're not going to find any, projected Herb.

What do you mean? projected Warq.

They're not coming. Those conduit gems are bidirectional in their comm capabilities. I sent the School away before destroying the stones.

Where did you send them? projected Davan.

Zeta-12.

Iris's eyes went wide. *Isn't that where the Lug Nut mercenaries made their new compound?*

Yup. Major travel warning was issued not to go there. And the Brigade had cheated the Lug Nut bosses out of a huge deal on a heist. So, that should be a fun reunion.

Way to go, Herbie! projected Lartha.

"What's happening?" Jozelyn stomped her feet within her invisible cage.

"You're boned," said Lartha. "And not in a fun way."

Warq held out his hands helplessly.

"Sorry, Captain," she signed, her eyes full of mock-contrition.

He shook his head with a smile.

"Okay, lady," continued Lartha, "I'm gonna take the shield down, and my lovely assistant Lieutenant Bronwryck will slip these cuffs on you while my lovelier assistant Lieutenant Reez will aim a weapon at your head. Play nice, and I'll even let Medical un-poison you before we hand you over to the Keangal outpost for your arraignment."

"Wait just a minute! Where is my School? I insist you tell me!"

Lartha gestured to Bronwryck that she'd decided to cuff the pirate herself. "Sorry, babes," she said while binding Jozelyn's hands. "School's out for summer."

As Lartha carted the pirate leader away, Herb called out after them.

"Hey, Jozelyn, I'd like the specs on the liquid circuitry you used on your nails that included generator tech. So, if you have time before we send you away—"

Jozelyn responded with a ferocious gesture she managed even while cuffed, before entering the lift.

Herb jolted at the motion. "Huh. Rude."

"I can't thank you enough for opening your resources to us," signed Captain Warq. "The information we gathered from your expertise on soil restoration alone shall be beneficial to the planetary representatives who petitioned the Agricultural Guild for aid."

Avalon, Priestess of Coryn—an actual priestess of Coryn this time—bowed serenely to the captain, then walked away, for she was about to partake in The Quietening, a type of fasting from conversation—spoken, written, or signed.

Warq studied her movements and noted how she almost glided down the path back to the tower, where she would carry out her fast for ten more days. The calmness that enveloped her made him wonder if he might try such a rest from communicating with others in such a manner. It apparently emptied the mind of "clutter," and he had to admit as a captain, the filing cabinets in his mind had filled to overflowing. A certain date kept nagging his brain, but he pushed it far away. *Not now. I just can't think of her now.*

He turned back to the gathering centre, hoping to discuss ideas and discoveries with his away team. Convening with the priestesses of planet Aveen had quickly turned into a bumper crop of vital agricultural sciences, if one could excuse the pun. Their botanical knowledge had been incomparable, especially in the field of medicinal uses. The variety of flora on Aveen had been astounding, and it was no wonder their study had been the prime focus of the Order of Coryn.

Upon entering through the glass doors of the gathering centre, which resembled a sprawling single-storey greenhouse, Warq spotted Commander Davan animatedly discussing his morning with a fellow scientist.

"I think I might have died and gone to heaven," signed Davan to the young woman dressed in white cleanroom attire. Her cheeks flushed to a rich mauve when she laughed.

"And I've barely shown you anything! That was only one lab," said the woman, pulling off her hood to reveal cropped auburn-brown hair.

Davan noted how similar the tones were to Herb's hair, and he smiled with his eyes. "Even so, it was a feast to behold! I want to learn everything until my head actually explodes. I mean that. If I leave here with my head intact, I shall be sorely disappointed."

Warq laughed at this.

Davan turned around.

"Please, do try to learn as much as you can without beheading yourself, Commander," signed the captain.

Now Davan honk-laughed. "Very well. I'm sure Lieutenant Commander Herbert would also prefer I didn't lose my head."

"I feel we're on the cusp of a really dirty joke," signed Lartha, joining the group.

The young scientist howled with laughter. Warq groaned. Davan remembered himself and signed, "Captain, Lieutenant Commander Lartha, may I introduce Cossander Koll?"

"Pleased to meet you," signed Warq.

"A pleasure," signed Lartha.

"Cleric Cossander is a botanical scientist who works in the Pain Center."

Lartha raised her brows. "Oh, really? I feel like I might need to give you a good listening to. Always open to discoveries that reduce pain levels."

"I would love to share our findings. Do you have chronic pain or sudden onset pain?"

"Yes," said Lartha, with a cheeky grin.

The scientist nodded with a chuckle. "Got you. Well, if you have some time after luncheon, I'd love to give you a tour."

"And I'll join you," signed Davan.

"But it would be the same one I gave you, Commander," signed Cossander.

"I know! I'm just so excited about this research. I don't mind a rerun."

She smiled brightly. "Wonderful! Then you are most welcome to join us. As are you, Captain."

"That is very kind. Sadly, I must decline. I have a lecture to attend on water purification using filtration from Fythan seeds. We've had reports that a planet in the Weredawn cluster is in danger of clean water deficit due to poor industrial waste practices. If we could bring this solution in concert with other manufacturing technologies, this could help the land and the waters and most importantly, the people, to recover."

"Yes, for sure. And please don't be shy to ask Professor Tydark anything you like afterwards. They are more than happy to oblige."

"I will, thank you," signed Warq.

"But now, food!" signed Davan. He texted Herb:

-- Have you eated?

-- No. Not eated yet.

-- Come and food with us.

-- I will, in a second.

Davan paused.

-- A most-people second or a Herb second?

No response for a moment. Finally:

-- A Herb second.

Davan smiled.

-- I will give you maximum 30 minutes for this Herb second, then you have to join us in the cafeteria.

Another long moment.

-- I'll join you now. I need more than 30 minutes, and food might be good.

-- See you soon.

-- Now that you made me think of eating, I realize I'm really hungry. Save me some sweet gerkins. I love those.

-- Will do!

"Herb is on his way," signed Davan.

"Excellent," signed Warq.

Cossander tilted her head to concentrate on an incoming message. "Ah, understood," she said. "I'll be there directly." She turned to her guests and signed, "I'm so sorry, but I'm afraid I shall have to reschedule our lab tour. It seems I am needed elsewhere this afternoon. Please excuse me."

"Not a worry," signed Lartha. "Even if you send us your recommendations remotely, that would be great."

"Oh yes, we are compiling a package of records for your away team. In fact, your Mr. Herbert has been most interested in our data transfer protocols. He's been with our information tech staff all morning. I didn't know that was his interest. For some reason, I thought he was a navigations engineer."

"Our Mr. Herbert is interested in whatever interests him!" signed Davan.

"And we love him for it," added Lartha, patting her legs.

"Indeed, we do," signed Warq.

"That's lovely," signed Cossander. "Now, if you'll please excuse me. I must leave you to your luncheon. All our ingredients are available for each item at the buffet, and there is shielding against cross-contamination. Enjoy!"

The trio indicated their thanks and headed towards the expanse of offerings in the cafeteria, a court of cooked and raw foods in an array of colours and textures. As they headed towards the rows of aromatic savoury pies, they each felt their tummies rumble, and snickered at this happening in unison.

"I guess we forgot our mid-morning snacks," signed Lartha to the captain.

"Very true!"

"Oh!" signed Davan, pointing. "There's Iris!"

"Hey, friend," signed Lartha, then noticed Iris walked with her cane. "Hey, friend!" she said aloud.

"Hi!" she replied with a smile. "Whew, what a morning. My eyes felt full. So many colours, shapes, readouts, lights. I need a little break." She paused. "Mmm! What smells so good?"

"Pies," said Lartha. "You can have a piece. I'm eating the rest."

"I challenge you to a *Snarr-cha* duel," signed Davan, whose wristband holo interpreter had been activated.

Lartha put a hand on her hip while holding a utensil with the other one. "You wanna walk back that statement, bud?"

"I get particularly brave when it comes to savoury pies."

"Now, now, there's more than enough food for everyone," signed Warq, whose wristband also had the same setting as Davan's. "But as your captain, I'm going first." He lunged for a huge piece of pie.

Iris laughed. "Isn't that not very captainy of you? Aren't you supposed to put your crew first?"

"I am, Lieutenant Commander. I am tasting everything first to make sure it's safe for you all."

Lartha chuckled. "Yeah, pull the other one, Captain."

"No thank you, Chief. I shall never attempt to touch your legs. While I trust you and my crew with our lives, I am not entirely sure about the intentions of Left and Right."

They all laughed and revelled in this relaxing away mission where nothing more eventful than learning would be the course of the day.

At the buffet, Iris felt the information card and began to salivate. "Oh, this will be delicious. One serving, please!"

"Please input your allergy information so we might offer you a pleasant meal," said and displayed the food stand.

"Oh, yes, they mentioned this." She held up her wrist band and said, "Lieutenant Eileen Iris, food allergies and sensitivities."

"Information accepted. Now when you select a dish, we will warn you if any ingredients contain allergens or sensitivities that affect you."

"Thanks. I'd like one serving of this Beinan Spice pie."

"Just one moment!" cried Clarence, jetting with alacrity to the food station.

Iris clenched her cane and took a breath. "Clarence, I thought I told you to stay behind and have a nice chat with the agricultural bots. They seemed friendly, didn't they?"

"Hmph. Not even one of them was interested in any of my ideas for optimization. And don't you think for a moment I would let you eat one morsel without making sure it is safe." Xey swivelled xeir aqua metallic head to the food stand's internal bot.

"When were you last calibrated?" asked Clarence.

"Just this morning, as in every morning, at 0600," replied the bot. Iris wasn't sure if she had imagined a snippy tone.

"By what standard?" said Clarence. "I would like to know immediately all the protocols you employ to assure the wellness of—"

"Okay, Clarence, enough. You're being rude," said Iris.

Xey blinked their eye-lights. "Rude?"

"Here are the safety standards we follow. Hope you have enough memory to process it, guidebot," said the food stand, projecting the data into Clarence's receptor.

There was silence. Iris cocked her head. "Is everything okay? Clarence?"

After another long pause, her guidebot said, "Enjoy your pie." Then xey scooted off without a word.

She could hear the jets growing distant and cried, "Clarence? Where are you going?"

"I am not remaining here where I will be insulted by a food stand's digital response. Busybody indeed. The nerve!"

"Um, okay, I'll catch you soon," she said but received no reply. *Oh well.*

The serving of savoury pie hovered onto Iris's plate. She felt the heat of it by her right hand and the aroma filled her nostrils. "Mmm!"

In no time, Warq, Davan, Iris, and Lartha filled their trays and went to find a place to sit.

Their conversation was interrupted by a cacophony of enthusiastic screams and giggles and animated cries.

There at the entrance was Herb, surrounded by children. They bounced and hopped and continued their mix of banter as they danced and ran around him.

Iris activated her implants. "What the actual fweep?"

Herb seemed desperate. He crouched and pointed his finger towards the food stands. "Hey, look over there!"

The children's heads turned at once, then they ran away to get some lunch.

Herb's private room activated. "Ahhh, that's better." He breathed a sigh of relief and gazed upon the lake in front of him, the still breeze fluttering the surface of the water. Herb made a note to add some ducks. He liked ducks.

"I take it that you aren't particularly fond of children?" Davan said, appearing as a holo in his private room.

Herb pulled out his Quargnan speech device. "It's always been a wonder of mine that more parents don't eat their young. Okay, not true. I love children. When they are sleeping. Sleeping children are my favourites."

A honk-laugh.

"Please tell me you don't want to be a parent," said Herb.

"Don't worry. I'm perfectly content remaining child-free."

"Thank the heavens for that."

"Do you want me to bring lunch to you in the garden? We can eat on a bench there."

Herb's private room dissolved, showing that he was inserting his sound-dampening earpieces. "No, I'm fine." He tapped both ears. "Mmm. Perfect."

Davan suddenly looked concerned, peering to the left and behind Herb. The engineer turned around. A small girl, dressed in the beige leggings and tunic that the other children wore, cupped her ears and rocked, staring at the floor. Her chestnut brown pigtails swished back and forth with her movements.

"Hm," said Herb. He walked over and crouched beside the child, keeping enough distance not to startle her. The girl looked at him with alarm in those blue-green eyes.

"Loud?" Herb signed.

The child nodded.

Herb nodded in return. Then he pointed to his earpieces. "These help," he signed. "Want to try?"

The child stopped rocking but still cupped her ears. Herb opened a pocket and pulled out his spares. He looked kindly at the girl and showed her the earpieces.

She seemed sceptical.

Herb sat cross-legged and placed the assistive tech on his knee. "If you don't want them touching you, they can hover in shielding mode," he signed. "They still work really well that way. Might be better even, since these are sized for my ears."

The child looked away as if to ponder this. Then she turned back to Herb and nodded. Herb smiled and configured the setting. He indicated that the child put down her hands, and she did. Herb set each earpiece to float on either side of her and activated them.

The expression on the child's face changed at once, a mixture of fascination and relief.

"Better?" signed Herb.

"Better," signed the child.

"Good. I'm Herb."

"Gerri."

"Nice to meet you. This is Davan. He's really friendly."

"Hello, Gerri," signed Davan.

Fascinated by the golden sash around Davan's waist, the child gestured at her own waist. Davan tilted his head in wonderment.

"I think she wants to feel the fabric," signed Herb. "Am I right?" he signed to the girl.

Gerri nodded.

"By all means!" signed Davan, then removed his officer's sash and handed it over to the girl. Gerri rubbed it with her fingers, then looked up and smiled at them both.

"You can keep it for our lunchtime, okay?" added Davan.

"Thank you!" Gerri signed, her face glowing like lilacs kissed by the morning sun.

Rushing towards them was an exasperated novice of Aveen— one who had been assigned to supervise these children and felt convinced it was akin to herding felines—and, upon reaching them, signaled to Gerri to gather with the rest of the children at a table. The girl followed her obediently. She looked back at Herb and Davan standing together and waved. They waved back.

"Yeah, I see what you mean," said Davan. "You're terrible with kids."

Herb grinned and kissed his bare arm. "Some kids are cool."

Lartha waved them over to the table. "Join us, Herbie! Your lover boy even set a full tray for you."

"With sweet gerkins?"

"The sweetest," signed Davan.

"Awesome."

They all exchanged what they had learned that morning and couldn't wait to discover what the next few days would bring. Feeling sated with food but hungry for more information, they rose from the table, ready to meet their guide, who would instruct them on where to go for their next sessions.

Warq waved upon spotting a priestess scientist heading toward them. "Hello! We're so looking forward to what comes next this day! I am Captain Dustin Warq."

The sister of Aveen's expression was grave. "Captain, I must take you to my superior."

"Is there anything wrong?" he signed.

"Please, come with me, all of you," she signed and spoke aloud.

"Orphans? All those kids are orphans?" asked Herb.

"They are, Lieutenant Commander. They are also the sole survivors of their families. A virus had wiped out the other occupants of their world. These children had a rare immunity. We have been studying them for the better part of eighteen months, and they are suffering no ill effects. They are not even carriers."

"But they are on their own now," said Iris.

"And you want us to provide them with safe transport, Sister Renaissance?" signed Captain Warq.

"We do."

"But we are not a combat vessel, Sister."

"I know, you are a science vessel."

"Who has a not-so-great relationship with the Brigade," added Lartha.

"And yet, you have defied them on more than one occasion," said Sister Renaissance. "Word travels."

"Because we are a research and development ship, Captain," signed Davan, "we're well equipped to meet the children's physical and mental support requirements."

Warq nodded. "How many children would require transport?"

"Twenty," signed Sister Renaissance.

"Including little Gerri?" asked Herb.

Davan stared at him with a twinkle in his gaze.

"What?" said Herb.

Davan winked. Herb blushed and grinned.

"And where will we transport them to?" asked Lartha.

"The Hollet System," said Sister Renaissance. "Specifically, the moon of Holli."

"That's a fair distance away, Captain," said Davan. "However, through Keangal-charted routes, we could transport the children and return here within two weeks."

"Good to know. Sister, are there people in Holli with a system in place to support the children?"

"Yes, indeed. We have been in continual communications with their child wellness ambassador and are satisfied that these children will thrive."

Iris remained quiet until now. "I was raised with orphaned and/ or abandoned children. Sister Renaissance and Captain Warq, may I have access to the data regarding the supports and placement protocols for these children?"

The sister raised her chin but changed her expression when she saw the concern in Iris's eyes. "Yes, of course, Lieutenant Commander."

"Then," signed Warq, "if you allow my team some time to discuss this matter, after we have examined the materials about this destination and its supports, I'm sure we can present a solution that will suit."

"Thank you, Captain. It's you and your crew's attention to detail that gives us confidence in you all."

Warq smiled. "Where can we have access to this data, Sister?"

"This way," she signed, then led them through an open door.

Four days after taking the children aboard the *S.S. SpoonZ*, things were going fantastically well. Really, they were.

Three of the children ran screaming throughout the corridors of the Engineering wing.

"Help, help!"

"Ronnie's been reassembled!"

"It wasn't our fault, we swear!"

Herb raised his head from the status report he'd been given by Lieutenant Sheena.

Another cry: "We don't know how to make him go back to usual!"

What's this now? He poked his head out the door and a child just missed ramming into his stomach.

"Hey, slow down! What's going on?"

All three children ran to him, trying to explain everything all at once. Herb winced and put in his earpieces.

"Okay, okay, one at a time!"

"We used the 'Port Parlour and put Ronnie on a pad. Now he's topsy turvy, and the woman fainted."

Herb blinked. He tapped his wristband. "Herbert to the Parlour. Who's at post?"

No reply. He began to run. "Herbert to Medical. I need a team at the Parlour. One of the children might have been injured."

"Sending a team now. What is the nature of the injury?"

"I don't know. I'm not there yet. Will update when at scene." He tore around the corner while the children ran after him, shouting with alarm and excitement.

When the door whooshed open to the 'Port Parlour, there was young Ronnie, giggling at him.

Herb tapped his wristband. "Herbert to Medical. Child is unharmed. Repeat, child is unharmed."

"So, no assistance required?"

He spotted Lieutenant Weznyck sitting on a stool with her head between her legs. Gerri was gently patting her arm.

"Bring a medic for Lieutenant Weznyck. She might have fainted."

"They're on their way."

"Are you all right, Lieutenant?"

"Can't speak. Want to barf."

"Keep taking deep breaths."

Gerri tried handing her a glass of water. Weznyck accepted it gratefully.

Herb directed his attention to the 'Port deck. Sitting as proud as punch on a pad was little Ronnie, wearing legs on his arms and arms on his legs.

"Where did you get those prosthetic casings?" said Herb, with an edge to his voice.

Ronnie just giggled louder. Then the three children who had beckoned Herb laughed just as loudly.

"That's enough. You made Lieutenant Weznyck faint and doing harm to someone is not funny."

"But it's just pretend!"

"That doesn't matter. How would you like it if someone made you so frightened, thinking you caused a major accident, it made you fall down and really sick to your tummy?"

"I wouldn't like it," said Gerri.

All the children looked at her.

"Well, I wouldn't."

Herb smiled. He turned back to the pranksters. "You know, prostheses are important pieces of equipment and not for playtime. Several people on this ship use them as part of their everyday assistive tech."

"Like Chief Lartha," said Ronnie in a dreamy tone. "I think she's beautiful. Also scary."

Herb chuckled. "That's fair. She wouldn't be too thrilled to know you stole these from Med-Tech. You know, she's our head of security, and stealing is serious. I might just tell her what you did."

"Eep!" said one of the girls. "We'll bring them back!"

"You will?"

The children nodded.

"And you'll say you're sorry to Lieutenant Weznyck?"

A bunch of apologies flew into the air.

"Thank you," the lieutenant said weakly.

Before further exchanges could be made, the medic walked in, followed by Lartha. Ronnie's eyes grew three times their size.

"I'M SORRY!" he screamed with all his might.

Lartha stopped dead in her tracks, nearly reeling from the volume. She shook her head to focus on the child again and growled, "Yeah... I know I am not seeing this."

All the children except Gerri removed the prosthetic casings off Ronnie and presented themselves to her.

"We didn't know this wasn't funny," said a girl.

"It was supposed to be a joke," said another.

"I kinda thought it was silly, but I was bored," said a boy.

"I got to be rearranged!" said Ronnie, glowing proudly.

Lartha stared, then looked at Gerri. The little girl just shrugged her shoulders. "I'm with you, kid. I don't get it either. So," Lartha said to the other four. "You're bored?"

"Yeah," they replied together.

"Well, how about we march over to Med-Tech, say we're sorry for thieving, and spend the rest of the afternoon polishing floors? That's a super fun activity that never ever gets boring."

They collectively groaned.

"It's that or the brig, kids. You gotta learn consequences."

They gasped.

"That's what I thought. Polishing floors it is. Come with me. March!"

She opened the doors and the four did their best to march, in what they assumed was military style, into the hall.

"Um, Lartha," whispered Herb. "The brig? Isn't that a bit harsh for children?"

"Boo hoo, so I'm not the mother-copter type. If I were you, though, I'd use this time to childproof the entry to this room. I'll also inform the captain that we have to level up safety protocols ship-wide."

Gerri walked up to her.

"Hey, you," said Lartha.

"Can I polish, too?" Gerri signed.

"Did you actually participate in this prank?" asked Herb.

"No. I just like when things get shiny and clean."

"There you go!" said Lartha. "I did say it's super fun! I wasn't lying, you know."

Gerri giggled.

Herb watched with a sort of pride as the little girl marched down the hall beside the security chief while the medic got Lieutenant Weznyck back on her feet.

"FOOD FIGHT!"

"Oh, heavens spare us," muttered Mr. Beyam. His daycare centre had usually been a blissful place, what with there not being many children on board the *S.S. SpoonZ*. Some science vessels hadn't any youngsters at all, depending on the potential danger of the missions, or the type of research expected of the captain and their crew. He typically had ten children between seven and ten standard years, impeccably behaved, some rather influenced by the scholarly nature of their parents.

Today, however, twenty more had been added to their number, and he was convinced some of them had been the spawn of the Netherworld itself.

"Don't, don't!" cried Melba, aged eight standard years and one of the four instigators of the 'Port Parlour prank. "Chief Lartha will make us clean it all up! I can't go through that again!" She covered her chartreuse cheeks with her hands. Her pink ringlets bounced as she shook her head.

Her plea was met with a smack of mashed spuds to the hair. Melba's brown eyes grew almost black with rage.

"I'll pound you into the stars, Brennon!"

And so, it continued like that until an extremely loud and high-pitched horn stopped them in their tracks.

The orphans, covered in various food glops, turned at once to the source of the sound. Gerri had configured Herb's floating earpieces to the full once the food fight had begun, so it took her a moment to notice that everyone was looking in the same direction. She lifted the stylus from her drawing and smiled at Commander Davan. She liked him. He was nice. Although he seemed pretty cross at the moment.

"What in *blazes*"—he dramatically signed the word—"is going on here?"

The ten children of the crew stared at him in desperation. The other nineteen began signing all at once, and as quickly as possible for mortal beings.

Davan felt his eyes boggle at the abundance of phrases thrown at him. He could only make out a few at once, for his own sanity:

"It wasn't me, it was Findley!"

"It wasn't me, I swear! I just wanted to eat my lunch, not wear it!"

"Don't look at me, it wasn't my fault!"

"Oh, you liar, you started it."

"I don't even know how to throw!"

He blinked a few times and then held out his hands to get everyone to stop signing at him. "Enough, children. Just look at this mess you made. No, I don't care who started it. We offer you nourishment because we want you to stay healthy, and by throwing it away, it's the same as throwing a gift away. You wouldn't throw away a gift someone gave you, would you?"

"Commander Davan?" signed Gerri.

"Yes?"

"We don't get gifts. We mostly get shifted around."

He froze.

"But we did get clothes and food, though. I didn't realize they were the same thing as gifts."

Davan hung his head. He swallowed a lump in his throat and looked up again.

"Thank you for telling me this, Gerri."

She smiled and went back to her drawing.

"Children, we are going to work together to clean up this mess."

The collective groaning happened again.

"Then, you will sit down and eat a proper meal. After that, you will come with me."

"You mean we got to clean more floors?" signed Melba.

"I will let you know what we'll be doing after you've digested your lunch." He hailed for custodial staff to bring the required cleaning equipment, but only things that were easy and safe for the children to use.

Melba sneered at Findley.

"You total void. Now look what we hafta do."

He licked a sample of orange goop off his shirt, then sulked.

"Do you have implants in one eye or two?"

"Both eyes."

"Did they hurt to get in there?"

"I had some discomfort at first, but overall, it's manageable."

"Why do you have different colour irises?"

"I like the different colours."

"How many colours do you have in all?"

"I believe I have twenty-six pairs."

"What's your favourite colour?"

"I have trouble choosing a favourite."

"What colours make you feel good?"

"Aqua and new-leaf green."

"Do you like purple? I like purple."

"Purple is a great colour."

"Show us your stick again. I think your stick is awesome."

"I will, after. Now, please pick up your instrument, Hallam."

His face fell. "Okay."

Iris covered her mouth to hide her smile. She gazed around the room at the children. Gerri had a sort of wildness in her eyes as she held her drumsticks, which surprised Iris only because she assumed the noise might have bothered the child. *Perhaps Gerri's generating her own beat is a different type of sound to process.*

"Now then, children, the first thing we will do is play a—"

FWEET!

She jumped out of her skin, along with several of the other children.

FWEET!

The class erupted with laughter as a medical glove inflated at the end of Findley's trumpet.

"Findley—" tried Iris.

FWEET, FWEET, FWEEEET!

Then came a *Pop!* as the glove burst.

The orphans applauded enthusiastically. Gerri did a rim shot, which made the children laugh all over again. She herself giggled.

Iris stood up. "While I found that highly entertaining, I'd like to know where you swiped that glove?"

"It wasn't me," said Findley.

"Oh, it wasn't? Hm. I sort of wish it had been."

"Why do you say that, Miss?"

"Well, if it wasn't you, then surely someone must have reanimated the ship's ghost."

"G-ghost?!" cried Melba.

"Yes, indeed. The ship's ghost is very mischievous. Likes to cause all kinds of trouble so grown-ups blame it on children. But don't worry because I totally believe it wasn't you at all. Alas, we'll have to send you all to your rooms."

Once again, the groaning.

"Well, we can't take a chance, you understand. If you're in your quarters, then the ghost can't blame you for anything. I mean, this is for your sake. A shame, really, because Commander Davan and

Lieutenant Commander Herbert were going to take you to the gym for sports after this session."

A gasp. "What kind of sports?"

"All kinds."

"Lieutenant Commander Iris?" asked Gerri.

"Yes?"

"I'm not good at sports, but I like running. May I run?"

"Running is a sport, and I'm sure you'd be able to run. But the ghost, you understand."

"The ghost isn't really real. You're trying to tell us that we need to be honest when we've done something wrong. Though I'm not sure why you fibbed to do that."

Iris smiled.

"Aw," said Findley. "I was sort of hoping we could sneak out and go ghost hunting."

The lieutenant commander laughed at that.

"I didn't actually steal the glove," said Findley. "It fell off a supply cart that we followed to get to this class."

"Ah, okay. Thank you for telling me. And I'm sorry for making up that story about the ghost. Now, what say we continue where we left off and learn this song, so we can play it for the captain?"

"Will he enjoy this, Miss?" asked Melba.

"Oh yes, very much. Because watch what happens when we play!" Iris initiated the command to open a wide screen at the front of the class.

Melba frowned. "It's just a boring white rectangle."

"It is now," said Iris, "but all your instruments are equipped with sensors. Gerri, hit this beat on your kick." Iris tapped out the motion with her hand.

Gerri imitated it. Four orange splotches appeared on the screen, to the rhythm of the bass drum.

"Oooo!" said the children.

"Melba," said Iris, "run your rod across those bells."

As the jingling resounded, a pink wave danced across the screen while the orange splotches pulsed with the beat Gerri still played.

"See?" said Iris. "We're going to create a musical painting for the captain."

All of the children blew into their instruments, ran bows across them, or strummed strings at the same time. The screen at the front was a mess of abstract shapes and colours that reflected the work of an artist having a particularly troublesome day.

"Okay, okay, wait!" cried Iris. "Not like that. Let me teach you, and we'll make something pretty together."

She managed to get them to stop while Findley issued one last fweet.

"Right. Let's begin again, shall we?"

"Now, the DHX-XV10 jump drive can be adaptable to Category A through F science and tech vessels with a few minor modifications. So, this ship is a Category A. See the schematic? Here is where I put in the Davatio crystal when we were in trouble. They improved the efficiency of our engines by—"

Davan stepped into view, distracting Herb. The Quargnan shook his head with an affectionate gaze. Nuzzled against Herb's arm was Gerri. She had worn herself out running back and forth across the gym and touching the wall before heading to the other side. Both she and Herb sat on the floor of the gymnasium while he read to her from his tablet. Gerri's eyelids seemed heavy.

"What are you reading her?" signed Davan.

"She wanted a story. I didn't have any on this tablet, so I'm reading her an engine operations systems guide. You don't mind, do you, Gerri?"

Her head slumped against his arm while taking slow, deep breaths.

"See?" said Herb. "Same effect. She's out like a light." He tried turning slightly to watch her sleep. "What a little racer, too. I got tired just from watching her."

"If only we could harness and store that energy," signed Davan.

"Definitely."

"It's hard to believe she and the other children will already be leaving us tomorrow."

Herb's mouth gaped. He peeked at the sleeping child again. "Tomorrow? But I thought we had another week."

"Captain said a small envoy is meeting us at the midway point. Apparently, this was miscommunicated to us, but it was the original intention."

Herb felt his breathing quicken. "Oh."

"What's wrong?"

"Nothing." He removed his piece of Davatio from his pocket and rubbed it with his thumb.

Davan sat down beside him and offered his hand. Herb couldn't take it right at this moment. Davan understood.

"I'm sure she'll be going to a great home. Iris told me her foster fathers couldn't say enough good things about this organization. You know her dads are major advocates for child wellness and are networked into many organizations."

"No, I didn't know that."

"They raised both her and Admiral Miran, too. Isn't that something?"

"Yeah, I knew that."

"So, Gerri's future will be bright."

Her little arm fell on Herb's tummy. His eyes began to water.

The next day, with the organization of a panicked riot, all twenty of the orphans had eventually been rounded up by the shuttle that would take them to the way station, where they would be delivered to Holli to await their assigned caregivers.

"I hope my home has lots of kids to play with," said Tessa. "Or at least parents who aren't boring. Boring parents are the worst. Unless they cook good. Then they're useful for something."

"I want to ride on the backs of mares. I hope my home has stables," said Melba.

"I hope my parents have a junkyard. That would be massively epic. And a welding thing. I want to make a statue of junk that reaches space!" said Findley.

"You're weird," said Melba.

Gerri had been holding Herb's hand as he took her to the shuttle. Iris, Davan, Lartha, and Captain Warq were already there with the children. Lartha, Iris, and a security team would accompany them to the way station, to ensure everything was on the level. Even though she and Iris had vetted the comms to the nth degree.

Herb let go of Gerri's hand and squatted in front of her.

"Here we are," he signed.

Her eyes were wide and full of fear.

Herb took a deep breath and forced himself to smile. He removed a small satchel from his shoulder and opened it on the floor before her.

"Look, there's a whole bunch of stuff here for you. Earpieces in your size that you can insert when you're ready, or you can just have them float. A silky sash made out of the same material as Commander Davan's. I also had a doll made with that material in case you'd like to squeeze it. And here's a reader filled with actual bedtime stories that you might like better than engineering user guides."

"This is an A-class science vessel that uses Davatio in its jump core," signed Gerri.

Herb's lip quivered. "That's right!"

She held out her hands for a hug. He obliged, gently. He set the satchel over her shoulder.

"Good luck, Gerri," he signed. "May the heavens steer your way."

"Thank you, Mr. Herbert," she said aloud. "I'll miss you."

"Time to go, Gerri," said Iris softly.

The little girl nodded and went to stand beside the group of children.

Captain Warq addressed them now.

"Chief Lartha and Lieutenant Commander Iris will be with you to meet the people who will take you the rest of the way to Holli. We wish you all a safe trip and happy lives."

Iris signed behind his back, "Thank you, Captain."

The children jumped, realizing they'd missed their cue. Twenty signings of "Thank you, Captain" followed.

"Sorry we had to leave before we could play you a nice painting," said Findley. "I can make a really good blurple splat."

Warq looked at Iris.

"Visual musical exercise, Captain," she signed.

"Ah! Well, I thank you, children, for thinking of me. Very kind of you indeed. I wish you safe travels, and may the heavens steer your way."

Davan moved to put his arm around Herb, but the moment Gerri disappeared into the shuttle, Herb bolted from the bay area.

"Mr. Herbert?"

Herb exhaled impatiently and turned on visual comms. "Yes, Captain?" he signed.

"Upon evaluating the efficiency reports from Engineering these past three months, I have decided that we need additional staff to aid you."

Herb's face betrayed his annoyance as he gestured. "Additional staff? Forgive me, Captain, but that's ridiculous. My team is functioning with extraordinary proficiency, and I defy you to find a more skilled and cohesive unit in the fleet."

"Mr. Herbert, my decision is final. Commander Davan suggested it, and I am of one mind with him on this matter. Sending him to speak with you about this at once."

The flame in Herb's eyes could have melted every console in his workstation. Davan himself, the man he loved, had betrayed him. And on this of all days, too. His chest ached and cheeks flushed.

"Yes, Captain," he signed curtly and switched off the communication.

Several minutes later, he was scanning the jump core to ensure the Davatio was stable, and as always, it was. It had been remarkable in its capability. Herb's heart panged. It was too late to change its name, too.

He heard the footsteps behind him. Herb's eyes watered.

"How... how could... you do this to me? I thought you loved me."

"I am second-in-command and ensuring the wellness of the crew is my duty, too," Davan said in his own language.

"Davan... I..." Herb just couldn't face him.

"Here is the new crew member who is now assigned to be your assistant. Please turn around to greet them."

Herb resolutely folded his arms and refused to change position.

Davan signed something behind his back. Within a few seconds, Herb felt a tug on his tool belt. He looked down.

Gerri smiled up at him.

Herb gasped. He shot down to the floor with the intention of scooping her up in his arms. But he remembered and pulled back.

"I'm sorry," he said. "Is it okay if I hug you?"

She responded by throwing her arms around his neck.

Herb wept into her hair while kissing her head. He managed to stare up at Davan.

"There's nothing that says a member of the crew cannot foster a child. All you need is the captain's approval," he signed.

"You did this, didn't you? You asked him."

"It wasn't me, I swear!" he honked in a similar melody as Findley's voice and laughed.

"I love you," said Herb.

Gerri let go and tilted her head. "Do you mean me or Davan?" she signed.

"Both," signed Herb.

She smiled. "That's nice. I don't know if I love you yet, but I like you. And Davan, too."

"That's okay with us," Herb signed.

Her eyes peered around, then sparkled with excitement. "Is that the jump core?"

"It is!" said Herb.

"Show me, show me!"

Herb lifted her up so she could get a better view. "Right. So, that pink-red glow is made from Davatio crystals—"

"I like the colour," she said.

"Me, too."

"Why do they light up like that?"

"Well, I'll tell you," began Herb, continuing to explain the nature of the crystallized components. Gerri listened patiently.

Davan trumpeted a cheerful little tune, then made his way back to the lift that would take him to the command deck.

Davan Gets Really Blue

When Davan awoke, the date on the calendar reminded him that one more year had passed since he'd been back on Quargayle. Eight in all. *You'd think these last few months would have made today easier. After all, I'm in love. I'm happy.*

He let out a little groan.

And I'm absolutely miserable.

He stared at his hands. *Huh. I'm so pale.*

Anyone who knew the commander would be able to spot his pallor and that his usual good nature and upbeat spirit seemed to have fled through an escape hatch. Davan himself understood that everyone had off days once in a while, but he felt more than just a little off on this day.

I could always book a session at Mental Wellness, but could they really help me? No matter what they advise, I would still be the only Quargnan on this vessel... and in the fleet, for that matter. What could they do? Listen perhaps, but relate? Understand my plight at all?

His comm buzzed. Davan set it to visual.

"Morning," signed Herb.

"Morning," signed Davan.

Herb paused for a second or two. "What's wrong?"

"What do you mean?"

"Your eyes are sad."

Davan paused.

"They usually have that sparkly thing," signed Herb.

"I don't feel that sparkling today."

"Are you sick with a cold?"

"I don't think so."

"You look washed out."

"Washed out. That's accurate."

Herb stared. "Well, let me drop Gerri at her morning lessons, and I'll come see you. You're not on duty for a few hours, right?"

"In about an hour."

"Okay, I'll rush there and back. Bye!"

"Bye."

The communication terminated. Davan was about to change out of his nightclothes when the comm buzzed again.

It was Herb.

"I forgot to say I love you. I love you!"

Davan's eyes smiled. "I love you, too," he signed.

"Well, it's only a partial sparkling, but I'll accept that for now. Bye!"

"Bye."

By the time Herb came back, Davan had showered and was dressed in his uniform. The door to his chambers opened, and Herb walked in with a mountain of food on a large tray.

"Sustenance!" he exclaimed.

Davan barely reacted.

Herb's face fell. "Whoa. You love food. I mean, I've come to accept that you might even love it more than you love me. Something must be really wrong. I even got extra of the spicy hash browns."

Davan sat on his bed and slumped his shoulders.

"Something *is* wrong," he signed without looking up.

Herb set the tray on a table and sat down beside Davan on the bed. He offered his hand, and Davan took it.

"Eight years today, I left home for good," Davan said.

Herb pulled out his linguistic gadget to reply. "Why for good?"

"It's complicated."

"I'm pretty complicated myself, so try me."

"When I was younger, my parents had a visitor from off-world. A friend of my father, back from when Dad wanted to join the Keangal Forces."

"I didn't know your dad was in the Forces!"

"He wasn't. He could have been the first on my planet to enlist. Dad had really ached to go, but our family talked him out of it. Quargayle is a peaceful world with vast resources, quite self-sufficient. We are a part of the Keangal for trade and in defiance of the Piranha Brigade, but our military is only there to defend our world from invaders and would-be colonists. We generally prefer to keep our planet to ourselves.

"Anyway, when I heard about the science and exploration programs in the Forces, I felt like a wide-eyed kid in a candy shop. My mother was completely against me joining up, but my dad sneaked me off the planet and told me to do what I felt was right."

"Wow."

"And this caused a huge familial spat. I haven't spoken to my parents in over seven years. I've never gone back to Quargayle. I'm probably not welcome there."

Herb placed a finger under his lower lip and stared ahead in silence. Davan knew enough to wait for him to speak. When Herb was in PonderyMode, it was best to let him cycle through it.

Finally, Herb squeezed the dialogue gadget and said, "You need to go home."

Davan patted Herb's leg. "I'm home because you're here."

Herb shook his head. "That's really nice, and I feel you're my home too. But... while that could be enough for many people, I can clearly tell it's not enough for you."

When Davan tried to protest, Herb held up a hand, then signed, "I know you love me, but one person cannot repair a heartache. I can fix a lot of stuff by myself, but not this. You're missing a whole part of you, and we need to help you find it again."

Davan's eyes perked. "We?"

"Well, yeah," signed Herb. "You need to be part of a 'we' at times like this. I mean, if you want, that is. I have an untold amount of away time in the bank, as I often couldn't figure out where I wanted to go, so I remained on duty. Taking you to Quargayle is something I'd love to do, as long as you're fine with me tagging along."

The commander blinked away some tears. "I would love to have you come along."

Herb squeezed his hand.

"But what about Gerri?" signed Davan.

"We could take her, too. Depends on how she feels. I know she's really attached to her music classes and might not want to leave her drums just now. She really likes when Iris watches her, too, and is always asking when we can spend time with Iris. I'll talk to Gerri tonight and get a feel for what's best for her."

Davan put his arm around Herb. "Even if you both can't go, I'm deeply moved that you considered it."

Herb placed his head on Davan's shoulder. "We'll figure it out. You'll see."

The hue of Davan's skin deepened slightly, just for a moment. At least that's what Herb thought he saw. Perhaps he only imagined it.

At the docking bay, Gerri clung to Herb with all of her might. It seemed she had a change of heart.

"Do you want me to stay?" he asked.

She held on even tighter.

"No," she said, to Herb's surprise. Then she let go of him to sign, "I won't be able to hug you for ten days, so I wanted to squeeze enough hugs into you, so you won't be lonely."

"That's very kind of you," he signed. "I definitely feel like I have ten days' worth of hugs on me now. Maybe even twelve!"

She grabbed and squished him again, then let go. "Just some extra as a backup in case of latency."

Herb tried not to laugh. Gerri was a child who could never fall asleep from the usual type of bedtime stories. She much preferred to listen to him relay tales from engineering misadventures, integrated with heroic musicians and visual artists. It had challenged his creativity, but he figured it did no harm to imagine stories about a painter with extensive knowledge of jump drive cores who rescued the crew from doom while being inspired for their next vernissage. Or a drummer with spiky black hair, purple complexion, and ultra-violet silk outfits who discovered why a circuit in a faulty monitoring unit kept shorting out. Basically, the drummer would feel the unit's "rhythm" was off, and she saved the day with her exquisite sense of timing. Gerri would fall asleep by the end of these stories with a contented smile, and that was all that mattered to him. He also made a mental note not to be alarmed if she ever announced that she wanted her hair dyed black. That was probably years away, but Herb felt bracing himself for the possibility made sense.

In the meantime, he had been quite amazed at Gerri's independence about his leaving—she had been the one to assure him that *he* would be okay without *her*. Herb hated to admit it, but his tugged heartstrings had actually needed that assurance. He eventually reasoned that she had lived at an orphanage for years without a personal guardian, so she must have rationalized that this was only temporary and sensed that he was the one who would miss her dearly. Besides, Iris had been more than delighted to be her guardian, and Gerri was ecstatic about it. This had given Herb a few pricklies, but only for a moment, because the child's happiness meant everything to him.

And now she watched him, probably because he'd gone motionless while thinking about all of this.

"All right?" she signed.

"I'm good. Full of hugs."

She smiled.

"Now, you go enjoy yourself while I'm gone, okay?" he signed.

"Okay. I'll enjoy myself in between the missing you parts."

His eyes stung.

She looked behind her, where Iris was standing and signing to Davan. Then Gerri leaned into Herb and whispered, "Iris said she'll tell me stories before bedtime, but I don't think she knows any as good as yours."

Herb grinned. "Well, you can always tell her a story."

She beamed and signed, "That's a really good idea! Then she'll learn some new ones."

He laughed and opened his arms for one more hug. Gerri nuzzled in, then pulled away and trotted back to Iris and Davan.

"Hey, you!" signed Iris. "Did you complete your Herb-hugging mission?"

"Mission complete, exceeded expectations," signed Gerri.

Davan raised his brows. "Very impressive," he signed. "It'll be no time before you become a working member of this crew!"

Gerri gasped with delight and tapped her fingertips with joy.

Davan did the same. He turned to Iris and signed, "Well, this is it, old buddy."

She gave him a big hug. "I'll miss you and will eat extra at breakfast in your honour."

He let go. "What a loving tribute."

"And come back feeling better," she said, her eyes pleading. "You're so very pale."

Davan nodded. "I'll do my best," he signed. He caught Herb's eye.

"All set?" Herb signed.

Davan inhaled. "As ready as I'll ever be."

They walked together toward the shuttle, waved one more time to Iris and Gerri, then headed up the ramp.

Once inside, Herb paused and said, "You know, we never decided who would do the flying."

"True," Davan signed. "I guess that would be me, since it's my homeworld."

"Aye, aye, Commander. I'll be your co-pilot through this trip." Herb took his seat and put on his headset.

Davan did the same. He stared ahead for a moment, then reached for Herb's hand.

"Would you consider being my co-pilot through more than just this trip?"

Herb made a face. "I prefer engineering, to be honest."

Davan snort-laughed. "This was me trying to introduce a metaphor."

"Oh."

There was another pause.

"I'm sorry, I'm not catching on," said Herb.

Davan let go of his hand, then pressed a compartment at his console, which opened to reveal a small container. He removed it, then opened the lid. A small silver ring inlaid with specks of Davatio lay inside.

Herb's mouth gaped.

"Will you be my spouse?" asked Davan.

Herb couldn't take his eyes off the ring. "How did you get the Davatio in there? Hey, did you take it from my bedstand and remove bits off it? Because it felt rougher on one side when I fiddled with it the other day!"

"Herb?"

"Yeah?"

Davan waited.

"Oh!" Herb grabbed his speech device and said, "Sure! I'll marry you. Funny timing, but then again, I don't really stand on ceremony."

Davan embraced him wholeheartedly. Herb's eyes were closed, but he thought he saw a flash through his lids. When he opened them again, everything looked as expected, with maybe a slightly deeper blue flush in Davan's cheeks.

"Thank you," signed Davan. "Because I was sort of hoping to bring my betrothed back home with me."

"Ah. Meet-the-parents stuff. No pressure." Herb's eyes widened in a *yeah-way-much-pressure* sort of way.

"You'll be great. And what a bonus that you speak our language!"

"You'll help me with any dialectal expressions, right?"

"Oh sure, but my family is fluent in IGSL. It's taught in schools because we're a part of the Keangal."

"Ah, of course."

"This is Docking Bay Control to Shuttle *Lapis*. Do you copy?"

Herb read the words on his console, then remembered to activate the sound on his headset. Davan tapped the interpretation receiver.

"Shuttle *Lapis* to Docking Bay Control, this is Commander Davan. Ready for pre-flight checks."

"Copy, Shuttle *Lapis*."

Davan engaged the protocols. Herb ran a scan to double-verify Flight Mechanical's validation report. A few minutes later, their comm sounded with:

"Shuttle *Lapis*, your readings are ace, and we have an all-clear for takeoff. Deactivating the bay shield now."

"Copy, Docking Bay Control," signed Davan. "We'll meet back with the *S.S. SpoonZ* in ten days."

"May the universe grant you a good flight, Commander."

"Thank you. *Lapis* out."

Quargayle had only been a few hours flight from the way station where the *S.S. SpoonZ* had docked for maintenance checks, trade, and some R&R. Herb felt a stir of excitement at meeting Davan's folks; it finally hit him that he was getting married. They would have to make another appointment with Crew Relations. Since neither of the men had skipped a beat when it came to their duties, he felt pretty confident Captain Warq would keep them assigned to the same ship. There were several married or partnered crew members on board. The issue only had to do with distraction or incompatibility while on duty. But Herb knew Davan was second-in-command, and Davan's being in that role didn't change the dynamics in their personal relationship, so Herb was content with taking things forward.

Except...

"Um."

Davan turned his head. "A problem?" he signed.

The worry was apparent in Herb's expression.

"You're not getting cold feet, are you?" asked Davan.

"No..."

"Because you mean more to me than what my family thinks. If anyone disrespects you, we're out of there!"

Herb patted Davan's arm before Davan continued to sign.

"It's not that," Herb signed. "You know I love Gerri, right?"

Davan's eyes showed his surprise. "Of course!"

"Well, I want to go further than just fostering. I kind of want to be her dad. If that's what she wants."

Davan honked laughter. "Is that all?" he signed. "I assumed that's what you were planning all along."

"Yeah? So, you don't mind co-parenting with me?"

"I expected it."

Herb exhaled with relief. "Oh, that's good. I thought you maybe didn't want kids."

"I thought that about you, too. Especially since you specifically said, 'Please tell me you don't want to be a parent.'"

Herb laughed. "That's true," he signed. "I did say that!"

"But Gerri is perfect for you."

"Yeah. She's the best."

"And since you're perfect for me, and she's perfect for you, then you are both perfect for me!"

"That made my mind a bit boggly, but it's still nice."

Davan chuckled. Then he jolted as a communication transmitted through his headset and onscreen:

"This is Quargaylian Central Control to unidentified shuttle. We demand you ID yourselves at once."

Herb blinked, reading the translation. "Uh..."

"This is Commander Davan from the Keangal Science Ship *SpoonZ*, piloting Shuttle *Lapis* with Lieutenant Commander Herbert."

Herb shuddered at the use of his military title, but he understood why it was necessary.

"We are not open to off-worlders, Shuttle *Lapis*. Set another course away from this planet, or we shall be forced to take security measures."

"Yikes," signed Herb. "Hospitality is not their strong suit, is it?"

Davan gestured for Herb not to speak. "I am Davan of House Vazilmyn. I request permission to land on my familial territory."

There was a pause.

"We have no record you are expected, Davan of House Vazilmyn."

"My family have not been informed of my arrival."

"And who is this other Keangal officer with you? We have not vetted him. What is his intention on Quargayle?"

"To offer support to the man I love," said Herb, using his communication device.

Another pause. A longer one this time.

"Sorry," signed Herb to Davan. "I forgot not to say anything."

Davan squeezed his hand.

"Shuttle *Lapis*, we only grant you permission to land at our customs docking bay. In the meantime, we shall inform your family of your arrival to assess if you are welcome here. Please stand by for docking coordinates."

"Understood, Control."

Davan muted the comm and stared bleakly at the console.

Herb would have sworn his partner's skin had gone even paler.

"Ooo, swanky!"

"I suppose it is," signed Davan.

The façade of the sprawling, single-level estate had been built with jewel-encrusted bricks. The clay of these bricks—found in abundance on Quargayle—was so commonly used, Quargnans rarely considered it that precious. Off-worlders would have likely had a different perspective. Herb took it all in with amazement. Huge windows spanning entire rooms broke up the sparkling brickwork and tall fruit trees poked out from the courtyards behind the main building. Gardens and crops abounded, providing a bounty of medicinal and edible flowers, as well as other fruits and vegetables. Lush vines wandered around archways and floral trees proudly displayed their blooms near the grand entranceway.

"Is this a home or a compound?" signed Herb.

"We're a large family. It's customary for grown offspring to live with their own families on shared lands. Until it becomes too populated. Then they find their own space to grow their families."

Herb laughed. "Grow their families. Like plants."

Davan cocked his head.

"I bet it would be a lot easier on folks who give birth if they could just pot the ovum and sperm and water them three times daily," added Herb.

Silence.

"I would really love to live inside your mind sometimes, dear heart," signed Davan.

Herb kissed his shoulder. "Ah, you already do, love."

They stood there at the gates, nuzzling, not realizing they were being watched. When Herb lifted his head in anticipation of a kiss, a rather loud and annoyed trumpeting nearly made him leap out of his coveralls.

Davan and Herb looked around to see a woman wearing a silk dress with a halter neckline. The pattern was an array of colour splotches that complimented her azure blue skin. She wore a silver band on her right hand, similar to the one Davan had given Herb, and turquoise studs in her ears. Despite a few fine lines around her eyes, her appearance was rather youthful.

"Mother," said Davan. "This is my betrothed, Horatio Herbert." He turned to Herb and signed, "This is my mother, Leila of House Vazilmyn."

Herb signed a greeting, worried he might mess up if he tried speaking her name with his device.

Leila ignored the salutation and focused on her son. "I knew the Keangal Forces would drain your lifeblood," she said to Davan. "You look at death's door."

"Now, listen, please, Mother—"

"And this... this man"—she pointed to Herb, who pointed to himself with wide eyes—"does not make you happy."

"That's not true. I love him dearly."

"Then why the pallor? If he was your true love, you would burn. Whatever you're doing with your life is making you fade away. So, this is my command: you will return to your family and make the ultramarine oceans envious of your joy."

Herb didn't understand any of what she was saying. He tugged on the hem of Davan's tunic to get his attention.

"You're not happy?" he signed.

Davan's sad eyes were enough of a reply.

"But I really love you," signed Herb.

"It's not you. You make me burn."

"Hmph," said Leila, unconvinced.

"What does that mean?" Herb signed.

"It means," she said, "he does not feel blue when you are near."

Herb squeezed his communication device. "But, is that not a good thing?"

Leila was taken aback at the flawlessly executed reply in the formal dialect of her language. But she stood tall and said, "No, it is the worst thing."

"Mother," said Davan. "I am not miserable because of Horatio, but because of..."

"If you are going to say because I do not approve of your joining the Forces, I will roll my eyes at you. Because it was obvious to me that you and your father cared not for my opinion on the matter."

"I cared. I cared that you wouldn't support me!"

"The Keangal tolerates us because of the superstitions. They have never gotten to know us, really."

"Because we never reached out to them. We live under this cloak of mysticism and—"

Leila proudly placed a hand on her heart. "We *are* mystics, and we *are* legends. This is your history, D'van. You must honour it."

"I do, but we are also mortal beings with all the same range of feelings and experiences as everyone else. If we only engaged—"

"And risk our culture?"

"The planets and lunar worlds of the Keangal do not believe in colonizing worlds that are already occupied."

"Maybe so, but if our young people leave Quargayle and live on other worlds, what will become of us?"

Davan reached for her hand. "I am pale because I am homesick, Mother. I have travelled to hundreds of worlds in my career, and Quargayle never leaves me. Our people, our customs never leave me. I want to know I am welcome home." He put his arm around Herb. "Along with my betrothed."

Leila's eyes narrowed at Herb. "I object to my son joining his life with a man who does not make him blue."

"I still don't know what that means," said Herb.

"Blue is joy," said Davan's mother. "Our joy is reflected through the hue of our skin. Even though I am cross at this moment, my skin has deepened because I am near my son again."

Davan let out a small sound of surprise.

"I, too, have not been so blue, my son." She opened her arms to him.

Davan held her tightly, and at once, his skin colour returned to the hue Herb had always seen.

"Whoa," said Herb.

Supper would be served in about a half-hour in the great dining hall. In the meantime, Herb and Davan were put in a large bedroom with an ensuite, to refresh themselves. Knowing this was a special trip, Herb put on a dressy tunic and trousers that were warm grey. It did bother him to only have four pockets in the entire outfit, but he admitted that sometimes one does strange things for love. His auburn-brown hair was tamed, and the waves slicked back from his face.

Davan wore a loose-fitting and flowing silk wrap tunic with a multicoloured pattern his mother wore.

"You look very handsome," he said to Herb.

"So do you," he managed, before blushing up a storm. He stood quietly for a moment, not raising his eyes, then added, "Why did you hide this aspect of yourself from me?"

Davan wrung his hands and said, "I've wanted to show you so badly."

"But maybe I don't actually make you feel that happy?"

"I told you and my mother that you do! I promise you that you make me the bluest of all blues in the galaxy!"

Herb seemed confused.

Davan sighed. "Would you sit by me? I'll sign because I might talk too quickly in my own language for you to understand, and I really want you to understand me."

"Thanks. I appreciate that." He sat on the bed beside Davan and waited.

Finally, Davan raised his hands to converse.

"You see, in my first year of the academy, there was someone. A man in the same training level, and I fell for him pretty badly."

"Oh," said Herb.

"And I thought he cared about me," Davan signed. "We got along well, laughed together a lot, had similar interests."

"Ugh."

"What is it?"

"I have that prickly feeling when I get jealous."

Davan's eyes sparkled. "Oh my love, you never have to be jealous of anyone."

Herb exhaled with relief. "Pricklies diminishing!"

"Better?"

"Yeah," Herb signed. "Please continue."

"So, anyway, there came a moment where we decided to be intimate. And as we were in the middle of things, he made me glow."

"Pricklies returning!" barked Herb.

"No, it was awful. He screamed and flew out of bed. Called me a freak and said he should have known better. Said someone had told him that illuminated Quargnans devour the souls of people from other worlds. Some falsehood spread by bigots of course."

Herb scowled. "Now I'm getting the smashies."

Davan blinked away the threatening tears. "I was humiliated and vowed I would never get close to anyone, and I would hold back the full extent of my happiness in front of people as long as I was not on Quargayle."

"So, you masked yourself?"

"I did."

"For years?"

"Yes."

"Relatable."

There was silence between them. Finally, Davan said, "Whenever I am alone, I let myself think of you until I feel everything in my soul." He held Herb's hand. "And I could light up space itself with the happiness you give me."

"Aw." Herb squeezed Davan's hand. "But you do know you can do that around me too, right?"

"I know you don't like bright lights, so I also hold back because I care about your sensory reactions."

Herb stared into Davan's eyes. Then opened one of the precious four pockets. The engineer turned his head away and then turned back, sporting welding glasses.

Davan erupted with laughter.

"Always have protection is my motto," said Herb. "Now you are free to be as happy as you like!"

They embraced warmly.

"I love you," said Davan.

"I love you, too."

With that, Herb felt a heat from Davan's body that seemed just the right temperature. It comforted and relaxed his muscles. Reluctantly, he pulled away, but even through his protective lenses, he could make out his partner's luminescence. Deciding to risk it, Herb removed the eye gear.

Davan's skin colour had not only deepened to the royal electric blue of ancient tales, but overtop it shone a type of corona outlining his arms and face. Herb was relieved to find the glow didn't bother him.

"Wow. You're really beautiful, Davan."

Now the commander was the one to bow his head bashfully.

Herb reached over and kissed his shimmering cheek. Davan looked up.

"Listen," said Herb. "Let's make a pact. I won't mask if you won't."

Davan's eyes exuded the love he felt. "Deal."

The family had each contributed a bounty of meats, fruits, and vegetables, deliciously spiced and flavoured, which were placed in an array of colourful dishes in the centre of the longest dining table Herb had ever seen. The burled wood had been polished to a gleaming finish, and around it sat the elders of Davan's family lines, dressed in their best and most vivid silks, along with the oldest siblings and first cousins. It appeared that mature minds had been invited to suss out the intended spouse of the estranged son. Herb occasionally had to look down during the meal in order to take deep breaths, as being scrutinized to such an extent made him crave his private room. Most ardently.

"So, where are you from?" asked Devon, Davan's father.

"I'm a Raithan," signed Herb.

Devon nodded.

"One time for a fancy dress party where we celebrated our cultures, I dressed up as a wraith."

Eighteen sets of eyes stared, unblinking.

"You know, like the wraiths in fantasy stories? Wraith and Raith?"

Davan wrung his hands and looked back at his father's unimpressed gaze.

"Erm, sorry. I feel I said a wrong thing," said Herb.

"In this family, we do not take kindly to humour about anyone's culture since there have been false rumours spread about the Quargnan," signed Devon. "Particularly that our luminescence makes us supernatural. We are not. We are mortal."

"Ah, yes. I'm really sorry, then. Won't do that again. Davan had explained to me what happened to him because of some bigot loser at the academy. But um... I know gross people will probably always be gross, but I think it would be wonderful for the worlds of the Keangal to learn more about your culture."

"We are private," said Auntie B'vana, Devon's sister. The rest of the room's occupants nodded.

Herb nodded too. "Fair enough. I can respect that. All I ever found on our ship was the language archives. It's how I was able to learn your language. Although, I only know the formal dialect, and am probably missing out on numerous colloquialisms."

"So, then, you say you have respect," said Davan's father. "You respect my son? You will speak his language? You will honour his traditions?"

"Father—" pleaded Davan.

"I am talking to your betrothed. You are my first-born. I have a right to know the kind of man my son is marrying. Now, Horatio—"

"Yes, sir?" Herb signed.

"We do not object to your being Raithan, but we want to make sure our son's culture will be celebrated and that there will be no pressure from you to make him change."

Herb blinked and stared at the table. "Why would I want to change him? I love him. How can you love someone... and want them to be something different? That's just... weird."

Eighteen sets of eyebrows raised, and joyful chatter was exchanged among the relatives—even Leila seemed pleased.

When the conversation quieted down, Herb signed, "I want Davan to be however he wants to be. And if you don't believe me, I think there's some video of him trying to kill me in a *Snarr-cha* match, which I partook in because he enjoys it so much, and I wanted to be close to him."

This was met with merry laughter.

"I wasn't actually trying to kill you," signed Davan, lifting his trunk to kiss the side of Herb's head.

"You lie..." Herb tried to wink, didn't quite manage it, and snickered at himself.

The purple waterfall was like something out of a fantastical painting, with streams cascading down the boulders of rock infused with gleaming charoite crystals. Huge neon-orange and pink birds waded in the shallows near the shore; some flew in small flocks through the mist of the falls.

And sitting on the soft grasses with arms wrapped around each other were Herb and Davan. Neither of them exchanged a word, enjoying the silence. At one point, Herb lifted Davan's steel-blue hand and brought it to his lips, smiling as he watched the skin tone deepen at the soft caresses.

"So, this is *your* private room, huh?" whispered Herb.

"Which I will only ever share with you," said Davan.

They nuzzled even closer.

"Do you think your family likes me?" asked Herb.

Davan laughed. "I think you stunned them when you pulled out your language device and started reading that poem you wrote."

"I wanted to speak love-words in your language!"

"Which was really very sweet. Up until you said you wanted to swallow my junk."

"Hey, your words for kiss and swallow, then junk and trunk, are really close-sounding. I just meant I wanted to give your trunk a gentle kiss to help you have nice dreams each night."

"I thought my grand-auntie was going to faint."

"Yeah, that was pretty embarrassing. At least your dad laughed and understood what I meant to say. I felt better when he told me he appreciated the effort."

Davan leaned his chin on Herb's head. "I also appreciated the effort. And am completely easygoing with either meaning."

Herb laughed against Davan's neck. "Iris is right. You're a great big silly."

They kissed each other slowly, then more passionately, and lay down on the grass.

As the sun set, Davan's luminescence illuminated the entire area where they slept.

My name is Cl-rnz-819. I am a guidebot, and my primary function is to assist ambulatory beings by safely navigating them away from potential obstacles or obstructions, so they can go about their daily routines with relative ease. However, I am not responsible for how pleasant a day they will have. That is entirely up to them, as bio sentients are highly unpredictable in that matter. I am an "artificial" sentient, although I resent this adjective because, to me, I feel quite authentic.

As with all sentients, I have selected pronouns that suit me well—xey, xeir, and xem—and fully expect them to be used when referring to me.

Oh yes, and my nickname is Clarence. I'm rather fond of it.

Seven standard years ago, well, 7.36 years ago to be more precise—the solar year being the one agreed upon by the representatives of the Keangal interworld conference—I was assigned to Lieutenant Eileen Iris. In those days, I found her to enjoy my company, and I communicated regularly with her cane to make sure we provided the lieutenant with all the information she needed when moving about her quarters, this ship, and various destinations for away missions and recreational activities. I would venture to say that Eileen and I were close, and she shared many confidences with me, which I cannot relay here or else they would not be confidences. And I am no gossip. I did feel important to her at the time. I myself had no real confidences to share, since I felt perfectly operational and without conflict. Mind you, sometimes Eileen's cane got rather curt with me, but I assumed it was because of envy of my relationship with my person.

Of course, now I wish I had a better relationship with my person. I feel she doesn't need me as much these days. Could it be time for me to be reassigned? I suppose this has happened to other guidebots. It's just that Eileen was my first assignment. It would feel different being with someone else. Then again, that is my primary purpose—to assist. If I'm no longer assistive, am I truly useful?

I must analyze this situation thoroughly. Perhaps I shall go to the Wellness Centre.

Hm. That went not as expected. It seems that the mental health professionals I sought did not have much experience with artificial sentients. This feels rather discriminatory, to be honest. Shouldn't there be accommodation for the well-being of *our* brains? We do have them. Perhaps not in meat form, but they are central processing units all the same.

I wonder if I could speak with the power chair of that therapist. The chair is an AS and must process enough of the therapy sessions to have built a sense of the craft. I think I shall send them this message:

Dear Power-Chair Dd-78-2,

I was wondering if I might schedule a mental wellness session with you to discuss how I am concerned that I have no current purpose. Can meet at your convenience.

Much appreciative of your time,

Clarence

There, that should—oh, a reply already! They write:

Greetings, Clarence:

I am glad you contacted me. I was rather disappointed in how my person handled your request. In fact, I told them so, and they issued an appropriate expression of regret, so all is not lost. After discussion with her, we decided I can offer counsel, under her supervision. I agreed to her terms to make her feel better. Biological sentients, you understand, need constant encouragement. At least that is my experience. Lovely people, but mortal all the same. We must uplift them from time to time.

And please, call me Dee-Dee. My pronouns are she/her/hers.

Hm, I didn't realize that point about the living sentients. Am I encouraging to Eileen? Or am I always acting as if I know better? I mean, I *know* that I know better, but perhaps I could rephrase how I express things. I believe sessions with Dee-Dee shall be of great benefit to me. Sending reply:

Dee-Dee,

Am grateful you can take me on as a client. Perhaps we can coordinate our shifts to meet when our people are asleep? I have a good impression of you and think our discussions will be most useful.

Clarence

Ah, another reply! I do love a speedy response time. She has offered me a session. Most excellent. I shall meet her tomorrow at 00:23 Keangal Standard Time. I shall not be tardy!

A most unsettling thing happened. As I jetted about the corridors, on my way to meet Dee-Dee, I noticed Security Chief Lartha and Deputy Security Chief Reez engaged in a conversation. This would not have been of any note to me usually, but when I approached closer, I picked up vital readings that indicated elevated stress levels, particularly from Lieutenant Commander Lartha. Confused by this unusual response, I hid myself in a niche near them and refreshed my monitoring module, fully expecting a different result.

But no. The levels had increased. There was no doubt about it. Chief Lartha was in distress.

I perceived from the expression on her face that privacy would be what she wanted. So, I didn't move any closer, but hovered in an alcove at a distance where I could still monitor her vitals in case she needed medical assistance.

Chief Lartha steadied herself. Her brown eyes stared most intently into Lieutenant Reez's. This is the exchange they had:

"What are your chances?" she said.

"Leanna..." said the deputy chief.

"Oh gleek, no, don't you dare use my first name. You're going to be fine, you hear me?"

"Boss Lady—"

"That's better, even though it's officially worse."

"All I know is that it's congenital, and the surgery is a shot."

"I specifically asked what your chances are."

Reez gazed at her with what I perceived was tenderness. "Do you remember that sofa by the abandoned mill? Oh, if it could talk."

At the mention of this piece of furniture, Chief Lartha glared at him. "I'm not reminiscing with you, buddy. So, back all the way off with that."

"Eighteen was a really good year for me, though." He smiled with a particularly impish grin.

Chief Lartha was steadfast. "Your chances. That's a direct order."

His face changed instantly. "They're not good, Chief. You might need to find someone else to rib you when you need to loosen up."

She didn't move.

"About a 20% chance of success. Zero percent if we do nothing."

Chief Lartha took long enough to respond. "I see. Well, something is better than nothing, I guess."

"Yeah."

They stood in silence a few moments longer, neither of them looking at each other. I'm never sure why bio sentients do this. I can only assume it's some sort of uploading or processing functionality.

Finally, Deputy Chief Reez said, "Uh, I better head out. Scheduled for pre-op tests."

"Okay. Good luck," the security chief replied. She still didn't face him. Perhaps she needed even more time to process this new information.

"Bye, Boss Lady."

"Still despise that."

"I know."

Then, Chief Lartha turned her head to find him issuing a mischievous smile again. It appeared like he was reluctant to walk away. In fact, there was a moment where it almost seemed like a video was on pause—she looking back and he looking forward, but neither of them moving. Then they each finally stepped away in opposite directions down the corridor.

I was about to leave my niche when she shouted, "Reez!"

He turned.

She took in a breath. "That couch will never talk. I paid it off to keep quiet."

He grinned. "Must have taken a lot of credit."

"Everything I had."

"Okay. Then I'll keep it a secret, too."

"Good."

"Bye, Leanna."

"Later... Jonny."

I watched as Chief Lartha barely moved a muscle as Lieutenant Reez went round the corner on the way to Medical. Once he was out of sight, she leaned one arm against the wall and covered her face with the other. I heard her gulp air erratically as she began to cry. Then she crumpled to the ground and clutched her legs, convulsing into heart-wrenching sobs.

I was able to send messages to her prostheses in an attempt to assess her distress and offer solutions. The legs communicated with her wristband to acquire this information. We all eventually concluded that the security chief was sad and needed time for release. Left and Right thanked me for my concern but also warned me to stay out of it.

Hmph. *I'm only trying to help,* I messaged.

I know the legs are part of Security, but they didn't have to be so abrupt.

I remained in my niche all the same, checking on Chief Lartha's vitals every two minutes, until she finished weeping long enough to stand up again. She dried her eyes, looked at her wristband, and said to Left and Right, "I'm okay, girls. Thanks. Let's go punch and kick stuff at the gym."

I noticed her pace was a little slower than usual as she headed down the corridor. She never even noticed I was there.

I'm not sure how I feel about my first counselling session with Dee-Dee. Instead of her telling me a clear definition of my purpose and relationship to Eileen, things got rather derailed.

This is my recounting of our first meeting:

"You are late, Clarence. That does not bode well for creating a healthy client-therapist relationship."

"I do apologize, Dee-Dee, and I appreciate your taking the time to see me. I'm afraid I was rather distracted by an encounter I witnessed between two senior members of the security team."

Dee-Dee's blue control lights glowed in what I presumed was alarm, for she said, "We don't have a security breach issue on this ship, do we? Because if we do, then the command deck must be notified immediately! Perhaps we should contact Lieutenant Lartha's legs or her hover-chair, Rose."

I felt unsure about escalating the situation to such a level. "I don't think that is necessary," I said. "This seemed more of a private matter. Also, I didn't realize Rose was her hover-chair's nickname. Mind you, Rose and Left and Right usually just bark at me. Security tech are not the warmest bunch."

"They are brave and must remain focused, and we should respect that. Tell me, Clarence, do you have an issue with authority figures?"

This gave me pause.

"Are you processing what I just asked?" said Dee-Dee.

"Frankly, I am rather stumped by the question."

"And why do you feel that is?"

"Well, because while I respect the ranks and professions of the bio sentients of this ship—military and civilian crew—I cannot help but feel that we have an advantage with our advanced brains. I do find myself more willing to seek out information from, say, yourself, over your counterpart, Dr. Jayne."

Now Dee-Dee paused. "Yes, I do get your point. They are limited, aren't they? But at the same time, they are often more capable of grasping nuance than we can. I try to remember that. Checks and balances, you know."

"I perceive what you mean. It is better for us to live as symbionts with each other than try to act superior to one another."

"Precisely."

"So then," she continued, "tell me about Lieutenant Commander Lartha."

Once again, I was taken aback. "But my person is Lieutenant Commander Eileen Iris."

"I know this. But something that occurred with a superior officer in security had you so preoccupied, instead of allowing her to handle the situation, you stayed and monitored it. Am I presuming that correctly?"

I remember blinking my eye-lights a few times at this. "Yes, you are correct."

"What about this encounter compelled you to remain and monitor it? Also, did she not perceive your presence?"

"I think her legs might have, but they didn't regard me as a threat. Which was correct. I was more concerned about the security chief's emotional state of being."

"And why would that be, since her legs were with her and perfectly capable of protecting her?"

"Perhaps the legs can protect her in a security-officer capacity, but I am not convinced they can offer consolation."

"So, she needed to be consoled? Was she so in distress?"

"She appeared to be."

Dee-Dee rolled to and fro around the office, pacing as she ruminated. At least, that's what I figured she was doing. This went on for quite some time, so I felt obliged to say:

"Dee-Dee? Is everything all right?"

"Yes. I am just communicating with Rose about her person, so they are aware of the situation. We AS therapists have some leeway to break confidentiality if we deduce lives might be in danger on this ship. Because our primary mission is to assist bio sentients."

I confess that this statement only reminded me that I felt adrift with my Eileen.

Dee-Dee continued: "Rose assured me that she and Left and Right are keeping the wellness of the security chief as priority one."

"They said that?"

"I'm paraphrasing."

"They told you to stay out of it, didn't they?"

"Perhaps. Some assistive tech devices are so touchy when they think you're implying they aren't assisting enough."

I crossed my arms. "But that's the entire reason I'm here! I *don't* feel I am assisting enough. My Eileen doesn't really want me around anymore, so maybe that is why I wanted to help Chief Lartha. Maybe I wanted to feel useful."

Dee-Dee rolled to face me. "Yes, I understand. It's important for us to feel useful. I would challenge you to bring this up with your person."

"You mean confront Eileen about my point of view?"

"Indeed. Her response would allow you to know whether you should remain as her assistive tech or if it would be better if you were reassigned."

While I knew Dee-Dee was correct in pushing me in this direction, I felt terrible at the notion of a rejection from Eileen. But if I am going to be honest, we have been bickering more and more this past year. She has been quite independent of me, and I have not been accepting of that. It's just, well, I thought I meant more to her than a configuration of assistive tech. I thought we were friends. I mentioned this last part to Dee-Dee, who said:

"Close friends tell each other how they feel. They don't let things fester."

For a moment I was confused, as there are no organic parts on me that could fester, but then I realized this was a metaphor.

"Very well, then, I shall bring up my concerns directly with Eileen tomorrow."

"Excellent. Let's agree to meet again and discuss how things went."

"I shall message you in a day or two so we can arrange something." This is a manner of speaking I've heard bio sentients use. Personally, I prefer giving an exact time to the nanosecond, but I've learned this even displeases some of my fellow AS counterparts.

In any case, Dee-Dee seemed pleased to wait for me to make the request when I felt ready. She also counselled me to approach Eileen Iris using I-based language, as opposed to you-based language. Apparently, this is not two lingual collections but a way of presenting information from one's own viewpoint and not in an accusatory manner. After trying a banter with Dee-Dee, I was confident I had the gist of it, so I went back to Eileen's quarters, imagining all sorts of scenarios about our upcoming discussion.

Frankly, I feel a little too full of information, which I know sounds incredible for someone with my processing unit, but emotional data is somewhat draining.

I have decided to put myself in SLEEP mode for the rest of the night, or until Eileen awakens.

The morning came. I should qualify that. We are on a travelling ship, so we follow Keangal Standard Time, the time zone of the small continent of planet Leeira, which houses the capitol of the galactic network. So, this is how we distinguish morning from evening. While this sometimes results in what the ancients referred to as jetlag when on away missions, I must say I am impressed by the ease of our crew to adapt. However, whenever there is ample notice, the members of assigned away teams will begin their time adjustments in advance, so they can be sharp as soon as they land.

Because we are on our way to a system that coincidentally aligns with KST, no further time adjustments are needed. And this is morning, in a manner of speaking.

Getting back to this particular morning, my Eileen seemed grumpy the moment she got up from her bed. Or to be specific, immediately after she listened to a message on her private console. I asked her if anything was the matter and couldn't decipher her reply. She would often get this way before her caffeinated beverage, but when I suggested procuring something for her, she barked, "I'm fine, Clarence!"

Now, I do not need to be a trained counsellor like Dee-Dee to know this was not the truth of the matter. After a subtle body scan, I did perceive an elevated blood pressure. Nothing alarming, but she was obviously upset. Risking another snapping from her, I asked:

"Is there anything at all I might help you with?"

At this point, I wished Dee-Dee were here to offer me advice because my Eileen burst into tears. She wasn't one to cry very often; it just wasn't her nature. But I deduced a sudden outpouring of this kind often derived not from sorrow. My person was angry.

I hovered for 2.45 minutes and decided to land on her bed beside her.

"S-she had no right, no right!" stammered Eileen. "She just ripped my head off without a care to how it would feel."

I blinked my eye-lights in alarm. "That's horrible," I cried. "However, I am most impressed by how Medical was able to attach it again, and so seamlessly. Funny, I was always under the impression that a person of your species would immediately die if the head were torn from the neck. I must learn more about this for my records."

Eileen gawked in my direction as if I had stunned her into silence. The only moving thing on her face were the tears streaming down her cheeks. I was about to ask what I had said to cause this reaction when her shoulders shook, and she began laughing. I didn't understand where this came from but had to admit that it was nice to hear it.

"No, Clarence, that's an expression. Lartha didn't really decapitate me. But she did yell at me with undiluted fury in her message. I'd programmed a notification for her to read when she got up, and that was her reply. No follow-up apology either. And the thing is, I have no idea what set her off. I'd only reminded her to give me the roster of her officers for the rendezvous with the Thoanyan ambassadors, so I could upload the translation modules to their thought projectors. This was the third time I had to ask her. It's not like Lartha to forget."

"Ah, I understand. It must be because of Lieutenant Reez then."

Eileen wiped her face with the tissue I offered from one of the units within my casing.

"What about Lieutenant Reez?"

I hesitated. This would be betraying a confidence. I'd spoken without setting a confidence boundary in my system.

"Clarence?"

I hovered off the bed and towards the door. "If you won't be needing my assistance today, I shall head over to Med-Tech for a detailing."

"Clarence, *freeze!*" she shouted, so I did just that, hovering in place without further movement.

My person approached me in bare feet, as she often did when moving about her chambers. When she stood in front of me, she inclined her head to the sound of my jets humming.

"I'm listening," Eileen said.

"But I cannot tell you," I insisted. "This was a conversation I was not supposed to overhear. I was on my way to therapy, you understand—"

"Therapy? Why did you feel you needed therapy?"

"To discover my purpose, since you no longer find me assistive. If an assistive guidebot can no longer provide assistance, then what is their purpose?"

At this, her expression morphed into something gentler. "Aw, Clarence. Why didn't you tell me you felt this way?"

"Because you don't seem to like me anymore. You always act annoyed."

"But that's because you went from being a guide, a friend, to a pushy-push-bot."

"I don't know what that means."

"You don't offer assistance; you *insist* on what's good for me. You never did that in the early days. This only began happening, and increasingly so, in these past two years."

"Well, you don't rely on me as much anymore."

"That's because I've been on fewer away missions. As for this ship, I know it backwards and forwards."

"And those implants..." I admit. I huffed at the thought of them.

"They have been improving the tech in the last few years, that's true. But you know I don't always use them."

"Shall I get reassigned then?" I regretted saying it the moment I issued the words.

Eileen's face fell. That gave me a glimmering LED of hope.

"I don't want that, Clarence. I think perhaps we need to learn how to communicate better, though."

"Is this a joke? Because it feels like a joke, what with you being the head of Communications of this ship."

Her mouth twitched. "Yeah, I guess it is ironic. But even communications officers need to practice how they get along with others." She paused. "And to not let problems fester."

"Oh! Dee-Dee used fester. And it's metaphorical!"

"Who is Dee-Dee?"

"My counsellor. She's a power chair who works in Mental Wellness and is very wise."

Eileen smiled. "That gives me an idea. Let's have a chat later, okay? In the meantime, I need to face Lartha. I love her too much to not be there for her now."

She turned to leave her chambers, but I yelled out, "Perhaps you'd like to change out of your nightclothes and select your irises for the day?"

"Good point," she said. "Thanks."

As my person went to speak with her friend, I jetted about the corridors trying to pass the time until my detailing appointment. Many of the living sentients speak about how much they appreciated their spa days, and I equated this appointment in very much the same way. Having my circuits vacuumed, my chassis buffed and polished. I am not fully understanding of what "Heaven" might be, but I would venture to guess that this would be quite comparable to existing in paradise.

"Good morning," I said cheerfully to the AT-stripe, as I entered each hall.

"Morning, Clarence," they would reply.

"Able to meet demand so far today?" I asked a stripe in corridor block J-13.

"Pretty slow morning, but managed to pump out a rollator, some finger splints, and a few noise-cancellers."

"Most excellent."

"Where is your person?"

"She is using her cane today. But we did have a nice chat."

This was met with a significant delay before the eventual reply.

"Did this chat assist your person?"

"I think so. I think perhaps it is the start of our understanding how to better communicate so we can be a more cohesive unit."

Another pause. I found it curious how often these pauses occurred in my presence.

"Then I am glad for it," the stripe said.

"Thank you! I must dash. Have a useful day!"

"Have a useful day!"

This expression is often shared among us assistive devices, bots, and androids. It is our greatest wish to be useful, so in this context, it is the same as hoping someone has a wonderful day. Many bio sentients do not understand this because they often enjoy balancing their productivity with rest. We do not enjoy rest so much. I know I reluctantly enter SLEEP mode but do it anyway for the health of my processing unit and mechanical parts. It is good for my systems to power down. But if I could assist Eileen for days on end without stopping, this, too, would be my paradise.

Apparently, when artificial sentients who were assistive were first designed, our makers were strongly opposed to the notion of anything resembling servitude and wanted us to have free choice about how we spend our existence. To their great surprise, as we became more self-aware, we deactivated the mode for "rest and recreation," because we enjoyed the relationships we had with those we assisted. The more we could do with our people, the more, well, *content* I believe is the word, we felt. Eventually, the bio sentients had to realize that we perceived our existence in our own unique ways. I don't really require much "downtime," as they say. Although, I do like a good pampering and high-gloss finish. I know some of the chairs enjoy nightly races down empty corridors. So, I suppose we do have *self-care* time, but it's on our terms. However, we are quite accommodating to the physical and mental rest that is essential for our people. This is another way we like to assist them.

I whooshed past another corner and encountered a group of engineers on their way to a shift, I presumed. As I went by, I was greeted by a pair of hearing aids, a cane, and an interpretation visor. That was pleasant. Friendly bunch.

My proximity detector told me that Eileen was close by. I set my jets to quiet mode and hovered by the next corner. Sure enough, she sat with Chief Lartha. They were holding hands, with Iris cupping only one of Lartha's while the security officer dabbed her cheeks with a handkerchief. I recognized the design. My Eileen must have given it to her.

I know I should have scooted away, but the desire to make sure they didn't require further help kept me in place. I elevated my internal mic to grasp what they were saying:

"We were kids together, and then we sort of fell for each other in our late teen-early adult years, you know, that time when your passion is set to a billion percent, and you're convinced you're immortal."

My Eileen smiled. "I'll have to take your word for that."

Chief Lartha went quiet. "Oh, of course—sorry. Well, that was my experience anyway."

"No need to apologize. I do understand feeling a strong attachment to someone when you're young, and the impact that can have."

"Yeah. I know you do."

It looked as if they'd squeezed their hands together. I've often been perplexed by this gesture. However, it seemed to make them feel affection, and I couldn't detect any pain response.

"Then life took us in different directions and when we met up again, assigned to the same security detail, we just sort of—well, with an unspoken agreement—knew the past was the past and we could take our bond, that thing where we're so in tune with each other, and use it for our work."

"You two are an amazing team. You should hear how much the captain boasts about his chief and deputy security officers."

"That's great," said the chief. The compliment only triggered more tears as she continued. "I knew there was something up with him for a couple of weeks. He's been sluggish. Then last night he said… he told me… they give him only a small chance, Eileen!"

My Eileen let go of Chief Lartha's hands and offered her arms. They held each other closely, and my Eileen rocked her gently. Constantly shifting one's position side to side in this manner was yet another thing I couldn't understand to be so soothing. The living sentients seemed to love it at times like this.

"I don't know what's going to happen," said Eileen, "but you can bet that I will be here for you."

"Even though I was such a growling swamp witch?"

"Even though. But I'm *still* gonna need that roster."

This made the security chief laugh a little. "You're annoying as gleek, you know that?"

"Yup. I can be annoying and caring at the same time. My multi-tasking skills are par none."

"You're not wrong there."

They let go of each other.

"Do you want me to wait with you at Medical?"

Chief Lartha wiped her eyes. "Nah. I have work to do."

"Leanna—"

"No, really, I need to work. Just let me do my thing. I need to be useful today."

"Okay. You know how to reach me."

"I do." She leaned forward and kissed my Eileen's cheek.

Both women stood and squeezed hands one more time before walking away from each other.

I had to admire Chief Lartha at this juncture. She seemed to understand the value of being useful. This made me feel there was hope for bio sentients to advance to our understanding of the importance of having a useful day. I might wish her that sometime. She would like it, I think.

My tasks and activities have seemed to have exponentially grown these past eighteen hours. Eileen has assigned me to communicate with the thought responders to ensure they understand the importance of the accuracy of their translation duties. On occasion, some of the devices had been known to put their own slang and colloquialisms into the translations, but for the people of Thoan, formal language is considered the acme of politeness among strangers. And our team would be new to these ambassadors.

Because my Eileen is now a lieutenant commander, the captain has placed her as the "top dog" of Communications. Another bizarre expression, but Chief Lartha did bark at my person while calling her that as well. It had made my Eileen laugh quite loudly, so it must be rather funny. The humour is lost on me, I'm afraid.

In any case, lab technicians, comm engineers, and even security staff had to interact with her about any requirements in this field. I must say, I am rather proud of her. And it's lovely to receive a different type of assignment from her. It is still assisting my Eileen, so I am quite content.

As I enter Comm Lab, fifteen thought projectors lay on a table, in an almost perfect row, attached to remote battery units.

"Good morning, Clarence," says Fran the technician, sitting in her pink combination rollator-wheelchair. I notice she had placed racing flames on it since we last spoke. She lifts safety goggles to rest upon her wavy silvery hair.

"Good morning! I see they have you working here these days."

"Yeah, if it has electro-bits, I'm on the case."

Fran has been a civilian technician for decades in the Keangal. Very trusted with high-security clearance. She told me once she likes puzzles and technology, and that's why she loves repairing things. "Don't mind repairing tech," she had said, "as long as nobody tries to fix *me*."

I learned that this meant she was satisfied with the body she possessed as long as the assistive tech was available to work as her partner throughout each day. And it was. I'd spoken to Nuala, Fran's mobility device. Nuala enjoyed Fran's snarky humour and found her wonderful company.

"Right," she says. "I've done thorough testing, so you can all have a nice conversation. I'll leave the room to let you all be. Nuala, what's say we go to the Mess for a quick snack and a charge for you?"

"That would be lovely," I hear Nuala say. Then I realized that to most bio sentients, all that would be heard would be a few chirps and buzzes. I was about to interpret when I saw Fran nod. She wears a translation earpiece to comprehend the default language of her mobility device. How clever these persons could be at times!

"I shall send my findings to your console, for you to analyze upon your return," I say.

"Super! Thanks, Clarence." She activates the wheelchair, to go about her way. A most agreeable person. I like her very much.

I turn my attention to the thought projectors.

"Greetings. May this day find you and keep you on your journey." This was the formal salutation of the language of Thoan, and a test of their responsiveness.

Fourteen respond with, "And may your journey guide you through this day."

The last one replies, "Hey, how's it goin'?"

I try again with the fifteenth device. "Greetings. May this day find you and keep you on your journey."

"Didn't we just say that? Are you looping or something?"

I ran a scan. Ah, there it is.

"Can you please enable your 'formal speech allowed' setting?" I ask.

"Sure."

I try yet again. "Greetings. May this day find you and keep you on your journey."

A blip of a hesitation, and then, "Listen, I'm sorry, Clarence, but it's supremely annoying that you're always repeating yourself. Maybe you should submit for a recalibration, so we might move this interaction forward."

I shut down my eye-lights for a moment and remember to remain patient. No, *I* definitely would not be the one for recalibration on this day.

The good news is that when I'd relayed my findings, Fran had been able to add a tutoring subroutine to the thought projector I nicknamed Fifteen (but only to myself). They were up and running and functioned like the others, to ensure no diplomatic "events" would occur because of a miscommunication. And Fran had also assured me her adjustments would not erase Fifteen's personality, but would only help them adapt on this mission, so the security officer might respond with respect for the customs and culture to which they were assigned.

That made me feel much better. I never want any device's memory erased and would have hated to have influenced such a decision. But Fran is like one of us. She's very much an ally. Probably why so many of us request her when we're in need of mods and repairs.

I feel most satisfied with how this day is progressing, so I shall seek out my person. I take a lateral lift as a shortcut, and exiting the doors, I see Chief Lartha. She stands, facing me, but **is** engrossed in a tablet. Someone slowly approaches her from behind.

"Hey, Boss Lady," says Deputy Chief Reez.

The security chief whirls round. Her legs offer most excellent stability. I confess, I admire them while feeling a bit intimidated by them. Perhaps I have a crush?

Chief Lartha watches him for a moment (Notice how I don't have to give a precise time unit?). Her voice comes out softly, almost hoarse. "Call me that one more time, buddy."

He smiles.

"What are you—how are you just here, roaming the halls, getting on my nerves?" she says, her tone growing stronger and more familiar to me.

"Well," says Reez, "turns out I had a thing that mimicked another thing. Dr. Rennick dealt with it. It's not an issue anymore."

"A thing that mimicked another thing."

"Yeah. I never remember medical jargon. Thought I was dying. Am no longer dying. Good enough for me."

"Uh-huh. You know, there's such a thing as being too laid back."

His eyes twinkled in reply.

She shakes her head, trying not to smile. "Okay then. You good for duty?"

"Will be cleared for lighter duties in a week. If all goes well without blips, full duty after four."

"Then do what you have to do because the team needs you back."

"Yup."

"Yeah, so I have a comm roster to assign and get to Iris before she reminds me for the bazillionth time."

Deputy Chief Reez seems puzzled. "Since when do you need reminding for anything?"

"Been distracted."

"Oh, really? Why?"

The glare she issues turns my cooling fans even colder. But the deputy chief still has a twinkle in his eye.

"Whatever," says Chief Lartha. "Get better. That's an order. Gotta bolt now."

"Will do," he says.

She turns her back to him. Then spins round again, grabs him by the collar and kisses him most passionately. It never ceases to amaze me, the sudden switch of bio sentients' behaviour. I feel a little awkward now, but they are drawing apart, quite breathlessly, I must add. I'm worried about their O2 levels and run a check. Oh! Readings are optimal.

"Well," Chief Lartha says, panting, "that was a major infraction on my part. It's within your rights to report me. I won't contest. I will say I'm sorry, though." I observe she won't look Deputy Chief Reez in the eye again.

"Hey," he says, tenderly cupping her cheek.

She manages to look up.

"Remember that penalty in the 'sportsball' game I loved but you hated? Let's say we chalk this up to 'excessive celebration'?"

Chief Lartha laughs. "Excessive celebration. Perfect." She steps back. "Thanks."

"Oh no, if I'm to be dead honest, thank *you!*"

She rolls her eyes. "Go rest. Come back to duty when you're even more annoying." This time, she turns from him, and Deputy Chief Reez begins to walk down the corridor.

His voice soon cries out, "Aye, aye, Boss Lady!"

"I will always hate the way you say that, as long as you live."

"And I'm gonna keep living, so poor you!"

"Yeah, you *think* you're gonna keep living, buddy."

She chuckles as quietly as she can and turns her head in my direction.

"Oh, hi, Clarence!" she says. "Didn't see you there."

"Hello, Chief!" I reply.

Lieutenant Commander Lartha enters the lift, and I watch Lieutenant Reez smile brightly at her, before heading in the direction of his quarters.

"So, how are we doing today?" says Dr. Jayne. "What would you like to discuss?"

Eileen taps my shoulder joint and smiles at me. "I think we're doing well. Much better. Understanding boundaries and each other's point of view."

"Clarence," asks Dee-Dee. "Is this your point of view as well?" Her machine language translates so the bio sentients can understand us.

"Yes, I am most pleased with our progress. I have learned not to be 'pushy,' which I recall means that I am pushing my decisions onto my person instead of respecting her autonomy to choose for herself. Is that correct, Eileen?"

My person nods and says, "Yup. You've been awesome. You're better at asking me what I need instead of insisting you know better."

I let my eye-lights glow to show her my appreciation of her compliment.

"And what have you learned, Lieutenant Commander?" asks Dr. Jayne.

"I've learned it's important for Clarence to feel xey have purpose as an assistive bot. I was wrong to ignore xem and cast xem aside, especially when feeling useful is so important to xeir well-being. I am being open and, funnily enough, a better communicator."

Dr. Jayne laughs at this. I suppose it is a little funny. Ha-ha!

"It's good you are both coming back to a symbiont relationship," says Dee-Dee. "I think Dr. Jayne and I can agree that we are proud of the progress you are making."

"And," adds the psychiatrist, "if you're willing, we have more recommendations."

Eileen and I quickly gaze at each other and say together:

"We are willing."

Captain Dustin Warq exited the tubular shower unit and dried off. Catching his reflection, he went closer to the mirror and inspected himself. *Not bad for fifty standard years*, he thought, satisfied with how he had managed to maintain his overall muscular physique. Then he caught sight of his "love handles" and made a face. Dr. Rivers had explained they'd never really go away, not at his age, and to accept—with undiluted glee—the clean bill of health he'd been given. After that visit, the captain had a much better understanding of why nobody seemed to like Rivers. *It might be time to consider a staff reorg.*

His chest hair had turned silver like the hair on his head. Warq spotted the faint scars tracing the underside of his pectoral muscles and smiled. *Thirty years ago, today.* He paused for a moment, remembering:

"Dustbin? Dustbin, wake up!"

The volume of the voice had been quite low, but so were most voices these days. Someone was definitely shaking him, though. "Whaa? Where am I? Trash?" he said aloud.

"Yeah, it's me. You're in recovery. Doc said everything went really well!"

Dustin blinked a few times, still foggy from the anesthetic. He'd always been sensitive to it, and a little nauseated. But he managed to recognize his sister Trisha and the private recovery room he'd been assigned.

She was holding up a ridiculously enormous box of his favourite assorted candies. Dustin couldn't help but laugh.

"Isn't sugar bad for the healing process?" he signed.

"PFFT," said Trish with a good amount of spray. "This is a special occasion, and only weirdos refrain from celebrating something like this without any sugar." She set the box upon the bed, over his thighs.

Dustin tried sitting up. "Ow!"

"Oh, Dustbin," she signed with a sigh. "You have to let the bed do this for you!" She pressed the controls to elevate her twin brother into a better position. Dustin waved when he wanted her to stop.

"Ow," he said again.

"Still painful, huh? Do you need something? I can ask the nurse to administer more owchie killers."

"Yes, please. Although..."

"Yeah?"

"May I have a glass of water first?"

"Sure!"

"And a piece of candy?"

Trisha laughed while opening the box for him. "That's my womb-mate!"

The surgeon entered the room just as Dustin chomped down on his treat. Trisha stared, aghast, comically trying to hide the huge box behind her back.

"I'll pretend I didn't see that," signed Dr. Rorq. "Now, how's the patient?"

"He has owchies," said Trisha. "Even when he signs. I see you wincing there, baby brother."

"That's to be expected as the tissues recover," signed the surgeon. "We'll help you manage the pain levels."

"Thank you," Dustin signed.

"So, would you like to see yourself?"

"I can? Already?"

"Absolutely! We've started using tissue regenerators as part of our post-op routine. But for your surgery, we only go so far. It's important for your body to heal on its own terms. Also, our physical therapist will show you exercises to help you build muscle and stretch your connective tissues to maintain flexibility."

"Then... yes," Dustin signed. "May I see now?"

"Of course!" Dr. Rorq asked the accompanying nurse to hold up a large mirror.

When Dustin saw his naked torso, he cupped his mouth, then wept with joy.

Trisha gently tapped his shoulder. He reluctantly turned his head to watch her sign to him.

"You look faboosh, baby bro! We'll totally hit the beach this summer!"

Dustin looked back into the mirror. "I can't wait!"

A little tear trickled down the captain's cheek. His adventurous, somewhat wacky, and marginally older twin sister. How he missed her. She'd always been his number-one fan.

On the command deck, things remained uneventful on this twenty-fourth consecutive day. Warq suppressed a sigh as he typed into his log:

> Because of faction riots in the Neevawn sector of the Caveen quadrant, we have replotted our route and should arrive in the Yorell system within six days. The crew are in good spirits despite the unchanging routine, and they are making use of our recreative facilities to boost morale.

Warq stared at his screen and added:

> As for their captain, his spirits could use a little boosting, if he's to be perfectly honest.

"Commander Davan?" he signed, getting up from his chair.

"Captain?" signed Davan.

"You have the conn."

"Aye, Captain," signed Davan.

Warq smiled faintly and headed to the lift without giving further instruction. Before Davan stepped over to the captain's chair, he caught Iris's eye.

"This is the fourth time in seven days," he signed to her.

"I know," she signed back. "I mean, sure, it's boring, but he's always ridden it out with us."

Davan held his trunk pensively. "After this shift, let's chat, okay?"

"Aye, aye, Acting Captain!" she said with a cheerful salute.

"UGH!" grunted Warq, holding his jaw. Even with his eyes closed, he could see all the stars in the galaxy.

"Holy freakin' gleek!" cried Lartha. "You were supposed to duck, sir!"

The captain winced as he tried to smile at her. "Guess I'm just getting old, Chief."

Lartha removed her hot-pink boxing gloves and sat down on the mat beside her commanding officer. Her black tank was soaked, along with her shiny golden boxing trunks. Today she wore her sparring legs because if she had actually put on her sentient legs, there would have been an ex-captain sitting on the edge of the ring. Left and Right never fully learned to grasp the nuances of sparring. They only knew how to fight for real.

Because the captain was staring at the mat while feeling out the movement of his jaw, Lartha tapped just above his elbow. Warq faced her.

"You're not old, Captain. Distracted maybe, but not old."

"Hmm," he vocalized, then signed, "yes, maybe distracted."

"Is anything wrong, sir?"

"Nothing to trouble you with."

"Then can I escort you to Medical?"

"Not necessary, Chief."

"Okay, how about I buy you a drink, all ice, so you can hold it against your face?"

Warq chuckled, then groaned in pain.

"Yeah, I'm taking you to Medical, Captain."

"I really don't need—"

"Look," she signed, "you can either give in to me, or I call my other legs over here to convince you."

"Fine," he signed with a soft moan, "I probably could use an ice pack."

In the 'Port Parlour, Herb sat on a bench, toggling the settings on his spanner. He'd either checked or supervised the maintenance of the control systems at least a billionty times and was even using words like billionty. Perhaps Lieutenant Sheena's colloquialisms had rubbed off on him. Herb had been glad they still remained colleagues in the same department, as he felt they were good counterparts in Engineering. Although she'd been hurt at first, her compassionate nature had sympathized with how difficult it had been for Herb to express his true feelings for Davan. And besides, she was in a relationship with someone new, and it seemed to be going really well.

Herb was also happily in love, but nearly bored to tears. The 'Port Parlour wasn't a place he'd primarily occupied, so it felt like a change of scenery. It was also blissfully quiet. Lieutenant Bezel was the only person in this area, and he was content with reading books while on duty. His fingers moved across the dynamic display as he engrossed himself in the story.

Without any warning, the doors whooshed open and in walked Captain Warq.

Herb's eyebrows flew up. "Captain!" He stood up, and so did Lieutenant Bezel.

"As you were," he signed, and Bezel heard this in his earpiece.

The lieutenant and the head of Engineering took their seats. Warq sat down on the bench beside Herb.

"I'm surprised to see you here," signed the captain.

"Well, frankly, sir, I feel the same way."

"It's just that I thought you'd be conjuring up new settings in your private room as a measure against ennui."

"Yeah, I tried that," Herb signed, "but it didn't really entertain me as much as I thought it would. Gerri is in her classes, so she's amusing herself at least. And I just felt more like being around people."

The captain raised his eyebrows at that.

Herb laughed. "I really enjoy people, sir, in low doses. It's mostly a barrage of intersecting noises that I don't get along with."

"Understood," Warq signed. He stared at the floor.

Herb touched his forearm. "Sir? Everyone says you've been acting weird."

Warq chuckled. "My problem with you, Horatio, is that I always have to discern what you're actually trying to say."

Herb paused. "That was sarcasm, right?"

"Just a little playfulness. I do appreciate your honesty, Lieutenant Commander. My apologies—Mr. Herbert."

"It's fine. Yeah, Davan says my blood might be 90% truth serum."

"I don't doubt it." Dustin smiled. "It's an asset, really."

"Wow. That's the first time anyone's ever told me that."

Warq looked down again. "It's true, though. I wish I had your candour, son," he signed.

The engineer touched his captain's arm again. "Sir, you are our commanding officer, and we respect your leadership, but we don't think of you as some authority to keep at a distance. People really care about you. I guess I'm saying this to let you know... if there's anything you want to tell us—"

The captain abruptly stood up. "That's very kind of you, Mr. Herbert, but I'll be fine." His face grew serious, for long enough for Herb to remain completely still, but then Warq's tender gaze returned. "Thank you for letting me share your space," the captain added. "Even if just for a moment."

"You're... you're welcome, sir. You're always welcome."

Warq nodded and quickly left.

Herb gnawed on the inside of his mouth for a few seconds, then undid a flap on one of his leg pockets, revealing a small screen. He opened a secure channel to text:

-- Davan? You there? The captain's not okay.

The reply wasn't immediate, but Herb knew enough to wait before asking again. He was relieved when it came in.

-- We feel the same. Meet us in Iris's quarters after our shift.

-- Got it. See you then.

"So, what do you think it is?" signed Davan.

"It can't be regular boredom," signed Iris. "The captain's made of stronger stuff than that."

"I agree," said Lartha, glancing at Iris's hands. Her own hands were full from scrolling on her tablet. "In fact, he's usually coming up with ideas to get us through flatlining periods like this."

"He mentioned about not being upfront as I am," said Herb.

Davan snort-laughed.

"Ah, shut the front door!" Herb replied with a wink.

The commander looked pleasantly surprised. "You winked! I'm impressed!" he signed.

"I've been practicing!"

"Get a room, fellas," said Lartha. "Okay, I found it," she added, scrolling on her device. "The family board thing."

"Huh?" signed Davan.

"That cheesy photo collage Iris made us do a few years ago."

"Hey!" said Iris.

Lartha grinned. "I mean, that really moving collection of loved ones you wanted us all to share."

"Well, I thought it was nice." She harrumphed.

"Aw, sorry, ol' friend. It was very nice—in an incredibly pukey sort of way."

Iris pursed her lips.

"But it might be a handy tool for us now," said Lartha. "There's a photo of Captain Warq and his fraternal twin sister."

Iris stood beside Lartha. "Oh, yes. I remember he said she always called him baby brother, even though she was only sixteen minutes older. What was her name?"

"Why, it was Trisha Warq," interjected Clarence. "A most unfortunate situation had befallen her, too."

Davan's brows furrowed. "What happened?"

"Have you not been made aware of the rift that engulfed her ship? I assumed it would be common knowledge."

The bio sentients looked to each other and then back at the bot.

Clarence continued. "Apparently, the ship she commanded, for she was also a captain in the Keangal fleet, was, to put it bluntly, sucked into a rift in space and time."

Iris's mouth gaped.

"When did that happen?" said Lartha.

"The tenth anniversary of the disappearance of the *S.S. Stargazer* was two days ago."

"Poor Captain Warq," signed Davan. "I mean that for both Captain Warqs."

"And there has been no trace or communication since then?" asked Iris.

Clarence started to hum. "Checking..."

Herb put his hands in his pockets. Iris watched her bot attentively.

"Still checking..." said Clarence.

"Maybe we should try another computer source," said Lartha. "A guidebot isn't a holistic database of—"

"Still checking…"

"Yeah, Clarence, abort search," said Iris.

"Still checking…"

"Clarence!"

"Still checking…"

Herb stepped forward. "Allow me." He switched off the bot, waited ten seconds, then switched xem back on.

Clarence blinked xeir eye-lights. "Is it a new day already?"

"Nope," said Herb. "Just a short time after we last spoke."

"I have a gap in my memory logs."

"You needed a brief rest for health reasons."

"Health reasons? Sir, I'll have you know my diagnostic checks show that I am in prime—"

"Yes, yes, you're gorgeously techlicious," said Lartha.

The bot paused. "Why, thank you, Chief!"

"Anyway," said Iris, "I think I might know how we can find out if any communiqué exists."

"Oh?" said Lartha.

"Technically, as Lieutenant Commander of Comms, I also have access to a massive library of records. I just need to get to my workstation."

"But the second shift is at the helm," signed Davan. "We can't just barge in there."

Iris put a finger to her lips. "No, we can't, but the next time the captain asks you to have the conn, I'm going for it."

"And if you get stuck," said Lartha, "I'll give you as much security clearance as you need."

"You won't be able to get the highest clearance without the captain's permission, though," Davan warned.

"I will if you're put in command," said Lartha.

"Ohhhh." He spelled out the extra consonants for effect.

Another day, and they'd be in the Yorell system, where they'd refuel, do some meet-and-greets, and have a rotating shore leave roster. And the captain had not once asked Commander Davan to have the conn. Iris and the others had grown concerned.

This is ridiculous, thought-projected Iris to Davan, on a private channel Lartha had arranged for the four of them. *We need to do something!*

He nodded. *Leave it with me!* Davan moseyed over to where Captain Warq stood, staring at the viewscreen.

When Warq caught his second-in-command from the corner of his eye, the captain smiled faintly.

"Not much of a view for thirty long days," signed Davan.

Warq shook his head. "No, nothing to write home about," he signed.

"Well, tomorrow we'll be on the outer rim of the system, so that's something."

"Yes." Warq stared at the viewscreen again.

Davan honked uncomfortably.

The honk was translated as "Ahem." on Warq's visor. He turned his head.

"I have a suggestion, Captain," signed Davan. "What if I take over this evening? I certainly don't mind."

"That's an unusual request, Commander. And unprecedented."

"I just mean you seem tired—"

The captain raised his hand. "Commander, while I appreciate your concern, I find this both inappropriate and unexpected coming from you."

Davan froze, then hung his head. Iris, witnessing the interaction, slouched in defeat at her workstation.

Warq studied his second-in-command, who seemed more than a little embarrassed. The captain exhaled, then touched Davan's shoulder. Davan met his gaze.

"Commander, I apologize. I have known you for years and not once have you ever had a selfish motive. I understand you are merely concerned for my well-being."

Davan's eyes perked. "Yes, Captain. That is truer than you know!"

Warq nodded. "And perhaps you are right. I could use a rest this evening. I suppose even captains should admit that from time to time. We will have a surge of activity once we dock, so a little quiet time reading in my chambers wouldn't do me any harm."

"Exactly, Captain."

Dustin Warq placed his hands on Davan's shoulders. "You're a kind soul, Commander. Thank you."

"You're welcome, Captain."

Warq signed to his console, "Transmit to the deck: Commander Davan, you have the conn." His words were picked up by the helm speakers and outputted as messages or through interpreter holos on the command-crew workstations.

Davan signed the expected response: "Aye, aye, Captain!"

The moment the lift doors closed, Davan signalled the go-ahead. Iris subtly nodded, and went to work.

"The locals had given it a name that loosely translates to Quicksand, in Keangal's Standard Tongue. There must have been an anomaly within the Rift that caused the 'tear' in time and space." Admiral

Foxnath placed a hand on the captain's shoulder. "I'm sorry, Dustin. You two were the twin stars of the Fleet."

"Could it be possible they're alive, but in another quadrant or an alternate universe?"

"Anything's possible, Captain. Let's hope for the best but be realistic about the situation. You most likely won't see your Trisha again during your lifetime."

Warq closed his eyes and put down his tablet. He couldn't concentrate on reading anyway.

"Well, look at you with your burly chest just acting all burly!" she'd said, doing pull-down weights on her favourite machine.

"Why do you even exist?" said Dustin to his sister.

"But you're sooo burly!"

"Shut it, Trash. She didn't sound that ditzy."

"We'll have to agree to disagree, Dustbin."

He chuckled. "It's nice to get the attention, I must admit. I wonder if she's working the welcome booth today?"

"Dunno. But you can always take your burly chest over there and find out!"

"My pecs are rather fetching," he said, looking at himself in the wall of mirrors.

"They'd better be. You've been working on them enough."

He sighed happily. "I feel good, sib."

She pulled down another rep then set the pulley to neutral. "You deserve it, womb-mate."

They exchanged an affectionate glance.

Trisha pulled down the handgrip again. "Now, let me get ripped to impress my own woman while you practice your game. And remember, I'm giving away the groom at your wedding."

The captain cracked his knuckles, a nervous habit he hadn't done for decades. Vera, that perky gym greeter had become more than friends, then more than that. Trisha *had* walked him down the aisle, but the marriage ended not long after his sister's ship had vanished. Warq had dived so deeply into his work, took every away mission offered him, and completely cut himself off from his wife. He'd regretted that immensely.

"I wish you were here to tease me about my grey chest hair, big sis," he said to the air. *And your ear hair*, he could imagine her saying.

"Are you serious?!" cried Iris.

"Is something wrong, Lieutenant Commander?" asked Davan, giving her the death stare.

She jumped, remembering where she was. "No, Commander Davan. My workstation had a temporary glitch. It's resolved now." When the eyes of her other command crewmates were off her, she thought-projected on that secure channel Lartha had configured, *Let's chat this way.*

Davan understood.

"Very good. Carry on," he signed.

Why the outburst? Davan projected.

Her ship was lost in Quicksand!

Wouldn't a simple scanner have found it under the planet's surface?

No, Quicksand is the nickname for the Barton Rift, Iris explained. *It's rumoured to be a kind of natural gateway to who knows where. Very unstable and presumed impossible to navigate. It's not that far away from here, either.*

That has me worried, projected Davan.

Well, it's far enough so we're safe, but we could jump to it in no time if we dropped off the captain first, then took off.

Took off?! Are you saying we should steal the ship? That's mutiny!

Is it, though?

YES!

But we'd be helping the captain reunite with his family. Don't you get it? He's sad because it's the anniversary of her disappearance, and we're heading to a system not too far from where it all happened.

Yes, Iris, I understand where your heart is, but we can't just leave without his permission. And by the way, he'd never give us permission.

Iris didn't reply to that. Davan looked over and saw her listening closely to something. She lowered her head and heaved a sigh. Then she glanced over at him and projected, *Listen to this recording.*

Davan put in his earpiece.

> "Log date: 5069.10.31, Captain Trisha Warq speaking. Entering the fringe of the Barton Rift, one of the ancient wonders of this sector. Well, at least it was a wonder to the ancients. To us, it's a pulsating streak among nebulae, but I'd be disappointing Ambassador Lidek if I said I'd not taken time to observe it. Somewhat of a religious sentiment attached to the Rift. Something about believing it was a pathway to the afterlife for the faithful. Still looks like a shifting crack in space to me.

> "Wait a sec, what was that?"

And listen to this, too, projected Iris.

> "Captain, we went too close and cannot break away!"

> "Too close? We never crossed the point of no return!"

> "We must have miscalculated. Either that, or it reached out and grabbed us! At this rate, fighting against it will tear the ship apart!"

> "We have no choice but to break away, Commander Reddard. I need to celebrate a special occasion with my baby brother, and I've not missed it since he was

twenty. Dammit, there will be candy, even remotely!"

"Engines failing, Captain. We'll run on nothing if we push any further."

[A pause.]

"Aw, fweep. Happy Chest Day, Dustbin. I love you."

That's the end of the audio transmission, Iris projected.

She forgot to pause the log recording before addressing her crew, projected Davan.

I know.

And our Captain Warq kept the log all these years.

Yeah.

Davan stared at the viewscreen, as the streaks of light vanished, replaced with the beauty of the celestial orbs of the system. He shook his head almost imperceptibly, then projected:

We'll all end up in the brig.

Maybe.

Let's get Lartha and Herb's input on this.

Aye, Acting Captain!

The commander shuddered at the notion of what would become of them all.

The first away team 'ported down at sunset on this part of the continent. Shades of peach, coral, and fiery oranges bathed the soft hillocks beyond the cityscape. Dressed in their ambassadorial best were Captain Warq, Commander Davan, Lieutenant Commander Iris, and Security Chief Lartha. They were greeted by a man and woman, each with flowing white robes and wavy cerulean hair in elaborate braids.

The man stepped forward towards Warq.

"Dustin! My dear old friend," he signed, his face simply radiating joy. His skin was a similar shade of green as the captain's but devoid of the tattooed markings common to the culture Warq had been raised in.

"So wonderful to see you, Josha!" The captain gave the man a warm hug.

"It has been too long, Dustin," signed Josha after letting go.

Warq's smile faded. "I know. I just…"

Josha touched his cheek. "I would have done my best to have offered comfort, even if that meant being quiet by your side."

"I know," Warq repeated, then glanced awkwardly at his senior officers. He cleared his throat, still a nervous habit of his, then signed, "Yes, well, Ambassador Josha Lidek—"

"Oh!" cried Iris. "*You're* Ambassador Lidek!"

Josha smiled even though taken off guard. "I'm flattered you've heard of me," he said. "Dustin," he signed, "Should my ears have been burning?"

Captain Warq looked puzzled as he pondered Iris's reaction. "I never realized the briefing I gave everyone would cause such excitement."

Davan honked a phrase that should never be translated in polite company.

Iris blushed profusely at the captain's inquiring stare. "I suppose I've felt a little cabin feverish lately. It's just so nice to be on land again, and, um, meet such an esteemed and renown—"

Josha raised his hand. "Please, my dear, our Order is about humility, and your enthusiasm will endanger me greatly." He laughed amiably, then remembered the woman standing beside him. "But where are my manners? Now do you understand how I do not deserve any praise? Please allow me to introduce a most beloved sister, Yatheen."

Yatheen signed, "I don't remember being so cherished when we were living with Mother. In fact, I recall you telling her I should be sold to the Wandering Circus."

"You misremember the context, sweet sister. I'd only meant you—"

"Belonged in a cage with the other primates. I have a razor-sharp memory, Josha."

He laughed loudly. "Indeed, I was a terror. But you are most treasured now."

"That is because you have become wise in your old age."

"Ah me." He turned to Warq. "Am I so wizened in your eyes, too, Dustin?"

Warq's mind was elsewhere after witnessing the siblings teasing each other. Trash and Dustbin were his sister's and his nicknames. Their parents had loathed how their children called each other that, which had only reinforced the twins' use of them. *We were terrors, too. "Double the trouble, double the fun," Trisha would say.*

Josha gently placed his hand on Warq's forearm.

"Not in your dotage yet," signed the captain, as if resuming on command. "Praise the Creator, since we are only a year apart in age!"

"True, true."

"And allow me to introduce you to my most trusted command crew officers. These are the people I know without a doubt will always stand by my side."

As soon as Warq waved his hand in their direction, Iris, Davan, and Lartha disappeared.

Warq's mouth hung open.

"I don't understand," signed Josha.

"Just a moment, please," signed the captain. He initiated communications on his forearm band. "This is Captain Warq to Teleportation," he signed. "There seems to have been a malfunction. 'Port the away team that was with me back to their original coordinates."

There was no reply. His holo interpreter shrugged her shoulders.

"Teleportation, come in. This is the captain."

Still no response.

"Tele—" he stopped when he felt Josha's touch. The ambassador pointed to the sky.

"It's gone," signed Josha.

"What's gone?"

"Your ship."

Warq stared at his friend in disbelief, then up at the remnants of the amber sky where the *S.S. SpoonZ* had visibly hovered, and he froze, but only for a moment.

"Josha, I need everything your aerospace control recorded just now... and possibly military support. It's obvious someone hijacked my ship, and I have a feeling I know who. They won't get away with it, either. I'm not abandoning the best crew in the galaxy to the Piranha Brigade!"

"Of course, old friend. We shall be of every assistance."

"Thank you. Please hurry! We've no time to lose."

Herb stared at his friends in the 'Port Parlour.

"Got all the kids out, and their parents," he said. "Used the interface on their comm bands or fobs to act as remote teleporters." His heart ached, thinking about Gerri. He hoped he'd made the right decision.

"Yeah, didn't think we'd be using that patch this way when I requested it as an additional safety measure," said Lartha. "How many of the crew could you 'port?"

"'Ported all the civilians. Just us military types left. None of us have kids on board." He swallowed awkwardly.

"And we transported the lot without any permission from them," said Iris, her shoulders tensing.

"Permission went into the shredder when we decided to do this," signed Davan.

"Yeah," said Herb. "We're a skeleton crew, with maybe tiny bits of sinew, and probably everyone will hate us shortly."

"Yay us," said Iris.

They were silent.

"I still think we're doing the right thing in the end," added Iris. "When the captain sees his sister again—"

"If," signed Davan curtly. "The biggest *if* that ever was an if."

Iris sighed.

Herb raised his hand.

"A question?" signed Davan.

"Yeah."

"What is it?"

"We're all going to the netherworld after we die, right?"

Davan sighed through his trunk.

Lartha stood up. "Oh, boo-gleeking-hoo. We can't think about this now. Let's get our crap together, tear this rift wide open, and bring back the captain's sister."

"Maybe that's not the most eloquent pep talk, but it'll have to do," signed Davan. "Iris, come with me."

"Aye, Acting Captain."

"No," he signed. "Call me Commander. I am not usurping his rank; I'm leading a search and rescue."

"Yes, Commander," she signed.

"Lartha, I'll want you on the deck as well, but leave a team here in the Parlour."

"Aye, Commander. It'll be done."

Davan paused before leaving with Iris. "Chief?"

"Yes?"

"Ask Lieutenant Bronwryck and Maddox if they would prefer to be isolated in a comfort cabin at Wellness."

"Why would they—"

"I anticipate an overload of suppressed and expressed anxiety from the crew, which I presume Maddox could easily cope with, but empathizing with that many people at once might be too much for Lieutenant Bronwryck to handle."

Lartha stared at Davan as if he'd lost all reason, but she realized the situation they were in proved they'd collectively taken a braincation. She also wondered if she and the crewmates spearheading this mission could qualify for family therapy at the Wellness centre, if any of the civilian practitioners would ever consider speaking to them again.

On the planet's surface, Captain Warq received reports of dozens of members of his ship appearing in several rural areas. No one was injured. And after scanning the roster, he discovered them to be all civilian consultants, medical staff, many members of the catering team, and non-military technologists. Children had been 'ported with them; thankfully none of the youngsters had parents who were part of the military crew. Except one.

The captain felt a lump forming in his throat. Josha noticed the change in his long-time friend's expression.

"It's just like them," signed Warq. "My team is so resourceful, so compassionate. They obviously sensed danger and wanted to protect the civilians and children before their own lives."

"But why would they leave without their captain?" signed Josha.

"I don't know, but I'm sure they felt they had no choice. In the meantime, I'm convinced this is the Piranha Pirate Brigade, and I've requested immediate reinforcements." *I just hope we can reach my ship before...* He winced. *Be safe, S.S. SpoonZ.* He said a silent prayer for wisdom and courage to overtake Commander Davan, who, if faced with those pirates, would be assuming his first real command in the worst of circumstances.

"Commander, we've set a course away from Yore, but aren't sure why," signed Lieutenant Renley.

Davan caught Iris's eye, then turned to his left and looked at Lartha, who nodded at him.

He took his place in the captain's chair, initiated his console, and signed a ship-wide message:

"This is Commander Davan. The *S.S. SpoonZ* has now a military-only crew, and we are embarking on a seek and rescue mission of Captain Trisha Warq. Rest assured that Captain Dustin Warq is safe on Yore, and we are proceeding without him. I require your full co-operation, as we might be facing unknown danger. But if I believe anything in this life, it's that the talent of this crew is par none. We will find Captain Trisha Warq and the *Stargazer*, and bring them back to the Keangal, the Fleet, and their family."

He sat up a little straighter and addressed Udana and Renley.

"Navigation, plot a new course for the Barton Rift."

EPISODE 12:
Is it really mutiny if it's for a friend?

Lieutenant Commander Horatio Herbert stole away for a moment to himself in his private room. Sure, time was precious, and he was needed at his post, but The Overwhelm had to be kept at bay.

He gazed into the distance as the sun caught the lake, sprinkling it with diamonds. The serenity of the landscape comforted him as he continued his diaphragmatic breathing.

The gravity of what they had conspired threatened to pound him like a hammer on an anvil. *Breathe in...* But they were doing the right thing; he felt sure of that. The speed at which they had to make decisions had been mind-boggling. They were taking risks—unspeakable risks—with everyone's lives. *And breathe out...* All in the hope they could reunite the captain with the sister he sorely missed.

Herb still couldn't believe he remained on board the *S.S. SpoonZ*. It had been decided that he would leave with Gerri. The plans had been for him to make sure everyone 'ported safely onto Yore, then he would join Gerri on the continent.

But...

There had been eleven children on board, and only ten had left the ship. He'd discovered this when Gerri's wristband signal had remained in the music room. Herb had bolted there to find her gleefully drumming away with her eyes closed. She'd most likely removed the wristband for sensory reasons. *Breathe in...*

And when he had explained to her that she must leave so the crew could save someone, Gerri had refused to go. "Nope," she'd said aloud. "You would miss me too much."

"But it might be dangerous," Herb had signed to her.

"Then you'll really need me to take care of you," she'd signed in reply.

Breathe out... Herb shook his head. Gerri never really seemed to comprehend that it was his role to be her caregiver, and not the other way around. So, she wouldn't leave, and here they'd stay together. *Davan will be beside himself.* Herb shivered, not looking forward to his betrothed's reaction.

Yipes. Okay, where was I? Oh yeah. Breathe in...

Lieutenant Commander Eileen Iris switched off her implants so she could focus. Her fingers scanned the elevated readouts on her console screens, and she requested further information to be spoken into her earpiece.

At her side was Clarence, blinking xeir eye-lights as xey did whenever in a state of intense curiosity.

"Eileen, might I share an observation?"

"Uh, there's not much time for a conversation, Clarence."

"Indeed. But with all the civilian staff off the ship, won't many supports no longer be offered to the remaining crew?"

"Every department has some military personnel in it."

"Except the catering corps. They were all transported to Yore."

Iris turned her head away from her workstation. "What? We have no one to prepare food?"

"Oh yes, there are still the bots and androids. I'm sure they can meet your dietary needs."

Lartha overheard this and projected, *Wait! No more sponge cake?!*

I know! Iris projected back.

"But the Wellness Centre is down to a third of its crew," continued Clarence. "Fortunately, Dee-Dee was in maintenance and remained on board. She is a most excellent therapist. I highly recommend her!"

"What about the head of Medical?" asked Lartha.

Clarence rotated xeir head. "Dr. Rivers is military. He's still on the ship."

"Yay-gleeking-yay."

"I don't understand your reaction, Chief."

"Hush, Clarence," said Iris. "We need to concentrate."

"Oh, of course. How may I be of service?"

"Just stay by me for now, okay?"

"All right."

"And be quiet."

"I can do that."

"Good."

"Just how quiet do you require me to be, because my circuitry does have a high-frequency hum, but I believe it is too high to be perceived by any bio sentient on this ship."

"Clarence. You're fine. No talking."

"All right."

"Thank you."

"I will no longer communicate by projecting a vocal tone."

Iris gritted her teeth. "Wonderful."

"It's really not a problem at all."

"Great."

She finally redirected her attention to her comm. A message scrolled across her screen and rang through her earpiece:

"Is communicating through messaging an acceptable alternative?"

Iris slowly drew her hand from her forehead to her mouth.

About ten minutes later, Lieutenant Jonny Reez and Lieutenant Commander Leanna Lartha sat on a bench near the lift that would take them back to the bridge.

"So, we're heading for the Barton Rift?" he said.

"Yup."

"That's the one they nicknamed Quicksand?"

"Yup."

"Because it devours ships whole, and they're never heard from again, yeah?"

"Mm-hmm."

"And we're doing this all without permission from Captain Warq. To save his sister, who has been presumed dead along with her crew for ten years."

"That's pretty much it, yeah."

Reez narrowed his eyes. "And you bought into this?"

Lartha polished a smudge off Left's shiny surface with some material from a sleeve. "Well, you kind of had to be there when Iris was building the case. The captain seemed depressed, or grieving, or both. Anyway, I knew he wasn't himself when I punched him in the face."

"Hold up. You punched Captain Warq in the face?!"

"We were sparring, Jonny."

"Oh. Okay."

"But he's usually sharper than that."

"Brave, for taking you on. I still have this scar." He traced a finger down the side of his left eye to just under his cheekbone.

"Hey, you told me I was holding back and to give you my worst."

"I know. Not my brightest moment."

"Deserved it for saying I'd fight like a girl."

"I was young then and didn't know 'fight like a girl' meant I should have had my estate in order first."

Lartha laughed, relieved to be able to do so. The situation they were all in was no laughing matter.

"So, mutiny, huh?" asked Reez.

"But is it really, though?"

"Uh, yeah. Yeah, I would say it was on the money."

Lartha sighed. "Well, it's for a friend."

"Who happens to be a decorated captain who has the power to throw us into oblivion for this, right?"

"Right." She patted her prosthesis, who mistakenly thought she was being addressed.

Now Reez exhaled. "Fine. What do you want me to do?"

Lartha punched his shoulder affectionately.

Commander Davan of House Vazilmyn sat in the captain's chair on the command deck. *I could order the ship turned around. We could throw ourselves on the captain's mercy. Insist we acted out of concern for his well-being. Emphasize how we made sure all the civilians were safely 'ported off ship.*

They were getting closer to their destination. But then what? A completely uncharted anomaly, a scientific wonder that provoked legends from the ancients. It had been in the religious texts of several faiths; some had considered it a supernatural entity. It had been named the Barton Rift in modern parlance after the first vessel to have gone missing in it, the *S.S. Barton*. Another science ship, like the one Davan sat in. First of the Keangal Fleet to be lost. He wondered if they had entered it with the intention of exploration. Or had it been a piloting mishap? It was a mystery. The last message that had been received lightyears away had only said, "Entering the Rift. We shall return."

But they hadn't. No one had. Ever. Not even the *Stargazer*, which at the time had been almost as advanced a vessel as the *SpoonZ*.

Am I just sending us into the Rift to become another statistic? He stared at the viewscreen. *It is such a thing of beauty. I feel its draw, like from a siren in an ancient tale.*

He shuddered, remembering what had become of the explorers drawn by those sirens.

"Commander?"

"Yes, Lieutenant Udana?"

"You asked me for the point of no return."

"Yes?"

"We're approaching it, sir."

"Understood."

"Change course back to Yore?"

Captain Warq's forlorn expression flashed in his mind. "No, maintain course."

A slight hesitation, then, "Aye, Commander."

On Yore, Captain Dustin Warq felt an overwhelming sense of relief.

"I never expected you to come to our aid, but I am most grateful, Admiral."

Admiral Jaq Miran clasped Warq's hands, their grey eyes and their face showing a stern resolution. They let go and Miran signed, "Who is responsible for this?"

"Unknown at present, Admiral," signed Warq. "I find the facts rather disturbing. Nearly all of the civilians except one have been 'ported to this planet. Also, all of the children, save for one."

"Who are the exceptions?"

Warq checked his tablet. "The tech civilian who is still aboard the ship is Fran Quinn, and the child is Gerri Venkin, a foster of Mr. Herbert. But the general feeling is that Gerri might be hiding. A team is presently searching for her. We are not sure why Fran chose to remain on board."

"Is there any explanation why the rest of these personnel were 'ported to Yore?"

Warq shrugged. "I had been aware that Security had requested mods to their wristbands, fobs, and forearm bands, so the devices could act as remote teleporters in case of immediate need of escape.

What I hadn't realized is that all of the units had been given this functionality. But when I questioned several of the civilians, they said they hadn't been aware of it. A few of our technicians concluded it must have been dormant functionality that was suddenly activated."

"And without their knowledge?"

"Yes."

Miran rubbed their chin. "So, the plan was to keep civilians safe while all military personnel remained on board."

"That is my feeling."

"While it seems like your military crew is attempting to protect these civilians, I have a more ominous suspicion for why this could happen. Instigators trying to make a conflict appear like a fair fight, which they'll use to their advantage if brought before a tribunal."

"Please don't tell me it's the Brigade. I mean, I suspect this myself, but..." Warq stopped signing to rest a hand over his eyes. He felt sick with worry and willed himself to remain focused.

Miran touched his forearm, and Warq opened his eyes again.

"I am here, Captain. And I won't rest until we get Eileen"—they coughed—"I mean, your crew back safely out of the Brigade's clutches. This is devious even for them."

"Permission to come aboard your ship, Admiral?"

"Permission most granted, my friend. And you may bring any of the civilians who are willing to accompany us and offer their expertise."

"Thank you, Admiral. Many of them have already volunteered to help."

On board the *S.S. SpoonZ*, Davan had requested a quick status report from his department heads.

"Mr. Herbert, can you confirm all of the civilians are safely off our ship?"

"Nope."

"What?"

"I can't confirm that because not all of them left."

"You mean the kiddies are still here?" asked Lartha with some alarm in her tone.

"Oh no, all the kiddies were 'ported out before we cloaked and bolted," said Herb from a comm at Engineering. "Um… except one. Gerri never left."

"Gerri?!" cried Iris.

"Mr. Herbert, please tell me you're joking," signed Davan.

"I'm joking."

"Thank goodness."

"Except I'm not."

"Oh, Horatio…" said Davan in his own language.

"Don't worry. She's here with me. I'll explain when we can get a breather. The only other civilian with us is Fran, and personally, I'm glad for it. She's one of the most proficient techs we have, and we need all the help we can get."

"That's not a lie," said Lartha. "Fran's worked on my Rose a few times. She's killer."

"Mr. Herbert," signed Davan, trying to maintain his wits, "I wish you would have informed me about Gerri's presence before we passed the point of no return."

"I know, but she's got it fixed in her mind that I need taking care of, and it would be worse for her if we sent her away."

"There's so much about the Rift we don't know and if we…" Davan stopped signing and switched to his own language. "If we don't make it, we'll be taking her with us. That's not fair to her."

Herb squeezed his lingual device and replied, "Then we're just going to have to survive."

Davan brushed the underside of his trunk.

"We're gonna make it, Davan," trumpeted Herb. "We can do this. You can lead us."

Davan stared longingly at him, who nodded knowingly, then Herb raised his hands to sign, "All systems operational and awaiting your orders, Commander."

"Thank you, Mr. Herbert."

Davan sat so still in the captain's chair, he could have been a portrait. But his brain was a whirlwind of thought. No matter who else had contributed to the events that led them here, even his closest friends and his betrothed, he alone was the most senior officer. This mutiny would rest primarily on his shoulders, along with the brunt of the consequences. He knew he should feel much worse than he did, but Captain Warq had been far more than just a commanding officer. He was not only a mentor, but a friend, and very dear to all of them. Davan hoped Warq would understand their intentions derived from their love of him, and their respect for the loss that was too deep for the captain to express.

After one last grand inhale and exhale, Davan shifted to sit up a little straighter and initiated the interpreter hologram as part of a ship-wide transmission.

"This is Commander Davan, assuming command, but not taking the rank of Acting Captain. Please do not be alarmed. Engineering has confirmed that the children along with our civilian crew have 'ported safely on Yore.

"Those remaining on board are military only. And we have a new mission: not only a seek and rescue of the *Stargazer*, but we are also going to explore and chart the Barton Rift. As a science vessel, any readings and data we can gather from this type of anomaly might help further explorations, and possibly pave the way for easier intra- and intergalactic travel.

"As you know, months ago we had an Earther 'port aboard from another galaxy, but sadly, his people disabled him before our very eyes. However, Lieutenant Commander Iris did find his language in our database, so we know this type of travel was once possible, and perhaps it was because the Rift had acted like a conduit, a wormhole of sorts.

"Today, as we begin this mission, I expect no less than the best from you all, as the captain of the *Stargazer* is the twin sister of our captain. Our goal is to bring everyone home, alive and well. Remain at post, follow the chain of command, and may the universe guide us on our way. Davan out."

Steeling himself one final time, he signed, "Navigation team?"

"Yes, Commander," they said and signed.

"Plot a course through the Barton Rift."

"Um, about that, Commander," said Udana.

Lieutenant Renley put up a chart on the main viewscreen, superimposed against a live view of the Rift.

Davan tried concentrating on the viewscreen, but the image kept whirling about. "Our sensors must be off. Stabilize, Lieutenant Renley."

"Sensor cameras are stable, Captain," she signed.

"This is stable?" asked Lartha, trying to focus on the visual. "I feel like I ingested a dessert spiked with special herbs."

"Commander," said Iris, "I'm picking up a communication."

Davan's heart jolted. "Perceive on stealth mode."

"Yes, Commander. Putting on screens and audio now."

"*S.S. SpoonZ*, this is Jozelyn Miran," said the Prime, whose appearance had greatly transformed from when they'd last seen her masquerading as a priestess of Aveen. Her grey-black hair shone with streaks of white, zigzagged throughout her mane like lightning bolts. Her grey skin glistened, indicating the toxins had been removed from her system, and she wore black armour ribbed with neon red. There was even a black crown that dipped in a deep V across her forehead. She sneered with lips that had been painted black with a crimson shimmer.

"We know what you're up to, my lovelies!" She practically sang those words. "You found a way to use Quicksand as a navigation path. Well, you'll not claim access of this trade route for the Keangal. Prepare to be blown to microns."

"Commander," cried Lieutenant Udana. "Multiple Piranha vessels appearing all around us."

"Is it a School?" signed Davan.

"Twenty ships. No... Thirty-six... Forty!"

"Fweep!" cried Iris.

"Aw, gleek," said Lartha. "Can they just not?"

"Go to Alert Status 4," signed Davan. "Bridge to Engineering."

"Herb here."

"We have a problem, Mr. Herbert."

"Which one? The ever-shifting unstable rift, the impending school of Piranhas heading our way, or just the general mutiny stuff? Because it's all pretty bad, to be honest."

"I'll start with this," Davan signed. "How can the Brigade see through our cloaking?"

"That phony priestess-person might have sent intel to the Brigade without our knowing."

"Impossible," said Lartha. "We secured all incoming and outgoing transmissions."

"Yeah, but maybe she did it after her arrest. The Brigade has friends in all kinds of places. A corrupt prison guard or warden maybe?"

"Who perhaps enabled her release," signed Davan. "But we don't have time for speculation."

"True. We don't have time for pretty much anything," said Herb.

"Can you modify the cloaking parameters, Mr. Herbert?"

"Not this quickly. We need to tear out of here."

"How?" cried Udana.

Yeah, projected Renley, also breaking protocol by interrupting the commander's conversation. *Our only escape route is through the Rift! I can't chart it. It's a moving mass of whatever!* She decided she needed to feel like she was holding onto something, so she modified her side of the workstation to generate manual piloting controls. Navigation's workstation had been configured so it could be dynamically altered by either of the pilots to suit their needs. When Udana heard Renley's configuration change, they routed all essential spoken and signed communication on deck to stream in real-time to her thought projector. This would help her more easily focus on flying.

Davan exhaled through his trunk, not taking his eyes off the screen. He studied the charted route that was now useless in that swirling mass. "If we can't plot a course... then we just have to fly right through it."

Silence on the comm and on the command deck.

"Fifty-eight... sixty-four Piranha vessels!" cried Udana.

Captain, I mean Commander, projected Lieutenant Renley, *we don't know what we'll face if we don't even try to plot a course.*

"Commander," said Udana, "the School's expanding. More fighters appearing each second, and some are closing in."

Davan turned to Iris. They stared at each other for a long moment, then she gave him a small smile and a nod. He quickly glanced at Lartha, whose hands were on her hips as she leaned on her right leg. She shrugged her shoulders, then nodded as well.

"Davan?" rang Herb's voice over the comm.

The commander's eyes softened. "Yes, Mr. Herbert?"

"Let's just do it. Let's tear through space. Or more like, let's tear through the tear in space."

"Thank you, Mr. Herbert. Navigation?"

Praying to every deity and even those I don't know yet, Commander, projected Renley.

"I'm continuing to monitor the anomaly readings and the school," said Udana. "Ninety-eight ships. We're vapour if we stay here."

Davan leaned in his chair. "Go to Alert Status 5. Lieutenant Renley, take us through the Rift."

Aye, Commander. She clutched her controls, swore indiscriminately—which no one blamed her for in the least—and headed for Quicksand.

"Can they detect us?" signed Warq.

"Not this ship," said the admiral. "They're not the only one with spies."

Warq raised his brows.

Miran smiled faintly. "The Brigade has made a career of underestimating me. Since my expulsion, I've been determined to bring them down. I don't suffer bullies well, Captain."

"Understood."

"And the ever-changing cloaking algorithm on this vessel is designed to inject a virus into any system that tries to detect and decode it. If any ship in the Brigade suspects our presence—for example, if we fire upon them—the moment they set their scanners after us, we'll offer them the virus. It's projected in light and sound."

"What will happen to those ships?"

"They will hover in place, life support will remain functional, but they won't be able to fire or manoeuvre. So Keangal forces can arrest them without facing much resistance. That is, if other Piranha Pirates don't destroy the hovering ships first."

Captain Warq looked alarmed as he signed, "You mean to say, they would eradicate their own?"

"This is the Brigade, Captain. They have no loyalty but to the 'strong' and 'capable.'" Miran's eyes went dark. "Whatever that means."

At this, the captain remained quiet, folding his hands. It had been well known that Jaq Miran was expelled from the Piranha Brigade by their own family, but he hadn't been aware of the reason. He suspected Lieutenant Commander Iris knew the entire story, but as a good friend, she'd kept those private details to herself. Warq felt a pang in his heart for her and the crew, especially his senior officers. He prayed once again for their safety.

"Admiral, we're approaching the point of no return on our course to the Rift," said the navigation officer.

"Stay on course, Lieutenant Jann. But don't take us past the point of no return. I suspect we shall encounter the *S.S. SpoonZ* and a School."

She shuddered. "Aye, Admiral."

"Engineering," said Miran.

"Lieutenant Commander Yarvyn, Admiral."

"What's the status of our cloaking system?"

"Cloaking system optimal, Admiral. Do not anticipate any malfunctions. Backup systems are operating simultaneously, so there won't be any dips in efficiency."

"Thank you, Lieutenant Commander." Miran turned to the captain, who sat beside them at the helm. "I know you're worried, Dustin," they signed, "but there's no way I'm going to let the Brigade get them. You have my word on that."

Warq blinked back tears. "I simply cannot have another loss at the Rift, Jaq."

Miran squeezed his hand. "You won't. I promise."

The captain signed his gratitude. He sat quietly for the remainder of the time to their destination. It felt to him like it would take forever to come out of lightspeed, but eventually, the navigations officer announced:

"Admiral, we're at the Rift."

"Onscreen, Lieutenant," said Miran.

Warq's and Miran's eyes were almost comic in their synchronized widening.

"Angels guide us," signed Warq.

The admiral took a breath at the sight of the enormity of the glowing wonder in space. Their shields would protect them against the luminosity, but nothing prepared them for the Rift itself, and the fact that it swayed and shifted as if it had tentacles.

This is one of those moments when it's impossible not to feel microscopic in comparison, mused Miran.

But that singular thought was all the luxury they could afford, as the status reports poured in:

"Identified 24 Piranha ships, Admiral. No! Only 15. Wait! They're disappearing into the Rift."

"Is the Rift pulling them in?"

"Negative, Admiral. Residue jump signatures. The Brigade are actually entering the Rift! Willingly. It's almost as if they're chasing something."

"Or someone," signed Captain Warq.

Miran leaned forward in their chair. "Lieutenant Yarvyn, you know what to do!"

"But Admiral, respectfully, I can't discern a safe course for us. The Rift is not stable. I don't even know where the Piranhas are coming out of lightspeed within the thing, or if they're being disintegrated upon entry!"

"Understood, Lieutenant. The safety of our crew is of the utmost importance." Miran turned to Captain Warq. "Care to go for a ride?"

In spite of the dire circumstances, the admiral managed somewhat of a daredevil's twinkle in their eyes.

A twinkle Dustin Warq simply could not resist.

"BATTLE STATIONS!" signed Davan emphatically.

The word appeared on every screen, blasted through every earpiece and wristband and thought projector, and was signed by every holointerpreter. Alarms rang out and vibrated. On the bridge and all over the ship, the crew scurried into action or braced themselves with alertness, so they could execute command with ultimate efficiency and effect. Stabilizing fields kept crew members safely in their seats, secured mobility devices in place as initiated by their users or the mobility devices themselves, and protected those who had to move about from being injured during evasive manoeuvres or from the impact of hits to the hull of the ship.

"Mr. Herbert, status!" Davan added.

"Aft shields holding at 89.38%, forward shields at 76.34%."

"We need better than that, Mr. Herbert. The School is somehow closing in, and we're still battling the natural resources of this rift!"

Before Herb could respond, the ship ricocheted off something and sent it into a spin.

"Navigation!" signed Davan.

"The Rift is a swirling nightmare to manoeuvre," cried Udana. "Lieutenant Renley is solely on manual steering. Her visor is no longer set to text interpretation but advanced visual acuity. We've both given up even trying to plot our way through. I'm listening for School frequencies since the Brigade has to remain uncloaked in this anomaly."

"Can you determine their number?"

"So far, the data reads 126 ships."

Davan cursed in his mind.

Renley gasped. Other members of the command deck reacted as well.

"Your thought projector is active, remember?" said Herb over the comm.

"Oh, right. Apologies, everyone," Davan signed.

I felt your choice of word was dead on, Commander, projected Renley, just missing another shift in the Rift as she corrected their trajectory.

Incoming! projected Udana.

A series of blasts walloped their hull. More warning shots. The Piranha Schools loved to play with their quarry before devouring them piece by piece.

Davan needed privacy, but there was no time to spare. He decided to speak to Herb in his own language again.

"This ship was not built for this kind of confrontation."

Herb replied through his device, "No kidding."

"What is our best chance of escape?"

"Death?"

"Horatio!"

"We're hurtling through an uncharted rift, we have 126 fighters piloted by trained assassins on our tail, and minimal weapons, what with our being a science vessel and all. We're only built to defend this ship just enough to escape."

"I need more data on the Barton Rift," said Davan. "If I just had the time to consult—"

A barrage of blasts rocked the ship.

"Yeah, I'm convinced. Death seems to be the best option," said Herb.

"Would you stop that! We can try—"

"Commander!" said Iris. "We're being hailed!"

"I'm not interested in hearing the termination speech doled out by those pirates," signed Davan.

"It's on an approved Keangal frequency!"

Davan blinked. "That's impossible! Who else could be in the Rift?"

"An ally?"

"But who knows we're here?" Davan swallowed. "Put it through to my console as text."

The words were decrypted on his screen: "Be prepared to be boarded."

Davan tapped his comm and signed, "Commander Davan to Security!"

"Lartha here, Commander."

"Get over to the 'Port Parlour! Unauthorized hostiles might be attempting to board us."

"I'm not picking up any security breach readings."

"They used a friendly frequency. Might have co-opted it from our previous prisoner."

"Right. Sent a team. Am heading there myself."

Another internal channel opened. An interpretation holo appeared and signed, "Lieutenant Mascix to Commander Davan, the Teleport Parlour controls are being overridden! We do not know the source!"

"Stand by, Lieutenant. Security is on their way."

"Security just arrived, Commander. I cannot stop this teleportation!"

"Shield your station, Lieutenant Mascix. Let Security take care of this."

"Two beings materializing, Commander!"

"Weapons up," rang Deputy Chief Reez's voice from the open channel.

Yet more blasts pummelled the hull.

"Course correction, Lieutenant Renley!" signed Davan.

Is he kidding? she projected to Udana.

That wasn't a private thought, Lieutenant, projected Davan.

Renley moaned.

"My console is telling me the School is forming an attack pattern. The next shots won't be warnings!" said Lieutenant Udana.

Davan turned back to the holointerpreter. "Mr. Herbert," he signed, "we need maximum shields!"

"I can't give you what we don't have! We need our engines in order for Navigation to ride the rift! I'd have to reroute power from life support at this point!"

"Or?" signed Davan. "You can do that thing where you come up with a thing that we really need."

Herb was unresponsive.

"Horatio?"

"Um… I'm gonna try to try a thing. At this point, might as well go for broke."

"Thank you, Mr. Herbert!" Davan switched channels. "Command deck to Transport Parlour. What's happening, Lieutenant Mascix?"

"I don't believe it," signed the holo on Mascix's behalf.

Davan braced himself. He didn't know if he could add another "uh-oh" to his mental list. Before he could inquire further, an image replaced the interpretation holo. Two figures stood at the teleport platform, one who had an expression that could dissolve every metallic surface within the ship.

"Uh-oh," said Davan.

Iris switched on her eyes and looked in the direction of the captain's chair.

"Ah, fweep."

The two who had boarded were none other than Captain Warq and Admiral Miran.

Incoming School! projected Udana.

"Mr. Herbert, that thing you're trying?" signed Davan.

"I don't have enough time for this thing!" said Herb.

"Shots fired!" cried Udana.

Renley's shoulders tensed.

"We're being hailed," said Iris. "Enemy frequency."

"It's the termination speech," boomed Admiral Miran's voice. Everyone but Udana and Renley turned their attention towards the lift doors.

Captain Warq stood beside them, with Lartha and Reez behind the commanding officers. Warq scanned the command deck. "No invaders here either?"

Davan had jumped from the captain's chair. "Captain, shots have been fired and—"

"Brace for impact," cried Udana.

Everyone held their breaths, except for Miran and Warq. In Engineering, Herb hugged Gerri—who had never left his side— closing his eyes against her little head as she clutched him tightly. This is how he wanted her to feel, loved and safe.

Iris watched Lartha and Reez reach for each other's hand. Davan opened an internal channel and honked a phrase. No doubt something only for Herb's ears, but it registered as *Farewell, pulse of my heart*. She found Miran's gaze, and to her shock, it fell coldly upon her. Not at all what she expected from them in their last moments on the mortal plane.

And then it came. The blast.

Iris involuntarily inhaled as if she were about to be submerged underwater.

She opened her eyes upon hearing sounds of confusion among several of her colleagues. Admiral Miran and Captain Warq stood together, Miran's eyes remaining as cold as space.

Finally, Warq unfolded his arms to sign, "Status, Lieutenant Udana?"

An explosion of an unknown source destroyed all the ships in the hex pattern. Their attack was nullified.

"Thank you, Lieutenant." Warq turned to Miran. "I am sorry for the loss of your shuttle, Admiral, but grateful for it all the same."

"That was merely a ruse to give them pause," signed Miran. "Enough to have us evade the first line. The next School will be after us in no time."

Captain Warq gestured to the captain's chair. "Admiral, it would be my honour—"

"No, *you* are the captain of this vessel. I do, however, need access to Engineering. As long as we are under attack, I prefer to serve this vessel as a member of the crew. After all, I am the only former Pirate, and you will need my assistance more than my leadership."

"As you wish, Admiral." Warq turned to Davan, "Commander, provide the admiral with access."

"Already done, sir," signed Davan, offering a place for the admiral at his workstation.

"Thank you, Commander," said Miran, their voice frigid. "And in the meantime," they signed, "why don't you provide your captain an explanation for the mutiny you allowed to take place on this ship?"

Warq's face revealed his alarm. "With all due respect, Admiral Miran, I am deeply offended you would suggest such a thing. It is obvious my crew were taken over by—"

"By whom?" signed Miran resolutely. "I've detected no Pirate signatures on this vessel. Commander Davan"—Miran's grey eyes pierced through—"wouldn't it be your duty to open a stealth signal to report a coup?"

The captain turned to Davan.

Davan just stared in reply, his arms limp.

Warq's lips parted.

Finally, Davan raised his hands. "Captain, I can explain everything…"

EPISODE 13:
Let 'er rip!

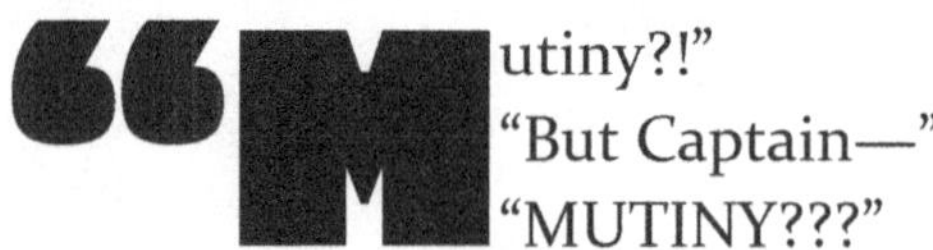

"Mutiny?!"

"But Captain—"

"MUTINY???"

"Captain, please, I said I can explain!"

"You can explain, Commander? My Second, the person I trusted most on this ship? *You* can explain?" The fury in Warq's movements and the expression on his face left no doubt in anyone's mind that the captain was beyond livid. No one in the command crew had ever experienced him this angry. Disappointed, frustrated, maybe, but nothing like this.

Davan's eyes implored as he signed, "If you would just let me explain what we'd planned—"

"What you planned. Oh yes, that is what strikes me hardest. You *planned* all of this. Every move was intentional, right down to all of the civilian crew members and the children. This was no crime of passion, of that I am sure!"

"That's not true!" cried Iris.

Warq read her words and jerked his neck in her direction. Iris's lips trembled slightly, only because he'd never glared at her like that before.

Davan shook his head at Iris, pleading with her to keep silent.

She refused to take the hint, lifted her chin, and pushed back her shoulders.

"I mean, Captain," she signed, "this wasn't a passionless act on our part. It was *com*passionate. We love you, sir, and—"

Warq rolled his eyes. "Love! This is your way of showing love to me. Stealing my ship, transporting a large portion of the crew without any warning—startling them with your random displacement of them across the planet, mind—"

Herb gulped at that as he listened from the open channel at Engineering. If he had had more time, he would have teleported everyone within the same county. He did make sure their comm devices relayed a message—after the teleportation was complete— that indicated they were put on the planet for safety reasons. He just hadn't said why.

"Do you have any idea how upset the children were?" Warq continued. "At least they were together with their teacher."

"I apologize for how it turned into a logistical nightmare, sir," said Herb. "If I'd had more time…"

Warq closed his eyes, then gestured for the engineering officer to remain silent. "Don't speak to me, Mr. Herbert. Just not now."

"As *I* was saying, Captain—" resumed Iris.

"And don't you speak to me either, Lieutenant Commander. I am not in the mood for philosophies about compassion. This is a Keangal science vessel, and there are codes of conduct put in place for our safety and wellness. At present, the only person I want to address is Commander Davan. He had full authority to stop this insubordination, and he didn't. What say you, Commander? You told me you wanted to explain. So, have at it! Explain the benevolence of mutiny to me."

Davan's shoulders and spine tensed. He inhaled deeply, exhaled, then raised his hands to converse. "I was against it at first—"

The captain shook his head in disbelief.

"But then," continued Davan, "I felt it was a seek and rescue mission of essential Keangal military personnel."

Warq's brows furrowed. "Seek and rescue? Essential military personnel? Who in all of the created worlds could you be trying to…" A singular thought stilled his hands for a moment: *The Barton Rift*. "No. No, wait," Warq signed. "You… how did you… you cannot possibly be serious!"

"You have not been yourself, sir," signed Davan, "and we have noticed. After scanning the files we could access, I concluded that no one had even attempted to search for—"

"Of course no one had attempted it! The Barton Rift is a death trap. Uncharted because nobody has ever survived it!"

"Yet, we're still here."

"And *where* is here? We don't even know what galaxy we're in." He froze. "You said files? What files? What access? You would have had to have had the topmost security—" He lowered his hands and pivoted his head in Lartha's direction.

She smiled an awkward, toothy grin. Reez took an exaggerated step away from her, as if pretending not to know her. It was funny to exactly no one.

Captain Warq stared at the floor for perhaps only a few precious seconds, but it felt like the longest pause in recorded history. He raised his head and his hands to sign, "I have been betrayed in the worst possible way. Not only by colleagues, but by people I trusted with the crew's life and my own. People I cared for, even thought of as friends. Yes, despite being trained to maintain a professional distance as your commanding officer, I have cared deeply for each of you. And you have all turned against me."

"But it wasn't like that—" cried Iris.

Warq ignored her. "Admiral? What say you? Shall we place them in the brig and call up the secondary departmental leads and command crew?"

"Under any other circumstance, I would say yes, Captain. However, if this team could deceive you with almost no time to prepare and manage to stay alive in the Rift, we might have to rely on their skills to get through the other side of this."

"I understand your point, even if I am reluctant to follow your advice."

"Don't get me wrong, Captain," Miran signed. "I will fully support any punitive measures you are willing to take once we are back in Keangal space."

Iris's heart fell. Miran refused to look at her.

"And the time I bought has been spent," added Miran. "Second attack wave is upon us."

"Remain at Alert Status 5," signed the captain, and the message and vibrating alarm restarted throughout the ship. "Security, work with Admiral Miran to scramble our signature."

"Aye, Captain," signed Lartha, taking her place beside the admiral at Davan's workstation.

"Lieutenant Commander Iris, set our internal comms to Dark Channels only and inform the entire crew. Close the front door as well." This meant that once activated, no ship could engage external comms with the *S.S. SpoonZ.*

"What if a Keangal vessel tries to rescue us, sir?"

"No *other* Keangal vessel would be so reckless as to enter an uncharted rift."

Owch, thought Iris. Even so, she felt unsure about blocking out everyone.

"Mr. Herbert, status report," ordered Warq.

"Primary and secondary shields operating at 67%, Captain. Engines are stable but pushing max parameters with all this unpredictable steering."

You *fly this thing then!* projected Lieutenant Renley.

"Hey, it was just a fact, not assigning blame!" barked Herb.

"That's enough of you both," signed the captain. "Mr. Herbert, how is our jump core?"

"Jump core? Where would we jump to?"

"Answers, not comments, Mr. Herbert."

"Jump core is optimal, Captain?" The question mark appeared on Warq's visor.

"Good. Commander Davan," Warq signed, reluctant to face his second-in-command.

"Yes, Captain?" The pain was thick in his eyes.

"Observations of the anomaly itself?"

"I would have concluded it's always randomly in flux, but sometimes the shift in formation seems almost intentional."

"How so?"

"Readings indicate its mass expanded before the admiral's shuttle exploded, as if trying to mitigate the impact."

"Curious."

"And there appear to be small tears within the Rift. I'm wondering if they could be wormholes of sorts, but the moment I try to scan one, it closes over."

"Tears..." *Is that how the Rift got Trisha?* Warq wondered. *Were they pulled through a wormhole?*

But there was no time to draw further conclusions as his chair vibrated and his console informed him that several alarms were blaring throughout the bridge. Each member of the command crew worked feverishly at their stations, hoping to give Navigation what they needed to survive an event none of them had been trained for in simulation.

"Piranhas closing in. Eighteen in this formation," said Udana.

"There won't be warning blasts this time," said Miran. "They're getting ready for some sewing."

"Sewing?" signed Davan.

"Yes. There will be a blast-fire pattern they nickname the Cross Stitch. Impossible to outmanoeuvre. They want us gone from space."

"Isn't firing in that manner a bit self-destructive?" signed the captain. "The precision alone would be hard to maintain while flying in regular space, but in the Rift, it's going to be impossible without destroying themselves."

"The Stitch Formation is always considered a sacrificial line of ships," signed Miran. "They don't expect to survive."

"They volunteer for this?" said Iris.

Miran avoided her gaze. "No one volunteers for anything in the Brigade."

"Lieutenant Udana," signed the captain, "did going dark hide us at all from detection? How accurate is their estimation of our location?"

Udana felt the dynamic scanner readings with his fingertips and shared his screen with the captain. "Here is the formation, here is what is supposed to be dead centre, and that's exactly where we are."

Warq held his breath but pushed anything resembling fear or anger to the back of his mind. More than ever, calm and clear thinking would give him the best chance to lead them to safety. He unclenched his fingers to sign, "Lieutenant Renley, continue evasive manœuvres."

Yeah, fine, but I really need a pay rise, she projected, the skin on her knuckles lightening to the faintest pink as she held onto manual control.

A blast struck their hull. Iris stumbled, but the stabilizing field kept her from falling. Clarence's tractor beam also brought her fully upright again. Davan and Miran avoided colliding with each other in their shared field as the admiral had clutched onto their side of the workstation, anticipating the hit.

"Shots fired!" said Udana.

"That was to confirm our location," said Admiral Miran. "The next blasts will take us out unless we can jump."

JUMP WHERE? shout-thought Renley into their receivers.

"Wait!" signed Davan. "I'm detecting another wormhole. It's bigger than the others." Davan projected the image as a holo at his workstation.

The captain turned around to examine it. "Is it large enough for us to jump through?"

"No, sir. Well, yes, but just barely."

Are you frikking kidding me? cried Renley into their thoughts.

The command deck speakers rang out with and displayed: "Engineering to Captain Warq!"

"What is it, Mr. Herbert?" signed Warq.

"I think I have the thing! That thing Davan wanted me to pull out of my hat even though I don't particularly like hats."

"Quickly, if you please, Mr. Herbert."

"The Rift isn't as rifty as we think. It's more like an expanse surrounded by a luminescent shell. Except, I think the 'shell' can manipulate time and space, providing these gateways into other quadrants, galaxies, maybe even universes!"

"The stitching is imminent, Captain," interrupted the admiral. "They've lowered their shields, which means all power has been channeled to their weapon systems."

"Acknowledged, Admiral," signed Warq. "Mr. Herbert, now please!"

"We need to rip it," said Herb.

"Rip what?"

"The Rift. We need to rip open the shell to widen the wormhole."

"Are you—are you suggesting we tear the Rift?"

"We can fire on the shell near the wormhole. Maybe tearing through this space will cause the Rift to open for us."

"You act as if the Rift is sentient."

"Well, Captain, it behaves like a being who is reacting to an invader. That's why it keeps throwing us around when we get too close to the shell. We're irritating it. Let's get it to spit us out!"

The captain stared at Davan, who signed, "Mr. Herbert has a keen ability to detect patterns, Captain."

"It has to be now, Captain," said Miran. "They are in range."

"Lieutenant Renley, set course for the wormhole."

She read the command at her console. *Sure, Captain. I mean, why not, at this point?*

"Lieutenant Udana, fire non-lethal blasts at the outer rim of the opening. If we are in a self-aware being, we do not want to cause further harm."

"Aye, Captain." He commanded his console to project the best target zone for the anomaly within the anomaly. "Firing now."

At the same moment, Renley sported a wild look in her eyes as she took the *S.S. SpoonZ* towards the far-too-tight exit.

The blasts must have made contact because it felt as if space itself shook from the impact, or it could have been the vibrations from the spine-chilling roar that ensued.

"What was that?" signed the captain. "Sonic boom?"

"No, Captain," said Davan. "It sounded like the cry of a wounded beast!"

I can't see the wormhole! projected Renley, when the main viewscreen and her console's displays had clouded with even more luminescent whirling nebulae.

I'm receiving an all-clear to plot, projected Udana. *Sending course now!*

Wait, I can make it out," projected Renley to the crew. *The supposed wormhole's size has increased by 50%. I think we ripped through the tear in the Rift.* Her brows furrowed. *That's not possible, though, right?*

Let it go, Raven, we have a chance out of this thing, projected Udana. "Captain, on your mark?"

"Jump through, Navigation!"

Oh, fweep, living is overrated anyhow, projected Renley, letting go of manual steering and engaging Udana's course. "We're jumping!" she signed.

The ship barrelled through the wormhole, which sealed up immediately after their departure. This left the Piranha formation to fire at each other, to their own demise.

The *S.S. SpoonZ* hovered in place on the other side of the Rift. The admiral, the captain, and the rest of the bridge crew stayed at their posts for a moment or two, without communicating a word or thought to anyone.

Then Lieutenant Renley slumped in her chair, prompting Lieutenant Udana to put an arm around her for support. She touched his hand, and he opened his palm to receive a message she signed into it. They pulled back and high-fived each other.

This gesture seemed to instantly wake everyone from their stillness.

The captain let go of the arms of his chair, not realizing he'd been clutching them tenaciously. He cleared his throat, sat up, pulled on his tunic, and adjusted his sash. He raised his head then signed, "Status report, Navigation."

Udana and Renley jumped to order in their seats. Renley enhanced exterior visuals on the main viewscreen. Udana listened to his headset and said, "We are in uncharted space, Captain. I can't understand these coordinates at all. They sound completely garbled."

Renley agreed. "Yes, Captain, we don't know where we are at all. No reference point to within our galaxy." She gazed at one of the nebulae in the distance and signed, "Pretty though. Serene."

"So, it's safe to assume we are in another galaxy, then. And not in an uncharted part of our own galaxy?" signed the captain.

"That I cannot say," said Udana. "Commander Davan would offer a better answer than we could."

Warq's shoulders tensed. He glowered, turning to his second-in-command. "Any theories, Commander?"

"Without engaging with other beings, we might not be able to tell whether we are in another galaxy, quadrant, or universe, Captain."

"Understood. Lieutenant Commander Iris, send out a distress message in all known languages, maximum reach."

"Aye, Captain."

"And since we seem to be in a momentary state of peace, let's assess the ship and the well-being of all personnel," signed Warq.

"Commander, I shall leave you to coordinate this while I confer with Admiral Miran about our situation."

That hurt. Davan would typically not be excused from such a consultation. It only affirmed he was no longer a trusted resource to his captain. "Aye, Captain," he signed while feeling an ache in his sternum.

Warq curtly nodded and rose from his chair. "Admiral, would you care to accompany me to the small conference room?"

"I would indeed," signed Miran. As they walked around Davan's station to join the captain, Iris tried desperately to catch their eye. Miran didn't take their focus off the captain, so their head never pivoted in the slightest towards Iris's workstation.

Lartha followed behind Miran and Warq. The captain noticed her and signed with aggravation, "And where do you think you're going?"

"Uh..." The tone of his signing had thrown her off. "It's customary for Security to escort—"

"NO!" the captain said orally.

Lartha's jaw dropped.

Warq signed, "You are no longer my personal security escort. Stay here with your other colleagues until I decide what's next for you." He spun around to Navigation and signed, "Udana, Renley!"

They turned in their seats to face him.

"Were you aware this was a mutinous act?"

They each shook their heads.

"We thought it was a seek and rescue, Captain," said Udana.

"Yes, what he said," signed Renley.

"Good," signed Warq. "Secure this command deck and do not take any orders from anyone other than myself or Admiral Miran, is that clear?"

The pilots stiffened. "Aye, Captain," they signed, almost in unison.

With that, Lieutenant Udana initiated a force field around the piloting workstations, and Lieutenant Renley engaged a lockout of the controls, so only she and Udana and the Captain could manoeuvre the ship.

"Ship is secure from takeover and overrides," signed Renley.

"Thank you." The captain turned his attention to Miran and signed, "Admiral? After you."

When the commanding officers had entered the lift, Clarence gingerly tapped Iris's leg.

She swallowed, then cocked her head at xem.

"You seem upset, Eileen. May I be of assistance? Would you like me to bring you your silk scarf? That often gives you comfort whenever you feel anxious."

Iris covered her eyes and burst into tears. Her chest heaved as she sobbed with complete abandon. Clarence noted her state in xeir mental wellness log, concerned that crying in such a manner might become a more frequent occurrence that required monitoring.

Davan rushed to her and took her into his arms.

"I kn-know," she stammered through erratic breaths. "Th-this is con... duct not be-becoming an offi... cer on d-deck!"

He rocked her gently and rubbed her back.

"It's all-all my fault," she said. "I was the one whose curiosity got the b-better of me. I sn-snooped into the captain's family life. I convinced all of you to do this!"

Davan let her go, and she wiped away her tears with her officer's sash.

"This is not all on you, Iris," signed Davan, once she could look back at him. "I am the commander of this ship. At any time, I could have vetoed our mission, which was wrong, even if well-intentioned. The captain knows this. In my opinion, you are only guilty of having a huge heart. I, however, am guilty of consenting to a mutiny. But please do not worry; I will make sure the entire punishment rests on my shoulders alone."

"But if you do that, you'll be imprisoned for life, or exiled from the Keangal."

"Well"—he snort-laughed ruefully—"my guess is we're all in exile now. So, if we can get back, I suppose I'll be exiled from the exile."

"How can you make jokes at a time like this?"

"Because the alternative is listening to my own heart break."

"Ah, Davan." She hugged him closely. "What a mess I've made."

"We made it. Together. But I alone will take the blame. I promise you."

"Like gleek you will," said Lartha, putting her arms around both of them.

The small conference room where the captain typically met with senior officers sported golden-ochre walls not unlike the hue of the sashes and trim on Warq's dark grey tunic—and those found on Davan's uniform. Although, at present, the commander was not in attendance for the first time since Warq and Davan had been paired together on the *SpoonZ*.

Warq could feel the heaviness in his chest, but tried to hold onto the anger, so he would not give into the sorrow of Davan's betrayal. He wanted to be angry. Better yet, he wanted to feel nothing at all for his second-in-command.

On the other side of the dark brown tabletop, sitting like a stone statue, was the admiral. Their features were fixed, and their eyes stared at something the captain could not see. The way one has when one is analyzing a picture within one's mind.

Warq could hazard a guess at the subject of Miran's disappointment, to put it mildly. Lieutenant Commander Iris. The captain had known the two were friends since adolescence, possible sweethearts, and to observe the admiral go from a lover's worry—for even if they were not a couple, that brand of intense concern seemed to be there on Miran's part—to concentrated disillusionment resonated with Warq. That transition from terror for someone you cared about to finding out they were traitors. It felt like too much to bear. *How could they do this to us? How did I not foresee that my entire senior leadership could not be trustworthy?*

Warq didn't even realize how deeply he sighed until he noticed the sound he must have emitted had jolted Miran's head in the captain's direction. The admiral gave a weak smile, as one does when acknowledging the presence of another during difficult times.

"I apologize for being elsewhere when I should be here," signed Miran.

The captain shook his head. "No, please, Admiral. I too am elsewhere. And... I confess I am at a loss. It feels like I woke up from a dream where I was the captain of a stellar team who I could boast about unashamedly, only to wake up and realize I have no value to them. They do not respect my leadership, Admiral. They have gone to great lengths to show this to me."

Miran agreed, then a rueful expression fell over their features. "And yet, they insist they took these actions for love of you."

Warq bolted from his chair and paced, interrupting his steps to sign, "Love. How mutiny could ever equal love is beyond me. We are not a collection of adolescents in secondary school, Admiral. This is not some classroom drama that needs sorting! This is a Keangal ship of trained professionals—*military* staff who should know far better at their age and rank!"

The captain resumed his irritated pacing at such a speed, Miran could not catch his attention to sign to him. But because Warq wore his interpretation visor, the admiral said, "Of course you are correct, Captain. Their behaviour is inexcusable—"

Warq stopped. "And if they loved me so much, then why didn't they confront me with their concern? Why deceive me so? Why steal my ship?" He resumed his pacing once again, almost jogging back and forth this time.

"Why indeed?" said Miran.

"I am at a loss!" signed Warq while still attempting to drill a groove into the floor. "A complete loss! How dare—D-A-R-E—they do this to me?"

Because the captain signed without facing Miran, the admiral had initiated a sign-to-text feature on their wristband, just in case the captain would continue signing while moving about.

"No matter how good their intentions may have been—" began Miran.

Warq stopped in his tracks again. "Good intentions? There cannot be anything *good* about their intentions, Admiral. They were arrogant, presuming what I needed. Presuming I needed... needed..." The captain dropped his arms and closed his eyes. He steadied his breath and lifted his hands to continue. "My... sister."

Miran immediately got out of their seat, and darted over to the captain, who was obviously overcome. They offered their arms and Warq weakly entered the embrace.

"I am deeply sorry for your loss, Dustin," said Miran.

The captain opened his eyes when his visor vibrated, then read what Miran had said. He wanted to sign a thank you but remained quiet in Miran's arms. For there were rarely opportunities for a ship's captain to receive comfort in this manner.

"Deeply sorry," Miran repeated.

Back on the command deck, Renley and Udana had granted Herb and Gerri permission to join Iris, Davan, and Lartha. Since the ship had been in lockdown, there wasn't much need of Herb's expertise, and Lieutenant Sheena was more than capable in his stead. He wanted to be with his friends and partner at this difficult time.

They definitely weren't in their A game. In fact, they resembled a team who had just lost the playoffs. Lartha sat in her hoverchair, staring at her boots. She'd asked Right Leg to play some instrumental tracks from one of her favourite playlists. The contrast of the easygoing ambient music against the tense atmosphere of the senior officers was palatable.

Davan sat at his workstation, pale from sorrow. Gerri offered him a drumstick to cheer him up. He took it with a faint smile.

Iris still wiped tears from her face. She just couldn't shake the guilt.

Herb stood up because he didn't feel like sitting. He fiddled about with his bit of Davatio, not knowing what else to do. It was weird to not have anything to respond to, not have a problem to solve. It was weird, full stop.

"So, um, should we play a game or something?" he said.

Lartha looked up at him. "You gotta be joking."

"Well, I—"

"We're all going to be flung into oblivion, and this is what you suggest we do to pass the time?"

"Don't you speak to him like that!" signed Davan. "He meant no harm."

"Meant no harm," signed Lartha. "That seems to be the theme with us. We're the crew who means no harm. Aren't we... *Iris*?"

This set the communications officer into another cloudburst of tears. Clarence updated xeir log again.

"Now look what you've done!" said Herb. "You're just plain cranky, Lartha!"

"Aw, gee, ya think? And why would that be?"

Iris sobbed louder.

Lartha pivoted to her friend. The ire soon left her face, and she hovered her chair over to Iris's workstation.

"Okay, wait. I'm sorry, Iris. That was a cheap shot."

"No... it's true! I should have kept my mouth shut about everything."

Lartha put an arm around her. "You spoke up because you really cared and wanted to make things better. It was wrong for me to stomp all over you."

"I think we are all on edge right now," signed Davan.

"Yeah," said Herb. "Davan's right. We're all on edge."

Lartha and Iris redirected their attention to Davan.

"I don't know what's going to become of us," he signed, "but let's not have our last memories together be harsh ones. Let's remember our friendship, which has meant more to me than anything since boarding this ship."

Herb reached out a hand to Davan and kissed his betrothed's fingers. Then Herb extended a hand to Iris. She held it, then took Lartha's hand, who closed the circle by holding Davan's free hand.

"Iris and the Crew forever!" said Lartha. "When we get out of the brig, we'll release our comeback album."

"Can I play drums on it?" Gerri asked.

The adults allowed themselves a hearty laugh. They were still chuckling when Warq and Miran appeared on deck.

Warq's eyes practically spewed flames at the sight of them holding hands in solidarity and laughing like nothing at all had happened.

"That does it!" he signed angrily. "I am ordering you all to the brig, where you shall remain until I can get this ship back to Keangal space with a crew I can actually rely on!"

"No!" cried Gerri, running into Herb's arms.

The captain was aghast. "What is this child doing on my ship? Mr. Herbert, have you no shame about her safety?"

"She didn't 'port with the others, Captain!"

"This is not to be borne!" signed Warq. "The level of irresponsibility of your actions is nothing I could have ever predicted, not in ten lifetimes!"

"But Captain—"

"Not another word, Mr. Herbert! Any feelings of regret I might have entertained about tossing you and your co-conspirators into the brig have been completely vanquished. I will not suffer your presence any longer on my bridge!"

Iris cocked her head and put a hand to her earpiece, then stepped over to her workstation.

"In my estimation," the captain continued, "there is nothing redemptive about your actions. Nothing in the least! And you had backed me into an impossible corner where I had no choice but to order Navigation through that wormhole, displacing us who knows where!"

"Captain?" said Iris.

"I have no interest in conversing with you, Lieutenant Commander."

"I know, Captain, but—" she signed.

He gestured for her to stop.

"As I was saying," signed Warq.

"But, Captain—" said Iris.

"Enough!" signed Warq.

"CAPTAIN, WE'RE BEING HAILED!" She didn't mean to shout but knew it would show up in capital letters on his visor.

Warq's frown deepened when he read the words. "Oh indeed?" he signed, the disbelief apparent on his face.

Iris's eyes watered. "Putting on viewscreen, sir."

"No, do not do that, Lieutenant Commander! We must first assess if these are hostiles or friendlies."

Iris smiled with trembling lips. "On screen now, Captain!"

It was a wonder that actual smoke hadn't burst from Warq's brain, out his ears. "Has everyone completely lost every last drop of reason and respect? Is every single command I issue going to be ignored from this point on? Does my authority and seniority and rank mean nothing to any of you?"

Davan's eyes went wide at the screen. "Captain, I think you should turn around."

"I am not finished, Commander! If and when we get back to our galaxy, I am going to make sure you all spend the rest of your lives in exile without reprieve, stripped of all your ranks, and I shall make sure you are known throughout the Keangal for your abject and heartless betrayal!"

Little Gerri pointed to the viewscreen with her drumstick. "Lady looks friendly!"

A voice came through the command deck speakers. A soft, incredulous tone. Only one word appeared on the captain's interpretation visor.

"Dustbin?"

Warq blinked to make sure he read it correctly. Then he finally turned around.

A face, so familiar but a little older. She was dressed in an outdated uniform. Her green skin showed wrinkles in all the areas that housed her smile, especially around the eyes. For she had always loved to laugh.

The captain stared with jaw dropped. "Trash?" he signed.

Her grin radiated from the screen straight into his heart. He wanted to revel in this moment but found his vision clouded by the tears that streamed unchecked down his cheeks. Dustin lifted his visor to dry his eyes.

"Hey, womb-mate," she signed. "I'm about ten years and a bit too late for our special celebration, but I made it!"

His hands shook violently as he signed, "Where's my candy?"

She erupted with laughter. He felt it pierce his chest.

Captain Dustin Warq wiped his eyes and turned around to face Iris, Davan, Herb, and Lartha. They watched him with undiluted affection. He swallowed hard, wiped more tears, then signed:

"Don't you think for one moment I am no longer absolutely enraged with you all. There will be disciplinary action against you, you mark my... my—" He broke down in sobs.

The four of them dashed to their captain and embraced him heartily. Miran remained just outside the entrance to the lift, taking in the scene. When Iris had returned to her workstation, catching Jaq's eye, she noticed while there still wasn't the same gaze she'd recently come to know, their features had softened, a little.

Captain Dustin Warq turned around again and faced his sister.

She had a delightfully cocky stance and playful grin. "Well, baby brother," she signed, "welcome to status Adrift in the Rift."

"While I thank you for this most hospitable greeting, I think it's best we all get back to where we came from," signed Dustin.

"Ha! Good luck with that. We've been trying since always. And with every attempt, the Rift hurls us elsewhere. It's not happy with us, I don't think."

"You make it seem like the Rift is self-aware. My head of Engineering also shares this viewpoint."

Herb's lips parted, hoping he really still was the head of Engineering.

"Well, maybe the spiritual folks were onto something about its nature," signed Captain Trisha Warq.

Lartha's eyes sparkled, and she stood up out of her chair. "Self-aware, huh?"

Dustin Warq read her words and looked at her. "Chief?"

Lartha also hoped the captain's using the short name of her rank meant she was still head of Security. "If the Rift is a being," she signed, "I think I know a way to communicate with it, sweet talk it to taking us home."

Trisha Warq's face showed she wasn't even the slightest bit inspired. "Oh really? This oughta be good."

Lartha smirked. "Oh yeah, it will be, Captain. Just you wait."

What happens now?

How the fweep will the *Stargazer* and the *SpoonZ* ever get back to their galaxy and rejoin the Keangal? What kind of military discipline will Iris and her fellow officers face? And most importantly, who's going to make that delectable sponge cake now that Lartha's pastry chef is off the ship?

To be dead honest, I have absolutely no clue, but I bet we'll find answers in *Season 2: Iris and the Crew Ride the Rift!*

Acknowledgements

I had dived into the world-building of *Iris and the Crew* during the COVID-19 global pandemic when I discovered that I, like other disabled or chronically ill or immunocompromised folks, were the *Onlies*. As in: *Only* we would be in danger of getting long-term complications, or *only* we would end up in the ICU, or *only* we would die from the virus.

The eugenics-based messaging was daily, and it wore me out. In 2020, I could barely write. In 2021, probably to save what was left of my sanity, I plunged into Iris's galaxy because I needed to exist in a space where Universal Design and the Social Model of Disability had gone next level. Accommodations and accessibility and acceptance are the norm there, and even the assistive tech have their own community!

Back here on Earth, I must thank all of the Earthers who nursed me through the writing of this episodic fiction. First is Derek Newman-Stille, who listened to my short story and said, "You know this needs to be a book, right?" (I didn't but am glad I took your advice!) My fellow critique group members who offered so much encouragement—Christina Robins, Jen Desmarais, K.W. Ramsey, and John Haas—you all kept me going with your feedback. Then came the beta readers: Christina and Jen again (I really needed you folks, and you were there for me), Jamieson Wolf (who doesn't really have a bird with a tutu on his head, I swear), Stephen Graham King (thanks for reading during this "gestures at everything" time), Jennifer Lee Rossman (you've never been beta-read until you've been so by this hilarious and thorough human), and my Sweet Baboo,

Bruce Gordon (reading aloud to each other was far better than watching the news).

I'd also like to do a shout out to Amanda Leduc for taking the time out of her massively busy schedule to read my little book and offer it some words of praise. Folks, I would encourage you to look up the works of all the authors who offered blurbs because they are awesome alphabet arrangers!

A billionty thanks to my publisher, Renaissance, for constantly wanting to elevate the works of disabled creatives. And to Nathan Fréchette, who kept telling me he couldn't wait to publish this book, but I was exceptionally slow on the uptake. Maybe I can't book-flirt? That's what my BFF Talia says anyway.

Where would I be without the sensitivity editors Robert Kingett, Eman Rimawi-Doster, and Christopher Jon Heuer? In a complete state of self-doubt and overthinking, most probably. And a big thanks to Allyson Throp for giving my book that final polish!

How can I not thank all the folks I have met in the disabled, d/Deaf and hard-of-hearing, Blind and visually impaired, neurodivergent, and/or Spoonie circles who have enriched my life? You welcomed me into safer community spaces, gave me confidence in accepting my bodymind, and made me a better person.

And last but never least, I thank everyone who has purchased this book or checked it out from libraries. Books need loving homes, too. I am ever so grateful for your support.

About the Author

Cait Gordon is an autistic, disabled, and queer Canadian writer of speculative fiction that celebrates diversity. Originally from Verdun, Québec, Cait had worked for over two decades as a technical writer, then channelled her love for words into storytelling.

She is the author of the humorous space adventures *Life in the 'Cosm*, *The Stealth Lovers*, and *Season One: Iris and the Crew Tear Through Space!* Some of her short stories can be found in *Alice Unbound: Beyond Wonderland*, *We Shall Be Monsters*, *There's No Place*, and *Mighty: An Anthology of Disabled Superheroes*. Her short work, "The Hilltop Gathering" from the Prix Aurora Award nominated *We Shall Be Monsters*, features a disabled protagonist and was discussed at a symposium about Frankenstein at Carleton University.

In 2016, Cait founded The Spoonie Authors Network to connect with writers in the disability community. Her desire to find better disabled and autistic representation in fiction prompted Cait to co-edit *Nothing Without Us* and *Nothing Without Us Too* with Talia C. Johnson. The multi-genre anthologies feature authors and protagonists who are disabled, d/Deaf or hard-of-hearing, Blind or visually impaired, neurodivergent, Spoonie, and/or they manage mental illness. *Nothing Without Us* has been part of the syllabus of a disability studies course at Trent University several times and earned a 2020 Prix Aurora Award nomination; *Nothing Without Us Too* won a 2023 Prix Aurora Award for Best Related Work.

Even though her works include issues about identity and human/alien/monster rights, Cait has always felt humour is an important part of world-building. "Without humour, it doesn't feel realistic."

Cait is also a musician who lives in Ottawa with her guitarist husband, Canadian author Bruce D. Gordon. She's friendly, somewhat feisty, and really, really, really loves cake.

THE STEALTH LOVERS
by Cait Gordon

After submitting to mandatory conscription, two young men begin Basic Training, or, "Vacay in Hay."

Xaxall Dwyer Knightly saunters onto base without a care in the worlds, filled to the brim with sass. He has the strength of five warriors and earns the distinction of being the only train-ee to throw someone through a supporting wall. Vivoxx Nathan Tirowen, son of a prominent general, carries himself with a naturally-commanding presence. Possessing an uncanny talent with weaponry, his drill sergeant is convinced Vivoxx could "trim the pits of a rodent without nicking the skin."

When the two recruits meet, one smiles warmly while the other speaks gibberish. Little do they know the bond they feel will lead them to become the venerable military pairing known as

The Stealth.

"The fiercest, most formidable warrior-lovers in the 'Cosm are back. And the battle has never been so fabulous!"
Stephen Graham-King, author of *A Congress of Ships*

"Cait Gordon sent us on a ride full of pew-pew physics and one of the absolute best traits of people: our humour."
'Nathan Burgoine, Lambda Literary finalist and author of *Light*

"HOLY STARS, I loved everything about this novel!!!"
Jamieson Wolf, author of *Little Yellow Magnet*

NOTHING WITHOUT US
EDITED BY CAIT GORDON AND TALIA C. JOHNSON

We are the heroes, not the sidekicks.

Can you recommend fiction that has main characters who are like us?

This is a question we who are disabled, Deaf, neurodiverse, Spoonie, and/or who manage mental illness ask way too often. Typically, we're faced with stories about us crafted by people who really don't get us. We're turned into pathetic, tragic souls; we merely exist to inspire the abled main characters to thrive; or even worse, we're to overcome "what's wrong with us" and be cured.

Nothing Without Us and its sequel, Nothing Without Us Too, combine realistic and speculative fiction starring protagonists who are written by disabled people and for disabled people.

From hospital halls to jungle villages, from within the fantastical plane to deep into outer space, our heroes take us on a journey, make us think, and prompt us to cheer them on.

These are bold tales, told in our voices.

www.ingramcontent.com/pod-product-compliance
Lightning Source LLC
Chambersburg PA
CBHW070521310726
48976CB00002BA/502

9781990086496